JUSTICE 4 WILLIS

RAY WEAVER

JUSTICE 4 WILLIS

The Fourth Novel in the Justice Series

RAY WEAVER

Sirena Press

For information:

Murmaid Publishing
Murmaid@tampabay.rr.com

Other books by Ray Weaver:
Tightrope to Justice
Miami Justice
European Justice

ISBN # 978-0-9856851-4-0

Cover and Book Design
theMurmaid ™
for Sirena Press

Printed in the United States of America

First American Edition

Dedication

This, my fourth novel, I wish to dedicate to
my wife of fifty-four years, Ellie. She spends
countless hours on the computer,
typing my articles and books.

My encouragement to continue writing, comes
from the support of my *Chicken Soup for the Soul*
family and its readers.

I feel that being published in this nationally
known series has helped to lend some
creditability to my efforts.

Once again a special thanks to all my family,
friends and neighbors who continue to
support and encourage me. Also, to my
publisher and dear friend, Nancy Frederich. It's
been a pleasure to work with such a perfectionist.

Contents

Chapter 1 1

Chapter 2 7

Chapter 3 11

Chapter 4 19

Chapter 5 27

Chapter 6 35

Chapter 7 43

Chapter 8 51

Chapter 9 57

Chapter 10 65

Chapter 11 71

Chapter 12 79

Chapter 13 89

Chapter 14 97

Chapter 15 105

Chapter 16 111

Chapter 17 123

Chapter 18 131

Chapter 19 137

Chapter 20 149

Chapter 21 155

Chapter 22 165

Chapter 23 177

Chapter 24 181

Chapter 25 189

Chapter 26 195

Chapter 27 205

Chapter 28 213

Chapter 29 227

Chapter 30 239

Chapter 31 247

Chapter 32 255

Chapter 33 263

Chapter 34 269

Chapter 35 277

Chapter 36 283

Chapter 37 289

Chapter 38 295

Chapter 39 301

Author Bio 313

Articles and Short Stories 314

Chapter 1

"Morning Dear—happy anniversary," Kelley said as she leaned over the bed, drew back the covers and planted a kiss on Phil's lips. "I can't believe it's been five years already and that we've got two perfect little kids from this blissful union."

He gave her a half grin, half grimace. "Well, I wouldn't say that Alan and Ashley are perfect. But thanks to you, they're doing great." He hopped out of the warm bed, slipped on a robe, eased his feet into a pair of slippers and followed her downstairs into the kitchen.

"You get the paper and I'll start the coffee," she said wrinkling her nose at him. "I'll be breathlessly awaiting your return."

"Yes Dear." He gave her a squeeze and headed for the kitchen door that opened into the garage. Looking around at the clutter, Phil frowned and mumbled, "Looks like Kelley will want this to be one of my Saturday afternoon projects." He pressed the garage door button and watched as the double door went up slowly and smoothly.

At least the door is working, he thought. But then, it should. Cost a hundred and fifty bucks for the repair last week.

He strolled slowly to the end of the driveway and

peered around for his morning paper.

"Okay kid, where did you throw it today," he sighed. "Ah, there it is. By the mailbox."

As he approached the mailbox, Phil heard a groan. Then, a voice called out, "Help. Help."

He looked around to see where the call was coming from. Suddenly, he realized that it was coming from next door. He stepped through the shrubs that separated the two properties, and spied his neighbor, Gary, lying face down in his driveway.

In the five years that Kelley and Phil had lived in the cul-de-sac, they had only occasional social visits with their quiet and somewhat reclusive next-door neighbors, Bruce Overton and Gary Toth. In fact, they were surprised when they had recently been invited to a birthday party for Bruce's elderly mother at the men's home.

Both of them were in their late fifties. Gary was tall and muscular and worked for an ad agency. And his partner, Bruce, who had just retired from his sales position at a furniture store, appeared to be the opposite. Short and heavy set, he looked as though he had never missed a meal.

Phil ran over to him. "Gary, Gary! What happened? Are you okay?" As he knelt down beside him, he noticed a large amount of blood on his neighbor's shirt.

Gary moaned softly and tried to crawl forward.

Phil leaned down and examined him closely. "My God man. You've been... stabbed? Stay calm, I'll get help pal." He jumped to his feet and raced back to his house.

He flung open the kitchen door, stepped inside and yelled, "Kelley, call 911."

Standing at the counter, calmly pouring a cup of coffee, she looked startled.

Phil's voice shook. "It's Gary. He's lying in his driveway. And he's been stabbed, I think. Hurry!"

Kelley slammed the coffee pot down, whirled around

and with trembling hands grabbed the phone from the counter by the sink. "Yes. I'm on it."

Phil raced down the hall to the bathroom, snatched several towels from the linen closet and ran back outside. He reached Gary, looked around his bleeding back for wounds and found what appeared to be three jagged knife wounds in his shoulder. He slapped a few of the towels over them, applied pressure to try to stop the flow of the blood, then gently turned Gary over.

The blood was flowing from a large wound in Gary's stomach. He took the last towel and pressed it firmly over the wound and again applied pressure. "Hang on pal. The rescue squad is on the way."

Gary's eyes flickered open briefly.

"Stay with me Gary," Phil whispered.

Still dressed only in her pajamas, robe and slippers and with her arms full of more clean towels, Kelley came rushing up. Phil whipped the blood soaked towel from Gary's stomach, grabbed a clean towel from Kelley and pressed it firmly onto the site. "He's got a couple of wounds in his shoulder but this one seems to be the most severe."

Kelley knelt down beside them, leaned over and looked at Gary's face, which was now an ashen gray color. She lowered her head, struggling to control her emotions. "I think he's going into shock. Just keep applying pressure."

She raced back to the house and quickly returned with a blanket and more towels.

She placed the blanket over Gary, then ran to the entrance of the cul-de-sac and watched anxiously for the ambulance. She heard the echo of a siren and then as the sound grew louder, it appeared, followed by a police car. At the sound of the sirens the other neighbors emerged to see what was going on.

Kelley waved the vehicles into the Willis driveway and

the paramedics jumped out. She pointed to the two men in the next door driveway. "Over there. It's our neighbor, Gary. He's been stabbed."

The paramedics grabbed their equipment and a stretcher from the back of the vehicle and raced over. They quickly pushed Phil aside and immediately began assessing Gary's condition.

The technicians worked as two uniformed officers exited the police car and walked up to Phil. "Who are you Sir? What's going on here?"

"I'm Phil Willis. I live next door. I came outside to pick up my newspaper and heard someone moaning." He pointed to Gary, "That's my neighbor, Gary Toth. He lives in this house with his companion, Bruce Overton."

After the paramedics stabilized Gary, they placed him on a stretcher and loaded him into the ambulance. As they pulled away with the siren blaring, another car pulled into the driveway. Two men stepped out. One of the officers looked up. "Hey Mason, what brings you and your partner here?"

The men sauntered up. "We heard over the radio there was a report of a stabbing. Thought we'd investigate. What is it? A domestic?" Mason asked.

"Not sure yet. Just got here."

"What hospital are they taking him to?" Kelley asked one of the officers.

"Probably Syracuse General. That's the closest."

Mason stepped forward. "And who are these folks?"

Phil stuck out his hand. "I'm an attorney, Phil Willis and this is my wife, Kelley. Next door neighbors. And you are?"

"Detective Sam Mason." He took a step back. "Can you tell me what you know about this?"

After Phil filled the detective in on what he knew, Mason asked, "Anyone else live with Mr. Toth? Wife? Kids?"

"Only his roommate, Bruce. Bruce Overton."

"Is he here?"

Phil glanced around. "Don't think so. His car is usually in the driveway when he's home and I don't see it."

"Well. We'll need you and the wife to come to headquarters and make a statement after you get dressed."

"Sure. Anything we can do to be of help."

Detective Mason turned to one of the officers. "Check the house to see if the roommate's inside. If he isn't we'll put out a 'bolo' on him. Lock the house and tape it off."

"Wait Detective," Phil said, "Before you put out your bulletin on Mr. Overton, I think that I might know where he is. He usually visits his mother on weekends. I'll bring him in if I can find him."

The detective stepped back and looked closely at Phil. "Say I think I recognize you Willis. I saw you in court last year. Guess I can give you some time to locate this Overton fellow before we put out a bulletin on him. Here's my card. I'll meet you folks at the station later."

Phil took his card and put it in the pocket of his robe. "Got it Mason. We'll see you later."

Their arms loaded with the bloody towels, they started back to their house. "The rescue squad took the blanket and some of the towels with them," Kelley said.

Phil put his arm around her and his voice became incredibly gentle. "They were so bloody you'd never get them clean. Just buy some new ones Honey."

She cut him off with a look. "But, they were my best towels."

"Not important now. Let's clean up and head for Bruce's mother's house. He stays overnight with her sometimes."

"Thank goodness the kids are at your folk's house this weekend. I wouldn't want them to witness this," Kelley said as they entered their house.

She put the bloody towels and their blood spattered pajamas and robes in the laundry tub. "I'll let this stuff soak in cold water to get the blood out. I'll run a load of wash later."

After a quick shower, they dressed, ate breakfast and headed to Mrs. Overton's home to look for Bruce.

Chapter 2

"Did I or didn't I wish you a happy anniversary this morning?" Phil asked as they headed down the street in their car. "With what we just went through, I can't even remember if I brushed my teeth."

She raised her head and smiled at him. "That's okay Dear. It was great of your parents to keep the kids for the weekend so we could celebrate our anniversary. But now, it looks like we may have to wait until next weekend for that special night out."

"I promise we'll have it next Saturday, for sure." A frown was beginning to deepen the furrow between his brows. "Right now, we need to talk with Bruce. I called earlier and told him we were on the way. Told him I had something important to talk to him about and it couldn't wait. Didn't want to tell him over the phone about Gary. I know how close they are."

"It looks like the road is closed ahead," Kelley said. "Take a left and go the other way."

He made a sharp turn. "How am I going to tell Bruce about Gary? Or does Bruce already know? God forbid, that he had something to do with it," he suggested.

"I doubt he could've done that to Gary," she glared at him as she tried desperately to corral that thought herself. "But, why don't you let me tell him what happened?

I think I can approach it in a more delicate manner."

"Good idea. Call the hospital now and see if they can give you an update on Gary's condition."

After Kelley made the phone call, she said with pain in her voice, "All the hospital would tell me was that he was in surgery."

Phil pulled into Mrs. Overton's driveway, exited the car and slowly walked up to the house. Before they had a chance to ring the bell, the door was flung open. Looking very distraught, Bruce ushered them inside.

"What's up Willis? What's so damn important that you couldn't tell me over the phone?" He seemed genuinely baffled.

Phil took him by the arm and gently led him to the living room sofa. Bruce's mother entered the room, wiping her wet hands on a towel, and rushed over to Kelley. Her voice deepened, incredibly concerned. "What's going on? What brings you two over here so early in the morning?"

"I think you better sit down too, Mrs. Overton," Kelley said.

Mrs. Overton took a seat on the sofa beside her son and both of them leaned forward, anxiously waiting to hear what they had to say.

"Something wrong at the house?" Bruce asked.

He looked at Phil and Kelley anxiously and a shudder appeared to ripple through him. "This is about Gary isn't it? I called this morning and he didn't answer."

"So you didn't see him this morning?" Phil asked.

"No. You guys know us." He appeared to be slightly embarrassed. "You've lived next door to us for a while. We had our once a month argument yesterday afternoon and I stormed out of the house. It was all over a dumb cruise. I booked a seven day cruise for us and he didn't think we should spend the money. You know we argue once in a while just, like regular couples."

"We understand," Kelley smiled faintly.

"Thank you. And you are such great neighbors," Bruce continued in a nervous voice. "Well, anyway I spent the night here with Mom. But I did call Gary last night to apologize and tell him I was going to cancel the trip." Bruce looked like he was ready to cry. "Something has happened to him. I know it. Tell me, please."

Kelley leaned forward and gently took Bruce's hands in hers. "Phil went outside this morning to get the newspaper and discovered Gary lying in your driveway. He appeared to have been stabbed several times."

Bruce jumped to his feet and wrung his hands in frustration. "But he'll be okay? Won't he?"

"We just don't know. He had several stab wounds to his back and a severe one to his stomach, but I managed to stop the bleeding," Phil said. "The paramedics said that he was stable before they took him away in the ambulance."

Bruce's mother started to sob softly. "Oh, my God. Where is he?"

Kelley sighed and replied gently. "He's in Syracuse General. I talked to the hospital a little while ago. Said he was in surgery, but wouldn't tell me his condition."

"I've got to go see him." Bruce stammered, his face pale with fear. He started to pace from one side of the room to the other.

Phil walked over, put his hand on Bruce's arm, and said calmly, "The police are looking for you Bruce. You know when something like this happens they always suspect the person closest to the victim. Detective Mason wants to question you. They were going to send out a bulletin searching for you. But I told them that I thought I knew where you were and that I'd accompany you to headquarters this morning. I think you should have an attorney present when you talk to them."

"Damn it. I'm going to the hospital, no matter what," Bruce shouted, his chest rising and falling in agitation.

Phil thought for a few minutes. "Okay. Here's what, we're going to do." He turned to Kelley. "You take the car and go to my folk's house. See how the kids are. Ask if they can keep them an extra day or two. Then head home. Check out what the cops are doing at Bruce and Gary's place. Give me a call and let me know what's going on there. In the meantime, I'll go with Bruce to the hospital to see what we can find out about Gary. They should give him the information since he's the registered domestic partner. Afterwards, I'll accompany Bruce to police headquarters."

Bruce's mother, sitting in a corner of the sofa and quietly sobbing, asked, "What can I do?"

Kelley replied gently, "Pray."

Bruce walked over to his mother, knelt down and gave her a hug. "Don't worry Mom. Everything's gonna be okay."

After Kelley left, Phil and Bruce climbed into Bruce's car and drove toward the hospital.

As Bruce drove along, Phil called Detective Mason. He explained that he had located Bruce that they were on their way to the hospital to see how Gary was. He promised Mason that as soon as they finished at the hospital he would bring Bruce in for the interview.

Mason replied that as far as he knew, Gary was still in surgery, but the sooner that Bruce came in for questioning the better it would look for him. Then he asked Phil if he planned to represent Bruce as his attorney.

"If he needs a lawyer, I'm there for him."

"Well, so far we don't know if Overton was involved in the stabbing," Mason said. "We've got a crime team going out to the house to search for clues."

Chapter 3

When Phil and Bruce arrived at the hospital, they learned that Gary was in the recovery room. The nurse informed them that Gary would remain there for a couple of hours and there was nothing that they could do for him.

Bruce wet his lips with a nervous darting tongue and pleaded, "Can I at least see him? I'm his partner."

"I'm sorry Sir, no one is allowed to see him at this time," she answered.

Phil laid a reassuring hand on Bruce's shoulder. "I think it's best if we go to see Detective Mason now. You can come back to the hospital after we talk to him."

After he asked Phil to represent him legally in case he had any difficulties with the police, Bruce reluctantly agreed to talk to the detective. They entered the police department and Bruce halted briefly. With a slight tremor in his voice, he whispered, "Please stay with me. I'm really scared."

"I'm here for you." He turned to the desk sergeant, "We're here to see Detective Mason."

A hand went up from the back of the room and a voice called out, "Over here Willis."

Detective Mason and another man walked up to them. "This is my partner, Detective Leo Purcell." Phil shook hands with both of them and introduced Bruce to

Purcell. After the detective acknowledged the introduction, Phil informed them that he was legally representing Bruce at this time.

Mason directed, "Follow us." The detectives led Phil and Bruce into a private room and motioned for them to have seats behind a small metal table.

Detective Purcell stood near the door as Mason took a chair across the table from them. He pursed his lips and pulled a sheet of paper out from the folder that he had placed in front of him.

His gaze settled on Bruce. "Your full name please."

"Bruce Herbert Overton."

"You live at?"

Bruce shifted in his chair, clearly uncomfortable. Annoyed, maybe even unnerved, he snapped, "Next door to my attorney, Mr. Willis."

Mason folded his arms, leaned back in his chair and looked at Bruce stonily. "Stay calm Sir. Just answer these simple questions, Mr. Overton, for our records. You're not under arrest. This is just customary procedure in a case like this."

Bruce, seething with frustration, cried out, "My roommate has been stabbed. He may be dying as we speak and you want me to remain calm."

"What I want Sir is to just obtain this standard information. Then, I want you and your attorney to accompany me back to the crime scene."

Bruce stood up abruptly and pushed himself away from the table, knocking his chair to the floor. He needed to move, to get out of this situation and put space between him and the cop. "Where's the bathroom? Think I'm going to be sick."

"Leo, please escort Mr. Overton to the men's room," Mason ordered. Bruce and Purcell scurried out of the room, Phil sighed and scooted forward in his chair. "You can see that he's quite upset about his companion."

Mason nodded. "I understand. I'll try to make this as easy on him as I can." He raised his eyes skyward. "But I must complete my investigation. We have a serious crime on our hands."

When Bruce returned, Mason went over a few more questions and then asked, "Did one of you drive here?"

"Bruce did. We came in his car," Phil answered.

"Okay then. I'll accompany Mr. Overton back to his house in his car. Mr. Willis, you can join my partner in his squad car."

Then, in a somewhat softer tone, he added, "I need to know more about your personal relationship with Gary."

"It's no secret Detective. Gary and I are both gay. He's my partner and companion. We've been together for years," Bruce responded with tears in his eyes.

Purcell and Phil arrived back at Overton's house and found Bruce and Mason already there, talking to a police officer who was standing outside. Walking toward the front door, Detective Mason asked Bruce, "Are there any pets inside the house, Sir"

"No. Gary had a greyhound, but the dog died two weeks ago. That was one of the reasons why he's been so irritable lately."

The four men entered the house to discover that it was in a state of complete disarray. Chairs, tables and lamps were knocked over and papers were strewn about the living room.

"Holy shit, what happened to our house?" Bruce shouted in apparent disbelief.

"It appears to have been ransacked," Mason replied. "Does it look like anything's missing?"

"How the hell do I know without looking around? Other than my coin collection, we didn't keep any valuables in the house," Bruce answered, wringing his hands. He ran down the hall to his bedroom with the other men following.

The top of Bruce's bed was covered with clothes dragged from the closet, contents of the dresser drawers were strewn about the room. Bruce rushed to his closet, stepped inside, looked at empty shelves above the clothes racks and exclaimed as his eyes widened in alarm, "I can't believe it—someone stole my big coin collection. It's worth thousands."

"Maybe, Gary walked in on the thief and that's when he got knifed," Phil suggested.

"It does look like a struggle took place in here," Mason said coldly.

Detective Purcell walked over to the bed; bent down and examined the throw rug on the floor next to it. "There appears to be blood stains on this."

Mason gave Bruce a doubtful look. "I have to ask you Sir. Are you sure that you and the victim weren't involved in some kind of argument here?"

Bruce became outraged. "Just take a look around Detective. Would I do this to my own house?"

"Oh, it's your house is it? Don't you own it with Mr. Toth?"

"No. The house is in my name alone. Gary just lived with me."

Purcell picked up a bathrobe that was lying on the bed. "This robe has blood on it too."

"That's my robe Detective." Bruce gritted his teeth in frustration. "But I don't know how blood got on it. Maybe Gary was wearing it?"

Mason took Bruce firmly by the arm. "I need you to step outside Sir while my men continue to investigate the crime scene."

When Bruce, Phil and the two detectives reentered

the living room, one of the crime scene investigators who had already been present in the house, walked up to Detective Mason. "Sir, I think I found the weapon. There was a large collection of gourmet knives in the kitchen. I found one of them in the sink with the dirty dishes. It has what appears to be dried blood on it."

"Well then, bag it and tag it," Mason commanded.

Mason led Bruce and Phil outside to the front porch. "Mr. Overton, you can leave now. But, I will have to ask you to stay out of the house until my investigative team can finish checking it out. You'll have to stay somewhere else for a few days. But don't leave town."

"I'm certain my client will stay close by," Phil said. "In fact, you can stay with us if you wish, Bruce."

"No. Thanks for the offer, but, I'll stay with my mother." He sighed, struggling to hide his distress. "She's terribly upset over this anyway and I need to keep an eye on her. Her health's not too good these days."

Phil took a step closer to Bruce. "Why don't you come over to the house with me now? Kelley can fix us some lunch. We can call the hospital and see how Gary's doing."

They started to leave when Mason yelled out, "Oh, Mr. Overton, we'll let you know when we can release the house back to you. And, you might want to contact a cleaning service to clean it up."

Looking over his shoulder at the detective, Bruce's mouth twisted in annoyance and he muttered, "Yeah. Good idea."

Phil led Bruce into the kitchen where Kelley was preparing lunch. "Just put on a fresh pot of coffee Honey," she said.

"Have a seat Bruce. We'll call the hospital after lunch. It may be a long afternoon ."

"I want to go to the hospital, try to get in to see him,"

Bruce said in a weary voice.

"We understand, but right now, you need to keep up your strength so you can be Gary's support when he wakes," Kelley said, placing a plate of bacon, lettuce and tomato sandwiches on the table. "Phil, grab the bag of potato chips on the counter."

After they finished eating, Phil called the hospital. He learned that Gary was still in recovery and he couldn't have any visitors yet.

He told Bruce what he had heard and persuaded him to stay there for a while longer. Sitting in the living room having dessert and coffee, they heard a loud knock at the front door. Phil got up, walked over and opened it. Detective Mason pushed his way into the room.

"Mr. Overton, you're under arrest for the stabbing of your room mate, Gary Toth. My men found evidence that incriminated you at your home. And the District Attorney has advised us to bring you in for more questioning."

Mason read Bruce his rights, pulled his arms behind him and cuffed him, then looked at Phil. "You're welcome to follow us if you wish."

Bruce stared at him in bewilderment and his eyes widened with fear. "I'm innocent. I would never hurt Gary."

Phil tried to comfort him. "Don't worry. I'll accompany you to jail; and, as your attorney, will be with you every step of the way. We'll find out who hurt Gary. I promise."

After Bruce left with Detective Mason, Phil walked over to Kelley and put his arms around her. "Don't worry Honey. Somehow, we'll help Gary and Bruce get through this. Right now, I'm going to head over to stay with Bruce. Why don't you drive back to my folk's house and see how the kids are doing. Tell them we'll give them a call on Monday."

"Okay. Sure you don't want me to come with you?"

"I think that it's best I handle this alone. Why don't you stop over at Mrs. Blake's house across the street? She usually seems to know what's going on in the neighborhood. Maybe she saw or heard something going on. Try to sound like you're just a concerned neighbor, see if she can give you any information."

"I'll do my best Honey." She took the dishes to the kitchen, rinsed them and stacked them in the dishwasher. After grabbing her coat, she headed out the front door.

Before he left , Phil made a phone call to a friend who was a criminal attorney and asked her for advice about Bruce. Phil arrived at police headquarters and discovered that Bruce was already seated in an interrogation room with Mason and Purcell. They looked up when Phil entered. "Now, that your attorney is present," Mason said, "we can begin."

Both of the men were questioning Bruce relentlessly, trying to get him to admit that he had stabbed Gary.

After the detectives grilled Bruce over and over, he finally broke down crying. "I didn't hurt Gary and I don't know who did it. Everyone loves him. It must have been the thief. You saw my coin collection was missing."

The detectives continued to question Bruce until Phil interrupted the conversation. "Bruce, I don't think you should answer any more of the detective's questions, until we have consulted a criminal lawyer. I contacted a friend of mine, Michelle Bain. She said she would be glad to represent you if necessary."

Mason jumped to his feet. "Okay. Okay. You're free to leave now Mr. Overton. Just be sure to be here Tuesday morning with your attorney for the arraignment. Don't go back to the crime scene. And don't leave town."

"I'll personally vouch for Mr. Overton," Phil said.

Still shaking, Bruce stood up and shook his head helplessly. "I'll stay with my mother until I can go back into the house. I have a razor, toothbrush and clothes over there. So I'm all set for a few days."

"Give us the address and the phone numbers where you can be reached," Purcell added.

Bruce gave the requested information, then Phil led him out of the interrogation room. "I'm not as tough as Gary is," Bruce said. "When Mom was sick I took care of her, but this is something else. Look, I'm still shaking."

"Well, this has been quite a morning."

"Please Phil; help me get through this thing."

"Kelley and I will be with you all the way. Don't worry. Just keep your cell phone charged so the police can reach you. That way they won't have to look for you."

After Bruce left the police department, Phil went back into the room to talk to the detectives.

Mason, who was sitting at the table, looked up. His tone of voice worried Phil; it was serious—very serious and rough. "What can I do for you now, Mr. Willis?"

"Just wanted to go over a few details with you." Phil said calmly.

"What's that Sir?"

"I've been neighbors with Gary and Bruce for several years and I want you to get a clear picture of just who these two men are. I feel fairly confident that Bruce had nothing to do with Gary's stabbing."

"Be that as it may Sir. We have to check out the men's activities for the last few days. And I need to tell you that the things that my men uncovered in the house led us to believe that Bruce may very well be guilty of the assault. That man in the hospital is in grave condition and we need to make sure that whoever is responsible for that, suffers the consequences of his or her action."

"I realize that Sir. And rest assured, I'll do all I can to help you achieve that goal."

Chapter 4

When Phil returned home, he found Kelley standing in the driveway looking over at Gary and Bruce's house. A couple of police officers were exiting the house with several paper bags in hand. Across the street, several television trucks were parked and a small crowd had gathered.

"The police have been over there for quite a while. Looks like they're getting ready to wrap it up now," Kelley said, as Phil got out of his car.

He put his arm around her and led her into the house. "Hasn't been the weekend that we planned, has it?"

She smiled up at him. "No. Have you heard anything more about Gary?"

"The last the police heard was that he was in intensive care and in critical condition."

"And what about Bruce?"

"The police decided not to hold him. He has to be in court at nine on Tuesday morning for the arraignment."

"Are you going to represent him?'

"Maybe." He grimaced. "I suggested that we contact Michelle Bain, who specializes in cases like this. But, so far, he hasn't asked for her. Right now, he's sitting tight at his mother's house. He can't get in to see Gary, so he's just going to check in with the hospital from time to time."

Kelley and Phil spent a restless night that evening. Neither could get much sleep as their minds kept reliving the events of the previous day. They spent the morning doing simple chores around the house, taking time to call the hospital occasionally, only to learn that Gary was still unconscious. Phil called Bruce several times trying to reassure him that Gary would be okay.

A Monday morning article in the local newspaper had featured Kelley and him as a new Syracuse powerhouse couple. They made an attractive pair and had no secrets in their closet.

Phil was now focused on finding who had attacked their neighbor, and why.

By two that afternoon, Phil had gathered all he knew about Gary and Bruce, as well as the information he knew about the stabbing. Kelley had talked with their neighbor about what she had witnessed, which apparently was nothing. "I told everything I know about those two sweet men to that nasty detective," Mrs. Blake said.

As he prepared to leave the office, Phil walked out to Mandy's desk. "Did you close out the last two cases we were working on?"

"Yes. I just mailed the clients their final bills."

"You know, you remind me of Radar from the old Mash Shows. Before I can ask you to do something, you've already completed it."

"Oh, I almost forgot to tell you, the real estate lady called again."

"I'll tell Mrs. Willis to give her a call."

She looked up from her computer, "Not happy in your neighborhood now?"

"No. Just looking for a place outside the city. Maybe a couple of acres for the kids. They want to get a dog too."

"Sounds neat." She smiled and returned to her work.

"After you're finished with what you're working on now, take the rest of the afternoon off, Mandy."

"Thanks."

Phil walked out to his car and called Kelley on his cell phone. "Hi Honey. The real estate lady called, so you might want to give her a call back. I'm leaving the office now. Heading to Herman's Bar to see if I can find out anything more about Gary. And don't worry about supper tonight. I'll pick up something for us. Just feed the kids after you get them home from day care."

"Okay. It sure was nice of your folks to keep them overnight and take them to day care this morning," Kelley replied.

Though Phil had spent most of his life in Syracuse and had witnessed the gradual decline of its south side, he was still shocked to see row after row of deserted buildings lining the streets on the way to Herman's Bar. It was tucked back on one of the narrow side streets and was nestled between a peep show and a small un-paved parking lot.

Parking his car, Phil noticed a 'For Sale' sign on the furniture store across the street. He wondered if this section of town could ever recover from the recent economic downturn. He put his head down in the slight drizzle that had begun to fall and hustled into Herman's Bar.

The establishment was nothing but a smoky, dimly lighted tavern with an old wooden bar placed in front of mirrors that appeared to have not been cleaned in years. Phil took a seat at the bar and glanced at his watch. Too early for the after work crowd. Seated nearby were a couple of middle-aged men who were dressed in faded blue jeans and dirty work boots. This appeared to be the hangout for local unemployed and for those few who were still seeking work.

Calling over to the bartender, who was standing at

the far end, Phil said, "A beer please."

"Sure. Tap okay pal? Two fifty. Otherwise it's three bucks."

"Tap's good."

The bartender wiped a cloudy glass on his apron, poured a beer from the spigot, grabbed a paper napkin and placed both on the bar in front of Phil. "I'm Leroy Coats. Don't remember seeing you in here before." He stared at Phil, who was dressed in a well tailored business suit.

Phil reached into his pocket, drew out a five dollar bill and threw it down. "Haven't been in here before. Gary Toth works here, right?"

"Sure. Weekend guy." He glared at Phil. "You're not a cop are you?"

"I'm Gary's next door neighbor."

"Too bad about him being stabbed. Paper seems to think his roommate did it."

Phil leaned forward. "Could I ask you a few questions about Gary?"

"Haven't got much time." Leroy wiped the bar down with a dirty rag, "Don't know too much about his personal life anyway."

Phil took a quick swig of his beer. "Do you know of anyone who might have had it in for him?"

"The guy is a bartender. We get nuts in here all the time, arguing with us. If you want to know more about Gary, ask Suny Chow, the Chinese guy in the kitchen. Gary liked to gamble on the ponies and Suny and his uncle used to place bets for him."

"Thanks. Maybe I can talk to him?"

"He's not on today. Say, what did you say your name was?"

"Willis. Phil Willis."

"Okay Willis. I see my other customers need some attention. You want something to eat?" He threw the menu at Phil and walked to the other end of the bar.

Phil nursed his beer along, picked up the menu and glanced through it. Out of the corner of his eye, he saw a large burly looking man in a black leather jacket slip onto the bar stool beside him. "Care if I join you pal?"

"Sure why not." Phil studied the menu. "What's good here?"

"Get the grouper sandwich. It's the best."

"I might take a couple of them home. I promised my wife I'd bring supper." He waved the bartender over and ordered a couple of sandwiches to go.

After the bartender walked into the kitchen, the burly looking man leaned over and looked closely at Phil. "Somehow, I got the feeling that you aren't here to grab a beer and order a couple of sandwiches."

"What makes you think that?"

"Heard you asking about Gary." The man extended his hand. "I'm Benny Lotts. And you are a friend of Gary's?"

"Gary's my next door neighbor. The name is Phil Willis." He shook Benny's hand.

"Gary's a good guy. Known him for years."

"That so?"

"Yup. Also I've lived in this end of town all my life. Know just about everything that goes on around here. What about you. You a cop? Or a lawyer?"

"A lawyer," Phil answered.

Benny's cell phone rang. "Excuse me." He swiveled around on the bar stool and turned his back to Phil.

"That's a bummer. Now its murder," Benny said as he switched his phone off.

He turned back to Phil. "Just one of my contacts. Said he heard from a source at the hospital that Toth just died."

Momentarily unable to comprehend what he had just heard, Phil just sat there, numb and in shock.

"Okay Willis. You said you're a lawyer. Whose lawyer?"

"Right now, I'm representing Gary's roommate, Bruce Overton."

"Yeah. I know Overton too. He comes in here when Gary works. Seems like a nice enough guy. Sounds like he's in a shit load of trouble right now. Likely to be up for Gary's murder according to the paper."

"You know both of them then?"

"Knew Gary better. Was well liked around here. I'm a former police officer. Got contacts everywhere,"

Benny Lotts had been on the Syracuse police force for years, until he was forced to take early retirement after being involved in a scandal regarding missing evidence—namely drugs. Now he was about fifty pounds heavier than when he had been active on the force. Also had a heavy gray beard and wore dark tinted glasses. He looked nothing like the dashing police officer he had been when he was on the force.

Benny thought for a few minutes. "Say, if you're representing Overton, you might want to hire me to help you. I work free lance as a P.I. now. Maybe, I can help you find out who murdered Gary."

Taken off guard by this suggestion, Phil thought for a few minutes before replying. "Sounds good. I think Bruce will need all the help he can get."

"Okay. We'll talk about a retainer later. Right now, you're looking for someone, other than Overton, who might have wanted to do Gary in. Right?"

Phil's response was curt and sharp. "Right."

"Okay. Overton will probably be brought in on murder charges. Retain me for a week. I'll find you the person who really killed Gary."

"How much do you charge?" Phil waved at the bartender to bring over a couple more beers.

"Hundred a day, plus expenses. In five days, I should be able to find the killer. I'm that good," Benny bragged.

Phil didn't flinch. "I guess I can put that much up for Bruce."

"It's a deal then. One week. Give me the address of your office and I'll meet you there tomorrow morning. I get five days upfront. Bill you for my expenses later. Trust me; you'll get your money's worth, in spades."

"Okay Lotts, it's a deal. But clean up a bit before you go out and question any of my neighbors."

Phil reached into his pocket, pulled out a business card and handed it to Benny. A small Chinese man walked up to them and handed Phil a big brown bag. "I assistant cook. Boss says man wants two grouper sandwiches to go. You pay bartender."

Phil took the bag from him and watched him scurry back to the kitchen.

"If you're going to work for me Lotts, you might want to start by questioning the cook, Suny Choy," Phil said. "The bartender mentioned that his uncle placed bets on the ponies for Gary."

"I know that," Benny grinned. "Handles mine too. Don't worry; I'll interview everyone who ever talked to Gary. I'm very thorough."

They stood up and shook hands, and Phil's phone rang. "Phil, its Bruce. The cops are here at mother's house. They told me Gary died and I've been charged with his murder. I really need you now."

Chapter 5

The next morning Phil walked into the office and greeted Mandy, who had a cup of coffee waiting for him. "Anything special on the calendar this morning Mr. Willis?"

He sighed with exasperation. "Yes. My neighbor, Bruce Overton, was arrested yesterday for murder and I'm going to handle the case."

"Oh my gosh. I read about the stabbing in this morning's paper. But I didn't realize that those men lived next door to you. Did you know them well?"

"Yes. We've been neighbors for several years. Yesterday I started a file on the case. Now, I want you to set up a section for the billing hours. I went into the police department late yesterday afternoon and arranged for bail for Bruce. Let's try to clear up some of my other pending cases as quickly as we can. I'm certain that Bruce is innocent of Gary's murder, but I need to focus as much of my attention as I can on proving it."

"I'm certain that you'll work your magic." Mandy smiled at him with confidence

"I hope so. Bruce's mother is really upset over her son being charged with his best friend's murder. And this also complicates matters for Kelley and me. We're planning to put our house on the market. This murder won't help our resale value. In fact, I expect to get another call from our real estate agent. She'll probably panic when she learns what happened."

He walked toward his office door, stopped and turned around. "Oh by the way, Mandy. I hired a private investigator by the name of Benny Lotts to look into the murder. Set up a file for his billing."

"Got it Sir." She whipped around in her chair and turned on her computer.

Phil went into his office, threw his briefcase on the desk and sat back in his chair, mulling over the upcoming case.

Shaking his head, he glanced at his watch and decided to make a quick call to Kelley.

"I took the kids to day care," she said. "I think Ashley's cold is a lot better. I gave her a couple of baby aspirin."

"What about the real estate lady? Did you hear from her? I expected her to call one of us the minute she saw this morning's paper. If she calls, tell her not to put a 'For Sale' sign up in our yard just yet. Let's wait and see what happens." Phil put his feet up on his desk as he talked.

"No she didn't call. You know, something bothers me about Bruce and Gary and I just can't put my finger on it. I'm going over to Bruce's mother's house this morning and talk to her. See if I can discover anything."

"Okay. But just play it cool Kelley. Don't upset the old lady anymore."

"Well, so far, the only suspect the police are centering on is Bruce. Maybe I can find out something that will help him."

"Okay. But be discreet." He shifted to a more comfortable position in the chair. "And let's plan on eating out tonight with the kids."

"Great idea. Love you Mr. Willis."

"And I love you even more, Mrs. Willis."

Shortly after he hung up the phone, Mandy buzzed him. "Benny Lotts is here to see you."

Phil placed his feet on the floor and sat upright in his chair. "Thanks. Send him in."

After a brief knock on the door, a clean shaven Benny walked in. He was dressed neatly in navy blue slacks with an open necked, light blue polo shirt.

Phil looked him over briefly. "Say, you really clean up nice." He reached into the desk drawer and pulled out a couple sheets of paper. "I've got your contract ready for you to sign and your five hundred dollar retainer check." He pushed the papers toward Benny.

Benny kicked a chair aside and plopped down in it. After looking briefly at the contract, he signed it, picked up the check, folded it and put it in his shirt pocket. "Guess you were pretty confident I would show."

Phil's eyes widened. "As a matter of fact, I was counting on you. "

"Glad you said that Boss. By the way, that's one pretty secretary that you've got out there. Does she have a special someone?"

"Not that I know of," Phil replied. "But tread carefully." His voice held a stern warning. "She's been around the track a couple of times, but I don't think that she's quite ready for someone as fast as you."

"I'm a nice guy, once you get to know me." Benny sat back and grinned. "Now for business. I think I've got a hot lead on our case. I should be able to hand over Gary Toth's killer to you in a day or two."

Phil looked at him, his eyebrows raised in question. "So you believe Bruce is innocent?"

"Seems like it. I heard that the police charged him with murder but you got him out on bail."

"That's right."

"Well, you'll soon discover I earn my fee. By the way, I'll keep track of my expenses each day and we can settle up at the end of the week." Benny stood up and kicked the chair back under the lip of the desk. "I'll keep in contact."

He strolled out of Phil's office and stopped at Mandy's desk. "You'll be seeing a lot of me in the future, Sweetie."

She narrowed her eyes at him and said nothing. "What a creep," she muttered as he opened the door and walked out.

After his brief talk with Benny, Phil turned his attention on a couple of pending cases. About an hour later, he decided to call Michelle Bain, who was a partner at his old law firm. She had second chaired about half a dozen murder cases and was proficient in that field of law. He knew that preparing to defend Bruce for murder would take him into a direction that he was not accustomed to. He could use all the help that he could get.

He placed a call to her private number. She did not pick up the phone and he was forwarded to her voice mail. "Michelle, its Phil Willis. I need your expert help. I talked to you briefly before about my neighbor, Bruce Overton. Well, I'm about to undertake defending him. He's been accused of murdering his roommate and partner. Give me a call as soon as possible."

He was deeply engrossed in one of his case files, when the phone rang several times. Realizing that Mandy was out for lunch, he picked up the call.

"Hey, Willis. It's Benny. I've been busy working on your murder case. Got a lot to tell you. I'll meet you tomorrow and explain everything."

Before Phil could respond, Benny hung up.

"He sure works fast." Phil shrugged his shoulders, and then returned to his paperwork. The next hour or so passed by quickly and when the phone rang again Mandy answered it. She buzzed him and said that Michelle Bain was on the line.

"Hi Michelle. Thanks for calling me back."

"So you're actually defending Bruce Overton. I read about the murder. You might have quite a challenge on your hands. But I'll be more than glad to help you in any way I can."

Phil spent several minutes giving Michelle a run down on what he was about to face. He knew that if anyone could offer him some assistance it would be her. She came from a long line of attorneys. Her mother and father were both tax lawyers in New York and her grandfather was a judge in Massachusetts. Michelle had risen quickly in the law field and was now recognized as one of the top attorneys in the state. She had tutored Phil with the state bar exam and had worked diligently to help him rise to a partnership at Tanner, Tanner, Jacobs and Willis.

After Phil explained his case to her, Michelle said in a teasing voice, "You know Willis; I still have a small crush on you. I was devastated when you got married."

"Thanks. I hope you've forgiven me by now."

She laughed. "You're still one of my best friends. Why don't we meet soon and go over your case together. I'll try to help you prove your client innocent."

"He is innocent."

"Keep on thinking that Phil. You'll need a positive attitude. By the way, how are the wife and kiddies?"

"They're fine. And how are you doing? Still single?"

"Of course. But, I do have a new love. Got to go now, Phil. Call me when you're ready to go over the Toth murder in depth."

Wednesday afternoon Kelley burst into Phil's office and found him talking on the phone.

"Hey, where's Mandy?"

He put his hand over the phone. "Late lunch." He motioned for Kelley to have a seat across from him.

Kelley waved her hand at him to stop the phone conversation. "Boy. Have I got news for you."

Phil hung up the phone and grinned. "Me first."

They giggled as Kelley stood up, reached across the desk and gave him a hug.

"You can't believe what happened," Phil said as he gave her a quick kiss. "That was Detective Mason on the phone. It seems that Benny discovered Gary's murderer and informed the police. They already arrested him."

That statement brought Kelley up short and she stared at him. "No kidding. Boy, was that Benny guy ever quick. Who was it?"

"It was Jung Soo, the uncle of the cook at Herman's Bar. He just admitted that he did it and signed a confession, Mason said."

Kelley threw up her hands, "Whoa. Something doesn't sound right."

Phil's phone rang, he picked up and listened for a few minutes. Then he put his hand over the speaker, turned toward Kelley and said, "It's Benny Lotts."

He took his hand off the phone and continued talking to Benny. "I know. Detective Mason called me. Good work. I'm totally amazed that you discovered the real killer so quickly. You really earned your five hundred bucks. Come into the office tomorrow. We'll settle up your expenses. And, I want a full report."

Kelley sat on the edge of her seat as Phil hung up the phone. "Tell me everything," she said with a doubtful look on her face. "How did this Benny character find the real killer so quickly?"

Before Phil could answer, the phone rang again. He waved his hand at Kelley, "Hold on a minute Honey and I'll explain everything to you."

He picked up the phone, listened for a moment and whispered to Kelley. "It's Bruce."

"Yeah, Bruce I can't believe it. I just talked with Detective Mason. He said my private eye discovered who really committed the murder. Said that he hauled this Soo guy into the police headquarters and Soo confessed. I'm on my way to the police station to make sure everything is cleared up."

"Thank you."

Phil hung up the phone, sat back in his chair and grinned at Kelley. "How about we grab some early supper after I take care of Bruce's affairs? Why don't you pick up the kids from day care? I shouldn't be long. Meet me at Norton's for a pizza. I've suddenly got an appetite. Oh, and I'm sorry, you said that you had some news for me?"

He could see that she was frowning, not smiling as he expected. "What's wrong Kell?"

"I hope you don't mind Phil. But, I think that I'm about to burst your bubble."

He got up, came around the desk and draped his arm around her shoulders. "I doubt if anything you could say right now would spoil this moment for me. But what is it?"

"Maybe, you better sit down again my Dear. I've got a headline for you. I think that Bruce did murder Gary, or had him killed."

"No way girl. Detective Mason said that they had the real killer. Case closed."

"Will you at least listen to me Phil?"

He sighed and sat down in the chair beside her. He looked at her with a slight feeling of unease creeping through him.

Kelley started to talk, when Mandy stuck her head in the door. "Hi. I'm back." Noticing Kelley, she added, "Good to see you Mrs. Willis."

"Same here," Kelley replied.

Mandy took a step inside the doorway. "I just wanted to remind you that I'll be here for about an hour yet, Mr. Willis. Then, I'm leaving early. I've got to get that wisdom tooth pulled."

"Sure. And take tomorrow morning off if you need to."

"Thanks."

He looked at Kelley. "Can your news wait until we get to the restaurant? We can talk things over quietly then."

Kelley looked perturbed. "Sure. You take care of business and I'll pick up the kids. We'll talk later."

Chapter 6

Kelley picked up Ashley and Alan from day care and headed over to Norton's, a small, homey neighborhood diner a couple of blocks from Phil's office. They sat down on a bench near the door and waited for him to arrive.

When he entered the restaurant, the owner escorted them to a quiet booth in the back of the room.

Their favorite waiter recognized them. "Hi there, Mr. and Mrs. Willis. Good to see you and the kids again." He placed crayons and coloring pages down on the table in front of the children. "What'll you have tonight Sir?"

"A couple of seven up's for the kids and iced teas for me and the missus. Two house salads with blue cheese dressing and an extra large pepperoni pizza with loads of cheese."

The waiter returned shortly with the drinks. When he left again, Phil leaned back in his seat and cocked a stern eyebrow at Kelley, "Okay, the kids are content for a while. So spill it. Tell me what's going on."

"Well, this morning after you left for the office, I sat down, had a second cup of coffee and thought about what happened. Finally, I decided to head over to see how Bruce's mother was doing. That sweet old lady was terribly upset. I thought I could reassure her that you were on top of the case and that everything would turn out okay for Bruce. Any way, when I got there she was full of questions and I gave her what I felt were reassuring answers."

"Excellent," Phil answered as their food arrived at the table. He picked up his fork and started to eat his salad. Stopping between bites, he waved his fork at her. "Go on."

"She said she was very worried about Bruce's mental state after losing Gary, so she talked him into staying with her for a few weeks." She leaned over and put a slice of pizza on each of the children's plates.

"Anything else?"

"Now, I'm coming to the interesting part. After we talked for a while she asked me to go into the spare room where Bruce stays and take down some boxes from a closet. She was cleaning out her things so that he could store more of his clothes, but she couldn't reach the boxes on the top shelf."

"So?" Phil finished his salad, picked up a slice of pizza and put in on Kelley's plate and grabbed a piece for himself.

"And, one was an old shoe box. It had some of her outdated tax records in it, and she decided to throw them out. I told her that we should look through everything carefully first and make sure that she didn't need to hold onto some of them." Kelley leaned over and wiped a piece of cheese from Ashley's mouth. She thought it was fortunate that the kids were busy eating—they didn't have time to interrupt their parent's conversation.

Phil stopped eating and looked at her. "I assume that you found something of great importance or else I wouldn't be listening to this story."

"Yes—there's more. Under all her old tax records was a pouch with an insurance policy in it. It was policy taken out over a year ago on Gary with Bruce as the beneficiary. It was for a million dollars."

Phil sat straight up. "Now that's really interesting."

"I thought so too. But, I didn't bring it to Mrs. Overton's attention. Just told her that it might be best to save everything in case she got audited. So we put the papers back in the box and returned it to the top shelf in the closet."

"That was wise. So you rushed over to tell me? Right?"

"No..." Her voice trailed off. "Something that you mentioned about your visit to Herman's Bar yesterday sounded suspicious to me, so I decided to go there next. But don't worry, I didn't give the bartender my real name. I told him I heard they were looking for a weekend bartender."

Phil responded with a teasing grin. "I should have known that you'd decide to play detective in this case."

"Just hear me out," she snapped back.

"Okay." He waved his hand for the waiter to refill their drinks. Then nodded to Kelley. "Go on."

"Well, anyway the bartender said the owner wouldn't be in for a couple of days, but he knew that they needed some help in the kitchen since the cook quit. I told him I didn't think I'd be interested in that position."

"So?"

"So anyway, while I was there, some guy sitting in the back of the room, yelled for three beers. The bartender said, 'It's that asshole, Benny Lotts again. He's in here all the time'."

Sitting back, Phil urged, "Continue." He took the empty plates from in front of the kids and piled them in the middle of the table.

Kelley reached down and picked up the coloring papers and crayons from the bench beside her and returned them to the children. She wanted to keep them occupied so she could finish telling her story without them interrupting constantly.

"I recognized Benny Lotts name, so when the bartender poured three beers and asked me to take them over to him, I did."

"Of course you did."

Kelley leaned forward and narrowed her eyes. "Now let me finish. When I approached the table I saw your pal, Benny, pass an envelope to each of the two men with him."

Phil sat upright, now extremely interested in her story. "What did these men look like?"

"One fellow was a short, middle aged, oriental man. The other was a skinny young guy wearing a Greek hat. The young guy looked inside the envelope and said, 'You've got to be shitting me. I thought we had a deal Lotts.' I put the three beers down on the table and started to walk away."

Phil's head was now spinning. "Then what happened?"

"Of course, I took my time going back to the bar so I could see and hear them. Peering over my shoulder, I saw Lotts reach into his pocket and pull out a wad of cash. He slammed it on the table and said, 'Here's an extra two hundred.' I walked back over and sat down at the bar. Both of the men drank down their beers, talked with Benny for a while, then jumped up and left."

"And then?"

"When I saw that Benny had finished his beer I walked over to him and introduced myself."

Phil looked at her warily. "You told him you were Kelley Willis?"

Kelley took a moment to praise Ashley's coloring before she continued, "No, I gave him a phony name too. Then I asked him if a lady could buy him a beer."

"And?"

"And, he asked, 'Why would you want to buy me a beer, pretty lady?' I told him I needed a favor and put the job application I had gotten from the bartender in front of him. Told him that I just blew in from Philly and needed a reference on the application. He wanted to know if I was applying for the cook's job and I told him no—the weekend bartender. He laughed and said that the chink in the kitchen was quitting and going back to China. Said that the chink's uncle was in jail."

"Very interesting." Phil was now intrigued with the story. "Mason said that a Chinese man by the name of Jung Soo confessed to Gary's murder. So Benny agreed to be a reference for you?"

Kelley sat back and grinned. "Well, it wasn't quite that easy. I had to turn on the old Irish charm. Gave him a short history about me. Told him I was single and used to work in a couple of bars in Philly. Moved here to be with my boyfriend. But we broke up and I'm into the dating scene once again."

Phil eyed her with curiosity. "And he bought that story?"

"Of course. He started opening up to me about his business. Told me that he was going to come into some big bucks in the near future and had booked a cruise in a couple of weeks. He even invited me to join him. He said, 'Hell, we could even share a cabin'."

Phil shook his head in amazement. "I guess you wouldn't be single long if we separated."

"Benny gave me his business card and wrote his home address on the back of it. Told me to stop by. And said if I needed a place to crash he would be glad to accommodate me."

"I can't believe that my private investigator was hitting on my wife," Phil responded stiffly. "What happened to your wedding band?"

Kelley laughed harshly. "Never wear it when I go undercover. After he said something about us making a good team he got up and left. I gave the bartender my application and told him I'd call in a day or two about the job. He seemed to care less one way or the other."

Suddenly, Ashley tugged on Kelley's sleeve. "I have to go to the bathroom, Mommy."

Kelley sighed, "Nature calls. Be right back."

A short while later they returned from the ladies room and slipped back into the booth. Phil looked at Kelley and grinned. "Sounds like you were a busy little lady today. All this is very interesting. Makes me wonder just who Benny is working for."

"Yes. Just think, if somebody else is convicted in Gary's murder, Bruce possibly could collect on the double indemnity clause on the insurance policy."

Phil's head was now spinning and his eyes widened. "Are you saying that you think that Benny and this Chinese guy are somehow involved in Gary's murder?"

"That's what I'm starting to suspect. What if Bruce conspired with Benny somehow? What if they setup up the Chinese uncle to do the murder or take the rap for it? Then Bruce could collect the insurance and split it with Benny."

"And Lotts is planning on coming into big bucks, he said. Certainly not from helping me with this case," Phil mused. "Well, young lady you've certainly caused a lot of questions to enter my mind. I thought when I paid Benny for his expenses and collected my fees from Bruce, this case would be over. But now, I'm starting to rethink the whole situation."

"Me too," Kelley sighed dramatically. "I'm starting to wonder if Bruce really is responsible. Maybe he did it or he hired someone."

"Perhaps you're right."

He looked over at both of the children, who were now bored with the coloring and were starting to fidget in their seats. "Right now, I think we need to get these two sleepy heads home and put them to bed. Then, first thing in the morning, we'll go visit Mason. Have to tell him about the insurance policy. It certainly would be a great motive for

Bruce to want Gary dead."

Kelley nodded. "And after that, we'll just step back and see what plays out."

"That's exactly what we do Mrs. Willis. No more undercover work for you. And you've got to stay clear of Benny Lotts. Promise?"

"Yes, Dear."

"Now, let's head for home. You need a good night's rest after all this detective work."

"Oh, I didn't tell you what I found in the pawn shop."

"Pawn shop?"

"Let's first get home and put the kids to bed. It's a long story and I'll tell you later."

Chapter 7

Kelley and Phil got home, bathed the kids and put them to bed. Then they sat down on the sofa in the family room with glasses of wine in front of them. Phil looked impatiently at Kelley, "Now tell me about the pawn shop."

"I watched Benny through the window of the bar after he left. He opened the back door of his car and took out two boxes. Then he walked across the street to the pawn shop. When he came out, he was empty handed."

"And you, of course, had to go over and check out the pawn shop."

Kelley's chin shot up an inch. "Well, I did walk casually over to the pawn shop and took a quick look around."

"I knew it. And what did you uncover there?"

"Well, this is the kicker. I asked the owner if he had gotten anything new in lately and he said 'no'. Then I pointed to the boxes sitting on top of the counter and asked what was in there. 'Oh yeah, just got this stuff in.'

He opened one box and pulled out some jewelry. One of the items was a small jewel encrusted brooch in the shape of a butterfly. I recognized it. It belonged to Bruce's mother. I saw her wearing it several times and remarked how lovely it was. She even let me try it on. So, I'm positive it was hers," she smiled confidently and continued, "The pawn shop guy offered to sell it to me for three hundred bucks. I said that I would pass on that."

Phil sat back in his seat as a stunned look entered his eyes. "Why would Benny Lotts have something that belonged to the Overton's?"

"That's a good question. Finally, I asked what was in the second box. He pulled out a nice eight piece set of steak knives with ivory handles. But, it had one knife missing. When I asked him how much, he said seventy five dollars. I told him that I would probably buy it if all the knives were there."

Puzzled, Phil looked at Kelley, "And why are you interested in a set of steak knives with one missing?"

She smiled smugly, "Because I think I recognized the knives. Remember when we hosted that neighborhood cookout last year? We needed some extra steak knives, so Gary went home and got a set of his. I'm pretty sure that those ivory handled steak knives belonged to him."

"All this is extremely interesting. I can't wait to tell it to Mason," Phil said. "Now, let's head up to bed. It's been a long day for both of us."

Early the next morning, as the sun was coming up, Kelley and Phil rose from bed, showered and dressed.

After each downed a latte and a muffin, Phil glanced at his watch and decided to call the police department. A pre-recorded voice announced the different options available. He pressed button "8" to get the operator. "This is Phil Willis, please put me through to Detective Mason."

A long pause, then a voice answered, "Mason here."

"Phil Willis. I've got to see you at once about the Toth murder."

"Hold on Willis. Your client Overton was released. We've got Gary Toth's killer. Jung Soo is ready to face the judge this morning. Or, are you going to represent this Soo guy?"

"No. You see Detective, I think you've got the wrong person."

"What the hell are you talking about Willis?"

"I'll explain it all to you when I get there. See you in about twenty minutes. Will you wait for me?"

"Sure. But it'll cost you a Starbucks coffee and two sweet rolls. Bring them with you when you come."

"Will your partner be there?"

"Yeah."

"In that case, I'll bring two coffees, and four sweet rolls."

"Don't rush Willis. The guy we got in custody ain't going nowhere."

Kelley and Phil walked into the station and were directed to the office where the detectives were waiting.

Phil knocked on the door and a voice yelled out, "Come in." Seated behind a desk was Detective Purcell.

"Where's Mason," Phil asked.

"Rest room. Back in a minute," Purcell answered as he stood up and greeted Kelley. "Nice to see you again, Mrs. Willis. Have a seat."

Phil placed the Starbucks bag down on the desk and he and Kelley sat down as Detective Mason entered the room. "Great. You remembered the coffee and rolls."

He opened the bag, pulled out the coffees and handed one to Purcell. Then he unwrapped the sweet rolls, threw one at his partner, opened his and started to wolf it down. "Very good. Thanks Willis. Now tell us what gives? What's your news about the Toth murder?"

Purcell took big swig of his coffee. "Yeah. It's solved. Suny Chow turned in his uncle, Jung Soo for the murder. Jung Soo signed a confession, but said it was self defense. Said Toth owed him a gambling debt."

Phil threw up his hand and rolled his eyes. "That's what we're here to talk to you about. My wife did some undercover investigating and discovered new evidence."

The two detectives eyed Kelley with curiosity. "Okay lady. You're on," Mason said.

Kelley cleared her throat. She knew what she was about to say would startle the detectives. "Yesterday, I went to see Bruce Overton's mother. She's a sweetheart and has become a good friend."

Purcell waved his hand at her impatiently, "We get the picture. Get on with it."

Kelley sat up straight in her chair and gave him a withering look. "Well. She said that Bruce spends a lot of time at her house. Going to move in with her for a while. His house is a mess you know."

Detective Mason nodded his head. "We know. We helped cause part of the mess looking for evidence. Please continue Mrs. Willis."

"Well. Mrs. Overton said that her Bruce wouldn't hurt a fly. Said he was going to help her find a nice retirement home because he didn't want her living alone and had her sign a lot of papers. She said her head was spinning at the time and she didn't know what she was signing. She said she also gave him power of attorney so he could take care of her business. Said she was getting so forgetful. Always losing things."

"Exactly where's all this leading, Mrs. Willis?" Detective Mason asked with frustration starting to creep into his voice.

Kelley glared at him, took a deep breath and continued. "I'm getting to the main point Detective. Finally, she asked me to help her clean out a closet in the spare bedroom so Bruce could store some of his things in there."

"And?"

"And on the bottom of a box in the closet, I found a life insurance policy. One on Gary Toth for a million dollars. And, Bruce Overton was the beneficiary. It also had a double indemnity clause, so he could possibly collect two million. Maybe he is responsible for Gary's death."

After a stunned moment when neither of the detectives moved, Purcell said, "That's a pretty drastic conclusion to come to Mrs. Willis."

"But you see Detective, Bruce never mentioned the policy when I discussed the case with him and we went over Gary's assets," Phil said.

"And it was hidden on the bottom of a bunch of Mrs. Overton's old tax records," Kelley added.

"That's certainly something to consider, but not enough to suspect Bruce of the murder at this time. Besides we have a written confession from Jung Soo," Mason said. "We don't want to cut you short, Mrs. Willis, but we do have a meeting this morning with the Chief."

"Oh, but my story doesn't end there," Kelley said nervously, sitting forward in her chair. "After I visited with Mrs. Overton, I headed over to Herman's Bar where Phil said that Gary used to work. Something about Gary's murder just didn't seem right to me."

Purcell grinned at Detective Mason. "Maybe we should have this lady on our payroll."

Mason nodded. "Go on please, Mrs. Willis. This is getting very interesting."

Kelley took another deep breath. "Here goes. Of course I didn't tell the bartender, Leroy, who I really was. I gave him a fake name and pretended I was looking for part time work as a bartender."

"Where's this going," Purcell asked.

"While I was filling out a job application, this guy in the back of the room yells out for a beer. Leroy tells me it's Benny Lotts and asks me to take the beers back to him and his two friends.

"So I did. Took my time of course so I could hear what he and the two fellows he was sitting with were talking about. Benny gave both of them envelopes with money in them. The younger guy started a fuss and

Benny threw a couple of hundred dollars more at him."

"Then, what happened?" Mason asked.

"After the two men got up and left, I went over to Benny's table and struck up a friendship with him. I gave him a fake story about applying for a job. Asked him to let me use him as a reference for it. He agreed. Over a beer, he even offered to let me stay with him."

"Sounds like you were heading into dangerous territory little lady," Purcell commented, narrowing his eyes.

"Don't worry. My wife can handle herself."

Mason looked amused and fought back a smile. "Is there more?"

Kelley nodded and continued, "Benny gave me his business card and put his home address and phone number on the back. I told him I might contact him. Then he said good-bye and left the bar."

"That's it then?" Mason asked.

"No. There's lots more." Kelley repeated the story that she had told Phil the night before about the pawn shop, the broach and the steak knives.

When she finished, Detective Mason jumped to his feet. "That sounds like the weapon that Toth was killed with. We didn't reveal to anyone that we recovered a steak knife from the bushes by the back door of the house."

He looked at the other detective and ordered, "Purcell, go to the property room and see if you can get that knife out of the evidence file."

Within a short time, Purcell was back in the room with a steak knife in a plastic bag marked 'Exhibit #15.' He placed it on the desk in front of Kelley. "Does this look like the set of knives you saw?"

She picked the bag up and turned it over, looking at the knife carefully. "I think that this matches the set I saw in the pawn shop. And, I'm almost positive that they belonged to Gary. When I remarked how lovely the ivory handles were, he pointed out that the handles had a lily pattern carved in them. Said that he had purchased the set in India years ago."

Phil's eyes widened. "You say you found this knife outside of Gary and Bruce's house?"

"Yes. And it had Gary's blood on it. No fingerprints though. Whoever used it, must have worn gloves," Purcell answered.

Mason looked as though lightening had just struck him. "Now, I'm starting to believe that Overton might be responsible. He certainly had a motive—the life insurance money. If he didn't do it himself, he might have hired someone to do it for him."

Purcell looked puzzled. "But, why did the Chinese fellow confess to the murder and what does Benny Lotts have to do with it all. And, how did he get the Overton lady's jewelry and the expensive knife set?"

Kelley leaned forward and calmly said, "Maybe Bruce hired Benny Lotts and the two of them paid the Chinese man to confess."

"Great detective work Mrs. Willis," Phil said proudly. "It's starting to sound like Bruce and Benny were in this together for the insurance money."

"And if Bruce was cold hearted enough to do away with Gary, he might decide to turn on his sweet old mother in the future," Kelley suggested.

Purcell looked at his watch. "Hey, remember Mason, we've got to meet with the Chief now."

Mason stood up. "Thanks for all your input Mrs. Willis. You can rest assured that we'll look into this further. After our meeting, we'll pick up Lotts and Overton and question them."

He turned to Purcell. "Let's see if we can get warrants. This case is now re-opened. We should question Jung Soo again. Let's press his hand. When we tell him that he's in line for murder and the chair, maybe he'll change his story."

Kelley and Phil stood up and turned to leave. Mason took Kelley's hands in his. "Good police work lady. I think your husband should put you on the payroll as his PI."

"And, here's a card from the pawn shop," Kelley said, handing it to him.

"Lady, you think of everything," Mason replied.

Leaving the police station, Phil said, "Let's stop by my office for a moment so I can check on a couple of cases. After that, I'll take you to lunch. But, I want you to know that I'm still a little angry with you, Kell. You really stuck your neck out on this one. Next time, let me know what you're up to."

"Yes Dear," she replied humbly, then smiled, "But the detective is right. Maybe you should put me on your staff."

"Right now you need to concentrate on just being Mrs. Willis and a mother to our children."

"Yeah. Well I wish I could be a fly on the wall when the detectives question Jung Soo," she responded sweetly, with a slight smile on her face. "I'll bet they'll crack him."

Chapter 8

The next few days saw a beehive of activity around police headquarters. Everyone was all abuzz with talk about the re-arrest of Bruce Overton and the arrest of Benny Lotts. The information Kelley had given Detectives Mason and Purcell, put them on a different track in the case.

They had also hauled in Jung Soo's nephew, Suny Chow. Suny was the suspected connection between Bruce and the 'confessed' murderer, Jung Soo.

The detectives believed the insurance policy taken out on Gary by Bruce, may have been the motive. After the new evidence had been presented to the district attorney, he decided to put Bruce on trial for orchestrating the murder. Jung Soo was indicted for actually committing the murder and Suny Chow and Benny Lotts were to be tried as accomplices.

After much questioning, Jung Soo admitted that he had received money from Benny to murder Gary. By confessing to the crime and agreeing to give evidence in Bruce's trial, Jung Soo, who was quite elderly, had reached a deal with the prosecution to spend the rest of his life in prison. Benny Lotts and Suny Chow also agreed to testify against Bruce in return for reduced sentences for their part in the conspiracy.

Bruce hired Michelle Bain to defend him and put his house up as collateral for his bail and legal fees. Benny hired a shyster lawyer he had used previously and public defenders were assigned to the two Chinese men.

In the following months, while the four men were awaiting trial, Kim Dashle, the Realtor had found a buyer for both the Willis' and Mrs. Overton's house. The court appointed a legal guardian for Mrs. Overton and she moved to an assisted living facility.

Kim had found a lovely Victorian house on an acre of land outside of Syracuse for Phil and Kelley. After some negotiating, it was theirs for a substantial reduction from the original asking price. Even though they had to take out a big mortgage on the property, Kelley thought that it was perfect for the family.

A fence surrounded the yard and was ideal for Alan and Ashley to play. With four bedrooms, three baths and a fireplace in the family room, Phil decided that it had ample room for his family. He planned to convert the fourth bedroom into a small home office. His computers and file cabinets would still allow room for a Murphy bed, to put up future guests.

As the Willis family prepared to move into the new home, the children once again pleaded for a dog. "Let's wait until after we make the move kids, then Daddy and I will think about getting a dog," Kelley answered their constant requests.

The next six months flew by. They moved into their new home; the children started at a new school and Kelley began working part time at the Syracuse Sentinel Newspaper. Her new job, writing the obituaries, developed from her previous experience at the Miami Herald years before. She dropped her volunteer work, deciding that the money she earned would be helpful with the educational funds for the kids.

Phil's case load started to increase. As the days went by, he started spending more and more time at the office. There was a rumor circulating around political circles that he might run for an office.

At the same time, the perfect love affair between Kelley and Phil Willis seemed to have hit a bump in the road. His five work days a week at the office, turned into six. And many a night, Kelley's knight in shining armor would return home around eleven in the evening. Then, he would spend the next hour sitting before the fireplace, with a drink in hand, and talking on the phone with clients.

Kelley would walk downstairs and plead, "Phil, please come to bed." She just wanted to feel his arms around her.

He would yell out in return, "Soon." But, he did not come upstairs and they grew further and further apart.

Phil was not pleased when his mother called him one day. "Kelley said that you're working long hours," she said in a reproachful tone of voice.

After this conversation, he screamed at Kelley. "Keep my parents out of my work ethics and our marriage." His eyes suddenly flared. "What do you want from me? You wanted this bigger house and I'm bringing in good money."

She stared at him, every nerve in her body raw and aching. "I just want a weekend alone. Just you and me." Tears started to fill her eyes.

"Okay then." For just a moment a shadow of remorse crossed his face. "Maybe a weekend in Atlantic City?"

But it never came to be and their love life rapidly disappeared.

Kelley had spent her afternoon preparing a special prime rib dinner for the family. Phil had promised to be home by five and the kids were excited as they helped her set the dining room table with the good china and linens.

Ashley got out the silver candlesticks and put them on the table. "Daddy promised to rent a good movie and bring it home for you tonight," Kelley said.

She could hardly wait for that evening. After the special dinner, she planned to make an important announcement to the family. Early that afternoon, she had visited her doctor, who confirmed her suspicions. She was, indeed, pregnant with the third Willis child.

She was not at all concerned that the doctor added that she would have to take it easy this time. "Plenty of rest, Mrs. Willis. Try to do some mild exercise, lots of walking, but no lifting. You did well with the birth of your first two, but you are not as young as you used to be."

She felt somewhat indignant at this statement, since she was only in her early thirties. "When can we tell the sex of the baby?"

"Another month, if the fetus is in the right position for us to see on the ultra sound."

"Well, I'm certain that my husband will want to be here when we do that."

"How did he feel when you told him that you thought you were expecting?"

"Haven't told him yet. I haven't had much morning sickness and he's been so busy with work lately that he didn't notice anything. I'm going to make a special dinner tonight and announce it to the whole family."

"Well, good luck to you. And I look forward to seeing you and your spouse in a month. Have the nurse schedule your appointment on the way out. Remember, try to take it a little easy this time," he cautioned gently.

Full of anticipation, Kelley left the doctor's office. She stopped to pick up Phil's shirts at the dry cleaners, made a quick trip to the meat market and picked the kids up from school. When they arrived home, she made a call to Phil's parents and asked them if they would like to join the family for dinner.

Kaitlin McLane said her husband, Dexter, had a bad cold and that they would make it another time. "Just prepare the meal for your family Dear. Light some candles and make it very special."

Kelley promised to call the next day to see how Dexter was. She did not want to tell her about the baby until after she told her Phil and children.

"Kiss the kids and your husband for us," Kaitlin said. "And tell Phil that he has been working too hard lately. We hardly ever get to see you and the kids anymore."

Chapter 9

Kelley planned for tonight to be extra special. Non-alcoholic wine before dinner would set the stage for the exceptional evening that she had planned: a prime rib dinner followed by her surprising announcement. She was confident that Phil would be delighted and the children thrilled to hear the news of a new baby

She glanced at her watch and realized it was time to dress the children in their Sunday best clothes. "Boy will Daddy be surprised to see us all dressed up for supper," Ashley cried out as she twirled around in her sequined blue dress.

"Tonight's supper is going to be really elegant. And I have a wonderful secret to tell Daddy and you."

Their eyes grew very wide.

"Can't you tell us now?" Alan asked.

"No. We have to wait for your Daddy," Kelley replied, smiling in anticipation.

Phil shut down his computer, picked up his briefcase and headed to the outer office where Mandy, was seated. "It's five-thirty. Let's call it a week."

Mandy paled a little. "Oh my gosh, I forgot to tell you we're scheduled to head for the local hangout. They're having a retirement party at 'The Final Verdict' for the Honorable Judge Walter Harrington."

"But I told Kelley I'd be home early tonight for dinner."

Mandy folded her hands across her chest and looked up at him with determination. "I accepted the invitation on your behalf already, you can't miss this opportunity to mingle with the in crowd if you want to be selected for a judgeship in the future. Just stay for a quick drink and then you can head home. The party has already started and the pubs within walking distance." Mandy took her purse out of her lower desk drawer and stood up.

Phil sighed, knowing that her reasoning made sense, but still he felt damn uneasy. After all, Kelley was expecting him home for dinner. He thought for a few moments, then shrugged his shoulders and said, "Okay, just one drink. And, we'll make it quick."

When they arrived at the party, they found the back room of the pub was filled with the who's who of the local legal system. It was evidence that Judge Harrington had been very popular with the Syracuse legal community. It would be tough for anyone to follow in his shoes.

One of the lawyers looked up and saw them enter. "Over here Willis. Grab a beer," he shouted. They sat down at the table, had a couple of beers and conversed with their colleagues.

A short time later, Judge Harrington was helped up onto a table by a couple of the men where he could voice his gratitude for the party. At sixty-five and with an ailing wife, the Judge had decided that it was time to hang up his gavel. "Thank you all for coming. Now, I want everyone to turn off their cell phones and all electronic devices. And I mean now. In my court, no business for the rest of the evening. Just good times and party."

The large group of attorneys, secretaries, judges and court personnel raised their glasses in honor of the judge. One of the clerks yelled out, "I'm glad that I never had to appear before you Judge. You're one tough cookie."

The crowd became more boisterous after a few drinks and sang a round of "For He's a Jolly Good Fellow".

As the party progressed, a slightly intoxicated young woman jumped up on the table yelling, "Where's a pole when you need one?"

However, the absence of a pole did not stop her from shedding most of her clothes and dancing wildly. All of the men and a few of the women waved their glasses in the air and screamed, "Go girl!"

From that point on, the drinks flowed like honey.

Judge Harrington walked over to Phil, sat down beside him and draped his arm around his shoulders. "Well, my boy. I want you to know that I've been keeping my eye on you. I want you to come into my office and see me in about two weeks. You might be interested in what I have planned for your future."

Phil wanted to believe that the Judge really did have plans for him; however, he thought that maybe it was the alcohol talking. Never the less, he smiled and said politely, "Thank you Sir. I'll be sure to put that on my calendar."

Now feeling no pain, the judge jumped up to wave his glass in the air and shouted, "Now, let's drink and party."

The next couple of hours went by quickly as Phil worked the room. He knew it was prudent to maintain a good relationship with the other members of the legal profession. It might lead to future business for him and maybe even that coveted judgeship.

Realizing the time was getting late, Phil turned to Mandy. "Time for me to go. The wife's waiting."

Now, quite inebriated, she put her arm around him and said unsteadily, "Not yet, Honey. That's the District Attorney that just walked in. Can't leave yet."

His face was flushed as he tried to stand up and

push himself away from the table. "Yes. But I think I'm starting to feel my drinks," he answered unsteadily.

"You can always crash at my place if you can't drive home," Mandy whispered in his ear. "Now, grab your glass. We've got more visiting and partying to do."

She winked at him and dragged him back into his chair. "And this may be your lucky day."

"Hey Willis," the DA called out as he walked up.

"How you doing Sir?" Phil responded as he reached out to shake hands.

"All's good. Been trying to reach you. Might have a big case lined up for you soon. Will you be in the office on Monday?"

"Where else?" Phil answered with a slight laugh. He slumped back down as the room started to spin a little around him.

Soon, Phil seemed to have forgotten that he had promised Kelley to be home by six and that he had not called to tell her that he would be late.

"Boy, these damn shooters are strong," Mandy said as she downed another one. She leaned over, put her head on Phil's shoulder and murmured in his ear, "See, you're glad you stayed. Right?"

By this time, most of the crowd had left the room and it was almost one in the morning.

"Now, my Dear. We've got to get you home," Mandy said, taking Phil by the arm and helping him out of his chair. She walked him to the front of the bar and asked the bartender, "Any chance to get a cab? I've got to get my boss out of here."

"I'm done for the night. Got my car outside. Maybe I can give you two a lift."

"I can't take my boss home in this shape. His wife would have fits. But my place is only a couple of blocks from here. You could drop us off there," she suggested with a seemingly innocent smile.

"No problem."

Mandy and the bartender put Phil in the car and he passed out. It didn't take long for them to drive to Mandy's apartment. The three hundred pound ex-bouncer was just what Mandy needed to help get Phil inside her place.

"Just put him on my bed," she said after he carried Phil inside. She led the way to her bedroom, where the bartender dumped Phil on the bed. "And here's ten bucks for your help," she said, extending a bill to him.

He folded his hands across his chest and grinned at her, "Lady, you can keep your money. Carting drunks home is just part of my job."

After he left, Mandy returned to the bedroom and slipped Phil's coat, shoes and pants off. Then she tucked the comforter around him. "I think you're good for the night, my friend."

Then she lied down on the bed beside him and fell asleep. It would be ten the next morning before they woke up.

Meanwhile, as six o'clock and then seven o'clock came and went, Kelley got more and more upset. The chilled non-alcoholic wine was now warm and the prime rib was tough and dried out.

Kelley felt a tap on her leg. "We're getting hungry Momma," Ashley said.

Kelley tried to reach Phil on his cell for the umpteenth time. Still no answer. He wouldn't have turned it off, she thought. I'll try the office phone. Maybe he's still working. No answer there either.

Finally, she fed the children, who had been patiently waiting for their daddy to come home. Kelley was too distraught herself to eat anything. After they finished eating, Alan said, "Remember Mommy, you said that we could watch a movie tonight."

"Maybe, tomorrow night." She took them upstairs, gave them a bath, put their pajamas on and settled them down for the evening.

Everything had been ready for her big announcement, except Phil was still absent. Kelley's mind raced as she went over how she had planned to tell him the big news.

Please Lord—make him happy about this new baby. In the past few months they had grown further and further apart, as Phil spent more and more time at the office and seemed distant when he was at home. The love making almost disappeared. Maybe the new baby and this coming summer's trip to Florida at a theme park would bring the family together.

Finally, at eight o'clock, Kelley put all the food in containers and put them in the refrigerator. She removed the fresh flowers from the table and placed them on the side board, put the china and silver away and pulled the lace tablecloth off the table.

She was extremely downhearted as she walked upstairs and read a story to the kids. She felt as if she had a knife thrust into her heart.

"Is Daddy home yet? "Alan asked.

Kelley tried to hide her feelings. "Not yet Dear, but when he does come home, I'll have him come in and give you a big kiss."

"I love you Momma," he answered.

"I love you too."

She took Ashley into her room and kissed her good night, then returned downstairs to sit in the family room in front of the fireplace.

It was now nine o'clock and still no sign of Phil. She suddenly felt cold and frightened. I hate to worry Phil's parents, Kelley thought. But maybe he's over there.

She reluctantly called, explaining that she had not seen nor heard from Phil in hours. "Sorry. We haven't heard from him either," Dexter said. "But, I'll make a couple of calls and see if I can locate him. Call you back in a little while."

Kelley sat alone and watched the flames in the fireplace gradually die out and become nothing but warm embers. Worried and upset, she started to cry. "Where are you, Phil?"

Finally, she extinguished the fireplace embers and shut the flue.

Kelley changed into her night gown and headed to the bathroom to remove her makeup and brush her teeth. Entering the bathroom, she hit a wet spot on the floor that had been left behind after the children's baths.

Down she went, striking her head on the bathtub.

Kelley lay on the floor, unconscious and bleeding profusely from a cut on the back of her head.

Chapter 10

"Did you say anything to Kelley about having the family over for dinner on Sunday?" Kaitlin asked Dexter after he concluded his phone conversation with Kelley.

"No. I didn't think about it," he wiped his hand across his brow. "She was quite upset because Phil wasn't home yet and she hasn't heard from him. Did you talk to him today?"

"No. I called him earlier, but he never returned my call." Her stomach contracted with anxiety. "Now you have me worried."

"He probably turned his cell phone off and didn't remember to turn it back on. Like I do, after church services. I'll try to reach him now."

A half hour later, after calling several of his friends and numerous attempts to reach Phil himself, Dexter decided to call Kelley back and see if she had heard from him. He dialed the land line at the Willis home and got the answering machine.

Taking a deep breath, he turned to Kaitlin, his eyes wide with anxiety. "Now, she doesn't pick up the phone."

"That's not like Kelley." She cast a quick pointed look at him. "She would be waiting for a call from either Phil or us. Try her on her cell. Maybe something happened to Phil."

Dexter inhaled sharply, then said calmly, "Slow down Kaitlin. I'll try her cell." He dialed that number. No answer.

He stared at Kaitlin as his skin prickled with alarm. "I can't seem to get her on either phone."

"I'm really concerned." She tried to keep her emotions under control. "Let's go over there and see what's going on."

"Okay, we're still dressed."

She turned to face him, her eyes wide. "I'm sorry to be such a worry wart."

"You aren't. You're just a typical mother."

When they arrived at the Willis house, they noticed that there were no lights on downstairs, but they could see a light on in the upstairs master bedroom.

"That's strange. If one or both of them are still up, they'd answer the phone." Dexter's chest felt tight and heavy as he rang the doorbell. No answer. He waited a while, and then rang again. Still no one came to the door.

"Now, I'm not only worried. I'm scared," Kaitlin said as she started to shiver with apprehension.

"Phil gave us a key to the house." Energy flowed through Dexter as he decided to take action. "Let's go in."

He opened the door, slowly entered, and saw only a dim light coming from upstairs.

Dexter's deep voice echoed through the entrance hall. "Phil. Kelley. Its mom and dad. Are you here? Are you okay?"

They paused. Waited. No response. With hearts hammering, they looked at each other. Without another word, Dexter ran up the stairs with Kaitlin at his heels.

Seeing that the light was on in the master bedroom, he threw open the double doors leading into it and rushed in. No Phil, nor Kelley.

Kaitlin scurried down the hall to Alan's room and threw open the door. Alan was sitting up in bed, rubbing his eyes. "Grandma, I heard noises. What's going on? I'm scared."

"Where's Mommy?" he asked her as Ashley came running into the bedroom. "Grandma, why are you here?"

Kaitlin put her arms around both of her grandchildren, who were now both startled and alarmed.

In the meantime, Dexter saw the light coming from under the bathroom door. Fear raced through him as he ran to the door and threw it open.

"Oh, my God. No." He spied Kelley lying on the floor in a pool of blood.

He swore under his breath and then out loud exclaimed, "Jesus, what happened?" Instinct kicked in as he rushed to her, turned her over and saw that the blood was coming from a wound in the back of her head. He pulled his phone from his jacket pocket and quickly dialed 911.

He explained to the emergency operator that he had found his daughter-in-law unconscious on the bathroom floor with a bleeding wound on the back of her head.

After asking him for the address, the operator told him to find a clean towel and to apply pressure to the wound until the rescue squad arrived. Then she told him to turn on the front porch light for the paramedics. While he was still on the phone, Dexter felt a hand on his shoulder.

"Dexter, what's happened?" Kaitlin asked, as she and the two children tried to look over his shoulder.

"Kelley had an accident. I've already called 911. Kaitlin, get the kids out of here," he ordered. "They don't need to see this. Take them downstairs and turn on the front porch light. The paramedics will be here soon."

Kaitlin escorted the children downstairs, turned on the porch light and sat down on the living room sofa with them. She tried to keep her own fear under control; comforting the children, as they waited for help to arrive.

The next few minutes were a nightmare as they waited for the ambulance. When they arrived, the paramedics ran upstairs with their equipment and assessed Kelley's condition. Within a short time, they placed her on a gurney, took her downstairs and loaded her into the ambulance. Kaitlin climbed into the ambulance beside Kelley while Dexter and the children stood on the front porch watching them drive away.

A neighbor, rushed out of her house and ran over to where Dexter and the now sobbing children were standing. "My goodness. What's going on?"

"Kelley had an accident," Dexter answered quietly, trying to keep his voice calm for the children's sake.

"Is she okay?"

"I'm not sure."

"Can I do anything to help?"

"I'm Dexter McLane, her father-in-law."

"Yes. I'm Edith Poole. We met once. What can I do to help?"

"Could you look after the children for a while? I would like to go to the hospital and support my wife."

"Of course. I watch the kids sometimes when their parents go out. They're such a lovely couple."

"That would be a great help."

He turned to the two frightened children. "Now kids, your Mommy had to go to the hospital for a little while and Grandma went with her. I want to go to the hospital and help Grandma so I need you to stay with Mrs. Poole."

"Where's Daddy, Grandpa?" Alan asked, his voice quivering.

"I'm not sure. Please be good and wait with Mrs. Poole until we get back." He knelt down and hugged them before Mrs. Poole led them away.

Dexter headed for his car and rang Phil's cell phone.

Still no answer.

Next, he called Kaitlin on her cell and asked her what hospital they were at.

"I'm at University Hospital. They have Kelley in the emergency room right now."

Dexter sped toward the hospital and blew out an exasperated breath. "Damn, I should have left Phil a note at the house. Please God, let this nightmare end soon."

Chapter 11

Dexter arrived at the hospital; parked the car and rushed toward the emergency entrance. As he raced into the building, he mumbled to himself, "Where is that stepson of mine!"

Looking around the lobby, he saw Kaitlin sitting at a desk across from the emergency room receptionist.

Kaitlin's head jerked up when she saw him approaching. Her voice shook. "Thank goodness you're here. Are the kids okay?"

He eased himself into the chair beside her and patted her hand gently. "Yes. I left them with the neighbor, Mrs. Poole."

"Still no word from Phil?"

"No. How's our Kelley?"

Kaitlin sighed, trying to keep her anxiety under control. "They have her in emergency and are working on her now."

"Can't we go in?" Dexter asked impatiently.

She shook her head. "They said not. I grabbed Kelley's purse on the way out of the house. I've got her insurance cards and doing the best I can to fill out this admittance form. I'm still shaky."

She rifled through Kelley's cards. "I think that her primary care doctor is Doctor Bales. Yes, it says on this card, Dr. Thomas Bales."

She sucked in a deep breath and tried to compose herself as she finished filling out the form and handed it to the receptionist who looked it over briefly. "This is great. No problem. The emergency room doctor's attending to her right now. Don't worry; we'll give your daughter the care that she needs. And I'll call you when we learn something definite about her condition."

After taking a moment to process her words, Dexter answered, "She's our daughter-in-law. And thank you."

The receptionist pointed over to a couple of chairs across the room. "Please have a seat over there. And help yourselves to coffee. I just made it."

Dexter linked his arm through Kaitlin's and led her across the room. "Want a cup?"

She shook her head. "No thanks. I'm almost sick to my stomach with worry."

They sat down next to each other and held hands, praying and waiting impatiently as the next hour and a half passed by slowly.

A doctor came out of the emergency room and walked up to the receptionist. After they exchanged a few words, the receptionist pointed to Dexter and Kaitlin. They jumped to their feet as he walked toward them.

"I'm Dr. Bales, Kelley's doctor. I came in when the hospital called me. I understand that you're Mrs. Willis's in-laws?"

"Yes," Dexter answered as the men shook hands. "We haven't been able to locate her husband," he added in a deflated tone.

Kaitlin grabbed the doctor's arm. "How's Kelley doing?" Her voice trembled, tryinhg to control her emotions.

"She took a nasty fall. We had to put in ten stitches. She's still unconscious. We're worried about the severe concussion that the CAT scan showed."

"Oh. My God." Kaitlin's knees buckled. "A concussion."

Dexter put his arm around her shoulders and supported her as Dr. Bales continued with deep concern in his voice, "Also, she lost an alarming amount of blood."

"From the head wound?" Dexter asked.

"No. She was about two months pregnant. We stopped the hemorrhaging but couldn't save the baby. As I said, she's still unconscious and we'll be sending her up to intensive care. The next twenty-four hours will be critical."

"Oh my goodness. No. She lost a baby. I wonder if Phil knew she was pregnant. Can we see her?" Kaitlin staggered slightly, as tears started to slide slowly down her face. Dexter tightened his hold on her.

"Just for a few minutes. There's a chapel on the top floor if you wish to use it. She'll need your prayers. Then, I suggest that you go home and get some rest. You can come back in the morning and see her."

The doctor led them into the emergency room, where Kelley lay in the bed with an IV tube, heart monitors and a catheter attached to her body.

Kaitlin blinked rapidly as she approached Kelley. She could hardly see through the mist of her tears. Getting control of herself; she knelt beside the bed, took Kelley's hand in hers and gently talked to her.

Not knowing if she could hear him or not, Dexter spoke quietly to Kelley for a few minutes. Even though he didn't know where his stepson was, Dexter told Kelley that Phil was on his way.

Kaitlin told her that Alan and Ashley were fine and staying with Mrs. Poole, in what she hoped sounded like a calm and collected voice.

After whispering to Kelley that they would be back in the morning, Dexter helped his wife to her feet, put his arm around her and led her out of the emergency room.

Before heading home, they took the elevator to the

fourth floor where the chapel was located. Kneeling down in front of the altar, Kaitlin lit a candle. "Please Lord, we need your help. Take care of our Kelley."

Dexter called Mrs. Poole when they got home. He told her that Kelley was unconscious and in intensive care and that he was still trying to locate Phil.

Mrs. Poole said she would be glad to keep the kids for as long as they needed her. After thanking her, Dexter tried once again to reach Phil. Still no answer. By now, it was after midnight.

The following morning, Mandy Parks awoke and saw Phil sleeping beside her, laying flat on his back and snoring loudly. She got up and went to the bathroom to throw cold water on her face and brush her teeth.

Phil suddenly woke up, blinked his eyes and looked around the strange bedroom. He sat straight up and called, "Where the hell am I?"

Mandy stuck her head through the open doorway. "You passed out last night Boss, slept it off in my bed."

He pushed himself out of the bed, looked down, and saw that he was dressed only in undershorts. Through his suddenly dry throat, he yelled out, "What the hell is going on? You mean I spent the night with you?"

Mandy walked into the bedroom, with her toothbrush in her hand. She chuckled. "Don't get all excited Phil. Nothing happened. We were both too drunk. In fact, we were fortunate the bartender agreed to drive us here. I was just going to get dressed and make some coffee. Then, you can take me out to breakfast."

"No. No." Phil screamed indignantly, "I've got to get my ass home. Kelley must be frantic with worry by now. I forgot to call and tell her where I was going."

As panic surged through him, he grabbed his clothes and shoes from the floor and threw them on. He reached into his pocket, pulled out his phone, turned it on and called his house. No answer. Then he tried Kelley's phone. Still no answer.

"Oh shit," he yelled. Now frantic, he raced out of Mandy's apartment.

Outside he looked around for his car. "Crap. My car's still at the office. We walked over to the pub and Mandy said the bartender drove us here." His face became grim.

He spotted a police car driving slowly down the street. In a combination of fury and desperation, he ran over to it and flagged it down.

The officer stopped the car and rolled the window down. "Hi there, Mr. Willis. Remember me? It's Tony. I met you at the courthouse last week." He stared at Phil's disheveled appearance with his shirt out of his pants and his shoes untied. "Looks like you had a rough night, Counselor."

Disgusted at himself, Phil grimaced and replied in a subdued tone, "You could say that. Say Tony, I need a lift to my office. Maybe you can help me out. It's only about six blocks from here."

"That's against the rules you know Sir." Then he grinned. "Hop in. I won't tell if you don't. Give me the address."

Within a few minutes, Phil was at his office. He jumped in his car and headed for home, talking to himself along the way. "Kelley's going to kill me. She had a special dinner planned. What a jerk I've been."

He pulled into his driveway, climbed out of the car and ran to the front door. He fumbled as he tried to fit his key into the lock. After a couple of attempts, he managed to get the door open. Inside, he called out, "Kelley, I'm here. Kids, Daddy's home." No answer.

He raced into the kitchen. No Kelley. No kids. Oh shit, it's Saturday. Maybe they went to the grocery store or they're still sleeping. He ran upstairs and looked in the children's bedrooms. No Alan. No Ashley.

He ran into the master bedroom. The bed wasn't made. Maybe, Kelley's in the shower. He ran into the bathroom and stopped dead in his tracks. There was a large puddle of blood on the floor and the towels in the bathtub were soaked in blood. His heart almost stopped cold with fear. He uttered a curse, turned and ran back out of the master bedroom.

Suddenly, he heard a voice call out. "Mr. Willis. Mr. Willis. I saw your car in the driveway. I've been looking for you."

Mrs. Poole was standing at the bottom of the stairs.

"Mrs. Poole, what are you doing here?" Taking two steps at a time, he rushed down to her.

"Your wife had an accident last night and was rushed to the hospital."

He took a step back in alarm. "When was that? Where are the kids?"

"Late last night. Your folks came to the house and found your wife unconscious in the bathroom. I guess she fell and hit her head. They went to the hospital with her and your children are at my house now. I kept them overnight and they're doing fine." Then she added in a low voice, "Your parents were looking for you Mr. Willis."

He gulped for air. "I was so anxious to get home this morning that I didn't listen to my phone messages. What hospital did they take her to?"

"Let's see. Oh yes. I heard Mr. McLane say University Hospital."

"Can you keep the kids until I can make other arrangements for them Mrs. Poole?"

"Of course. I was just feeding them breakfast when I heard your car pull into your driveway."

"Thank you," Phil said as he raced for the front door.

Mrs. Poole followed him out of the house. "Be sure to

call me, Mr. Willis, and let me know how your wife is doing."

"You got it." Phil jumped in his car and headed for the hospital. He gripped the steering wheel with sweaty hands. It seemed like he caught every red light. His heart threatened to beat right out of his chest as he prayed, "Please God. Let Kelley be all right."

Phil pulled his car up to the emergency entrance and jumped out. The parking lot valet walked up and handed him a ticket. Phil grabbed it and ran inside to the reception desk, where a heavy set female volunteer asked, "May I help you Sir?"

Phil was in a daze. "My wife came into the emergency room last night. Where is she? I need to see her."

"Her name Sir?"

"Willis. Kelley Willis."

She input the name in her computer. "Oh yes. Here she is. She was admitted last night through emergency."

Beginning to sound rather frantic now, he croaked, "Well, where is she?"

"In room three thirteen—intensive care unit."

To Phil, it seemed to take forever to reach the third floor. He dashed out of the elevator, saw a sign that indicated that Kelley's room was to the left, ran past the nurse's station and down the hall to her room. He threw open the door.

A voice said calmly, "Good morning son. We're been wondering where you've been, tried to. to reach you."

Phil stared at his mother standing next to the bed. Then he sagged, barely unable to stand, as he saw Kelley in the bed, with all kinds of tubes and wires attached to her. With her head wrapped in white bandages and an oxygen mask on her face, Phil barely recognized her.

He ran over to the bed, dropped to his knees and sobbing, laid his head on the sheet next to her. "Oh my God, Kelley. What happened to you?"

He felt Kaitlin's hand on his shoulder. With tears streaming down his face, he looked up at her.

She could see Phil's pain reflected in his face as he whispered, "Will she be all right?"

"She hit her head and has a severe concussion. The doctor said that the next twenty-four hours are very critical for her."

Chapter 12

Phil took Kelley's pale cold hand in his and kissed it gently. "I'm here Kell. I'll never leave you again." He bowed his head in prayer and his voice quivered. "Please God. Make her well."

Tears welled up in his eyes and slowly streamed down his face. "Please Kell. Forgive me for not coming home last night. I'm such a jerk. I'll change. You'll see."

With a heavy heart, Kaitlin watched her son pour out his love to his wife. Finally, he lifted his head and looked at her. A loud ugly sob flew from his mouth. "Mom?"

She fought a hard battle to put a courageous smile on her face, "Please Phil. Don't say anything more. You're here now and it's time for all of us to pray."

"I'm such an ass."

Kaitlin walked over to him, knelt down and put her arms around him. "Your job now is to stay with your wife. The nurse said she was stable. And Kelley is a fighter, you know. She'll pull through this."

Phil, laid his head on Kelley's chest and whispered, "The kids need you. I need you."

From the corner of his eye, Phil could see his stepfather approach him. Dexter put his hand on Phil's shoulder. "Son, your mother and I need to go pick up the kids from Mrs. Poole. We'll bring them to our house and take them to school tomorrow. Their routine should continue normally so they won't get too upset."

Struggling to keep himself under control, Phil looked up and bowed his head in agreement.

Dexter continued. "You stay here. We'll call you later and see how Kelley's doing. And, I'll bring your razor and some clean clothes."

His stepfather's thoughtfulness soothed Phil a little. He stood up and briefly placed his head on Dexter's shoulder. "I'm so lucky to have you two." Dexter gave him a pat on the back.

Kaitlin gave Phil a squeeze. "Don't worry, Kelley will be okay. I just know it."

She stepped back and looked at her son with a question in her eyes. Then, deciding that now was not the time to quiz him about where he had been the previous evening, she kissed him and stepped toward the door.

After they left the room, Phil pulled a chair up to the bed beside Kelley and took her hand in his. "I'm not leaving here until I can take you home with me," he said with determination.

The next few hours passed by slowly as he sat by her side. Nurses came in from time to time to check on her medications and to care for her.

After falling asleep later in the afternoon, Phil suddenly awoke as a nurse entered the room. He glanced down at his watch. "My God, its six o'clock."

She smiled. "Hi. I'm Lola. Signed on at three. I came in a couple of times to check on your wife and saw you were napping. Thought I'd let you sleep. You looked like you could use the rest."

"Thanks," Phil replied, with a sheepish look on his face. "I guess I just drifted off for a while."

"Visiting hours for intensive care are over now, so you'll have to leave Mr. Willis."

"No way," he said firmly, fixing her with a calm gaze.

"You can rest assure that we'll take good care of your wife." She tilted her head and tried to reassure him, "We will be constantly monitoring her condition from the nurse's station and we check on her regularly."

"Please nurse. I can't leave her. I've just got to stay," he begged. "She's my life."

The door opened and a tall thin man with gray hair and glasses entered the room. He looked at the nurse's badge and said, "Good evening Nurse Steward."

He raised an eyebrow at Phil. "I'm afraid visiting hours are over Sir. I'm Roland O'Malley, the hospital administrator. I'm making the rounds and thought I would see how some of our critical patients are doing."

Phil stood up, shot him a challenging look and swallowed hard. "I'm Phil Willis and this is my wife Kelley."

Roland paused and his eyes narrowed. "And how is Mrs. Willis doing, nurse?"

"I was just telling Mr. Willis that his wife is better at this point and that the visiting hours are over and he needs to leave."

Deep in despair, Phil looked at O'Malley and pleaded, "Please Sir. I just can't leave her. I've got to stay."

O'Malley put his hand on Phil's arm as understanding dawned in his compassionate eyes. "I think that we can make an exception to the rules this time. Nurse, call Charley from maintenance. I'm certain there's a cot around here that he can bring in for Mr. Willis."

Phil grabbed O'Malley's hand in his, as relief surged through him. "Thank you Sir."

"Call me Roland. Now, please come with me. I just finished up some of my paperwork. It never ends you know. And I put a fresh pot of coffee on in my office. You look like you could use a cup. Maybe, we can rustle up a sandwich for you too."

"That would be great."

"Let the nurse get her work done now." O'Malley

linked his arm through Phil's. "We'll return later."

Approaching O'Malley's office, they saw a man dressed in black and wearing a religious collar standing outside. "Father Donnally, you still here?" O'Malley greeted him warmly. "Thought you went home long ago."

"The Lord's work is never done you know," the priest replied. "I had to give one of my parishioners' communion and the last rites. Just getting ready to leave. I'll be back in the morning for my usual morning mass."

The priest glanced at the tired looking man in front of him. "Would you like to receive communion?'

Phil inhaled, released a breath and walked forward to shake the priest's hand. "Yes. If I could."

"Just follow me to the chape."

O'Malley patted him on the shoulder. "You go ahead with Father Donnally. When you're done, come back to my office. I'll have the kitchen send up a couple of sandwiches for us."

After they entered the chapel, Phil drew a ragged breath. "May I go to confession first, Father? I think I need to before I receive communion."

"Of course." He walked up to the small altar and Phil knelt down in the pew in front of him.

When he finished his confession, Phil received communion and lit a candle in front of the Statue of the Blessed Mother. "Please dear Mother Mary make Kelley well."

The priest gave him a reassuring pat on the back as Phil stood up. They headed back to the administrator's office.

Phil gobbled down the club sandwich that O'Malley had gotten for him; drank the cup of coffee and managed to eat a couple of donuts, while the other two men chatted.

After thanking them both, Phil headed to Kelley's room. He walked over to the bed, whispered a few words to her, and kissed her on the forehead before heading to the cot that had been set up in the corner. Within a few moments, he was sound asleep.

Although, he slept somewhat restlessly through the night, he did not awaken when the nurse came in.

She entered the room, opened the blinds and gently shook Phil on the shoulder. "Mr. Willis. I've got good news for you. Your wife is awake now."

His heart surging, Phil jumped to his feet, ran to Kelley, knelt down, and looked lovingly at her.

Recognizing him, Kelley rewarded him with a smile.

She tried to lift her arms to welcome him as he leaned over to hug her. Phil looked up to heaven with tears in his eyes, "Thank you Lord. You brought her back."

He showered Kelley with kisses. "You're looking mighty fine this morning Mrs. Willis."

She smiled weakly at him and whispered, "But, you don't look so hot, Mr. Willis."

"I'm so sorry that I wasn't with you when you had your accident, Let me explain what happened."

She put her finger over his lips. "Shush. Time for all that later. Just hold me."

A few moments later, Dr. Bales entered the room. Phil stood up and stepped to the side as he checked Kelley over briefly. Pausing, as he glanced at the nurse, he sighed and said gently, "Your wife is doing well this morning, Mr. Willis. But, I do have to tell you both that she lost the child."

Phil sagged, barely able to stand. He looked at Kelley, his anguish reflected in his face. "Child? We were going to have a baby?"

Now devastated at the news of losing her baby, Kelley started to sob. In between her tears, she whispered, "That's why I was planning a special dinner for us. I was going to tell you and the kids."

Phil knelt down and put his arms around her. "It's

all my fault. If I'd been home this wouldn't have happened."

"No. It wasn't your fault Phil. It was just an accident."

"There is no physical reason why Mrs. Willis can't conceive again," Doctor Bales said reassuringly. He turned to the nurse, "Call maintenance and have them remove the cot. I don't think Mr. Willis will need it tonight."

He looked at Phil with compassion. "Why don't we give the nurse some time to get your wife cleaned up? You can get some breakfast if you like."

Phil stood up and drew in a sharp breath. "Sure Doc. Sure."

The two men left the room and the doctor led Phil to a nearby lounge area and guided him toward a couple of chairs. Once they were seated, the doctor said, "I would like to give you a few words of advice, Mr. Willis."

Phil looked momentarily startled. "Yes. Of course."

"Your wife has had a very traumatic experience. Not only did she suffer a severe concussion; but, also lost her child. You will need to give her plenty of time and space in the near future, if you want her to recover mentally and physically from this."

Phil listened intently as the doctor continued, "You'll need to be there for her; but not too close. You might even consider not sharing a bedroom with her for a few days. Give her complete bed rest. She'll be on strong pain medication for both her head and her injured knee for several days."

"I understand."

"Try to spend more time with your children. When she sees how much you care for your family, it will endear you to her once again."

He sighed and asked, "How will I know when she forgives me for this?"

"Don't worry, she'll let you know. Just let your actions show her how much you care for her and the children.

Everything will work itself out."

Phil waited a few moments, before he replied. "Thank you for the advice, Doctor. I'm going to earnestly try to show Kelley how special she and the kids are to me. I'm one hell of a lucky guy and I'm sorry that I didn't realize it sooner."

The doctor stood up and they shook hands. "Don't worry. As they say, time heals all things." He turned and walked down the hall.

Phil sat slumped in his chair, quietly thinking after the doctor left. He picked up his phone and called his mother. "Kelley's awake and talking, Mom. She's going to be all right." Then he sobbed and held his head in his hands as he repeated what the doctor had told him.

In an attempt to calm him down, Kaitlin changed the subject, "Did you get the fresh clothes and your electric razor? Dexter brought them last night. Left them at the nurse's station for you."

"No. I'll ask about them. The nurse is with Kelley right now. Said to come back in about forty-five minutes. I'll clean up and head to the cafeteria for a bite."

He talked with his mother for a few more minutes, then walked down to the nurses' station and picked up the gym bag Dexter had left for him.

He entered the men's rest room at the end of the hall, washed up a bit, shaved and put on the fresh underwear and shirt that his mother had packed for him.

As he passed the chapel, Phil heard the sound of music. He entered and found Father Donnally saying mass for about a dozen members of the staff and several visitors. Phil stayed for the mass, took communion again, and told the priest the good news about Kelley.

Leaving the chapel, he saw Roland O'Malley walking down the hall. When the administrator spied Phil, he stopped and put his hand on his arm. "Just heard the good news about your wife, Mr. Willis. You're a very fortunate man."

"You're right. I'm very lucky. But, I know God must have been listening to my prayers." He reached into his pocket. "Here's my business card. If there's ever anything I can do to pay you back for your kindness, please call."

Phil stopped by the cafeteria, grabbed an egg sandwich and an orange juice and headed back to Kelley's room, where the nurse was just leaving. "She's doing just fine, Mr. Willis."

"When do you think I can take her home?" he asked impatiently.

"You'll have to check with her doctor, but, I wouldn't be surprised if he released her tomorrow."

Kelley was sitting up when he entered the room. Still, a little disturbed that Phil hadn't been there, when she needed him most, Kelley just lifted her head and gazed at him with little emotion.

Phil walked over and gave her a quick kiss. He picked up both of her hands and placed them on his cheeks as tears started to flow. She gave him a sad smile and whispered, "Please, no apologies."

"Just don't leave me Kelley. I love you."

"I know. I promise."

The door opened and a voice asked, "Can we come in?"

Phil spun around and saw his mother and stepfather standing in the doorway. Behind them were Alan and Ashley.

"We got special permission to bring the children up to see you," Kaitlin said.

Kelley looked at them and tears welled up in her eyes. "Alan. Ashley. Don't stand there. Come over here and give Mommy a big hug."

The children ran to her. "Grandma and Grandpa got us in, but the nurse said we had to be very quiet," Ashley whispered.

Phil picked up the children and put them on the bed

beside Kelley. She gathered both of them in her arms and hugged and kissed them.

"We love you Mommy," Ashley said.

"And Grandma said you're okay now," Alan added.

Kelley looked over the tops of their heads at her in-laws. "Thank you, Mom and Dad."

"Our family is together once again," Kaitlin said. "Now everything will be all right."

But silently she wondered if Phil could slow down and if Kelley's life would return to normal. She realized that some drastic changes needed to take place at the Willis home in the future.

Chapter 13

A couple of days after her accident, Kelley returned to the doctor's office to have the stitches taken out of her head. Before leaving the office, she and Dr. Bales had a long conference about her health. He suggested that she should have tests done to be sure that she would be able to conceive again after the miscarriage.

Later, several tests and a biopsy revealed that numerous tumors surrounded Kelley's uterus and that they were pre-cancerous. Dr. Bales recommended that she have a hysterectomy. This news, after losing the baby was extremely traumatic for her as she hoped to have another child. When she told Phil what the doctor had said, he insisted that it would be best for her to have the surgery

Two months later, Kelley's body was healing nicely and while her doctor gave her a clean bill of health physically, her emotions were still in turmoil. She knew she would never forget the child she had lost. To try to ease her anxieties, she had returned to working out at the gym and jogging every morning.

Phil's life had also changed dramatically. He did not renew the lease on his office, and relocated to a smaller space in a busy strip mall. At his request, his secretary, Mandy had resigned.

It was now a typical Sunday morning as Phil entered the bedroom with a tray in his hands. He leaned over and whispered to Kelley who was still snuggled under the warm covers, "Breakfast in bed for my Sweetie."

Kelley peeked out. "I hope you made enough for two. I could smell the coffee and I'm famished."

She sat up in bed and he placed the tray on top of the comforter. "You mean breakfast for four."

Standing in the doorway, were Ashley and Alan. Kelley looked at them and opened her arms for them to join her. They ran eagerly over to the bed, plumped up the pillows and climbed in.

"This is the first course," Phil said. "Toast and coffee for Mommy. Orange juice for kids. Pancakes and sausages for everyone later."

Alan took one look at the tray, bounced off the bed and ran out of the room.

Phil looked puzzled. "Where's he going?"

"Oh, I know," Ashley replied. "He always has to have peanut butter on his toast."

Kelley looked and Phil and grinned. "I think he's developing a lot of his father's habits."

"I eat peanut butter on bread, not toast."

"Well, Alan is starting to eat it on everything," Kelley said as she picked up her cup and took a sip.

Alan returned to the room with the jar of peanut butter, smeared in on his toast and settled in on the edge of the bed.

"Be careful, you don't get anything on the comforter. I just washed it yesterday," Kelley said.

Ashley sat upright trying to be very careful as she drank her juice and ate her piece of toast. After the last bite, she said, "I'm really hungry Daddy. I'm ready for the pancakes and sausage now."

Phil handed her another piece of toast and looked at his watch. "You know I have a terrific idea. It's almost nine o'clock. Let's all get dressed and we'll go to mass at ten. After that we can head over to a new Italian Restaurant that I heard has a big Sunday brunch."

"Do they have pizza?" Alan asked.

Kelley quelled the urge to laugh. "I'm sure they do. Let's all get dressed and let Daddy treat everyone."

After several trips to the buffet at the restaurant, Phil sat back in his chair and sighed, "I don't think that I could eat another bite."

"I didn't know that you like breaded veal chops that much," Kelley said. "You ate two big ones."

"Well, I don't have it often. And I did notice that you returned to the pasta bar a couple of times."

Kelley eyes widened a fraction and she looked over at the children. "Ashley did get her pancakes and sausage. And I was glad to see that they did have pizza for Alan at the pasta bar. You know, they really feature some unusual items here for a Sunday brunch."

"That's why I brought us here. I knew they would not only have the usual breakfast items, but I heard that they had a lot of Italian dishes." He leaned over and whispered in her ear, "Kids eat free."

"Then, we should come more often."

The two sat back, savored their second cups of coffee and talked about Phil's new office and his work. Alan suddenly interrupted the conversation, "Daddy you said that Miss Mandy doesn't work for you anymore. Are you going to hire a new lady?'

Phil sighed and released a breath. "I'm thinking about it."

Ashley looked up from her dessert. "Why don't you hire Mommy to help you? She says she doesn't have much to do at home now that we're getting big."

Both Kelley and Phil looked at her with startled expressions on their faces.

Phil debated the intelligence of that statement for a few moments, then leaned toward Kelley, "You know that's not a bad idea. But first, let me tell you about something that I've been thinking about lately. I want to go back to school and study tax law. Work out of the office mostly."

Kelley, amazed at this sudden announcement from Phil, managed a weak smile. "That sounds like a good idea."

"And do you know what would make it an even better idea? Why don't you go to tax school with me? That way we could work together as a team. You could handle the paper work while I take care of the legal side of it."

Indecision swept through her. Then shrugging her shoulders, she replied, "Sure. Why not?"

"Why not what? You'll go to tax school with me or you'll give up your part-time job at the newspaper and work with me at the office?"

Kelley grinned. "Yes to all three. We are partners aren't we?"

Sunday, was usually popcorn and movie night at the Willis household. That evening, Phil said, "Okay Alan, it's your turn to pick out the movie."

Kelley lifted a hand to her mouth to cover her smile. She couldn't help it. "I'll bet you're going to choose, 'Lion King'."

Alan clapped his hands. "Yes. Yes. It's my favorite."

"You line up the snacks Phil," Kelley said, "and I'll help the kids with their baths."

She whispered to Phil, "Good thing that Alan knows this movie by heart. He usually falls asleep before the end."

While Kelley escorted the kids to the bathroom, Phil headed for the kitchen. "Let's see. Where's the popcorn?"

He heard Kelley call from upstairs, "I hear the door bell."

"I'll get it," Phil hollered back as he walked through the entrance hall to the front door. Opening only the inside door, he saw a man, who looked vaguely familiar, standing on the other side of the screen door.

"Mr. Willis. I'm Roland O'Malley. We met at the hospital."

"Oh sure. I remember you. You're the administrator."

"May I come in? I need to talk with you if I may."

"Of course." Phil opened the door, stepped back and waved him inside.

Nervous, O'Malley spoke rapidly. "I know it's kind of late."

"Never too late for a friend. Follow me to the kitchen, we can talk there." Phil walked to the kitchen and motioned for O'Malley to have a seat at the kitchen island.

"My wife's bathing the kids. I was just getting ready to make some popcorn. Tonight is family movie night."

"I won't keep you long. And how is Mrs. Willis doing these days?"

"Just fine. All's great with the family. Now, what was it that you wanted to talk to me about?" Phil shot him a questioning look, opened a kitchen cabinet and pulled out a couple bags of popcorn.

O'Malley swallowed and leaned in closer. "I would like to keep our discussion private. I came to see you because you're a lawyer. And from what I hear around town, a pretty damn good one."

Realizing that O'Malley had something serious to talk about, Phil threw the popcorn down on the kitchen counter and walked over to the island, and sat down next to him. "This is starting to sound quite serious."

"You're right." O'Malley looked at him with a frown. "It is. Very serious."

"Well, you can rest assured that anything you wish

to tell me will be kept in strictest confidence," Phil reassured him.

He cleared his throat and continued. "Good. This is about my brother. My twin brother, Reagan O'Malley. Father Reagan O'Malley. After college, I became a hospital administrator and he joined the priesthood. And, now he's in trouble."

Phil's eyes widened as he calmly asked, "Okay. And what's the problem?"

He paused for a moment, took a deep breath and continued. "My brother has been charged with molesting a young boy in the sacristy of his church."

"That is quite serious. A church here in town?"

"Yes. St. John's on the other side of Syracuse."

Phil leaned forward, as his legal training kicked in. "And when did this alleged incident supposedly happen?"

"I don't know exactly. Yesterday he conducted the seven a.m. mass. After, he went to call on two of his sick parishioners who are in nursing homes. About four in the afternoon, when he was sitting in his apartment working on his computer, a police officer knocked on his door. He told Reagan that he had a warrant for his arrest."

Phil's eyes widened. "And exactly what was the charge?"

"Molesting a minor. It seems a young altar boy accused my brother of molesting him. Right now, Reagan's in jail downtown."

"Okay Roland. Because it's Sunday, your brother will have to spend the night in jail. Tomorrow, he'll probably be arraigned in front of a judge."

"Can you help us, Mr. Willis? Will you be Father Reagan's attorney?"

"Of course, I will. But call me, Phil."

"Will you need a retainer up front? We both have some money. Just name your price." Roland summoned a weak smile.

"Let's talk about that later. Right now, we'll take things one step at a time." Phil tried to sound optimistic. "I'll meet you at the court house about eight-thirty tomorrow morning. They usually start hearing the cases about nine. We'll have your brother plead innocent of course. The judge will set a bail. We'll post a bond and get him released."

Now shaking, Roland dropped his head, drew in a deep breath and tried to compose himself. "I know my brother would never do such a thing. And, why would some young boy accuse him of something like this? Even if he's proven innocent of the charge, this could ruin his reputation and career in the church."

Phil stood up and patted Roland on the back. "We never know why kids do crazy things. Maybe, this young fellow is just seeking attention. But, don't worry, we'll work our way through this. That's a promise."

Somewhat relieved, Roland nodded and got to his feet. "Okay. I'll just have to have faith in you and the good Lord. I hope I haven't ruined your evening with your family."

"Not at all. You know, I'm forever indebted to you for your kindness to me during Kelley's hospital stay. I really appreciated it that you made arrangements for me to stay in her room that night."

"It was nothing, believe me," he replied, as Kelley entered the kitchen.

Phil took a step toward her. "Kelley, look who's here. Remember Mr. O'Malley?"

"Yes. The hospital administrator. I remember him very well. " Kelley rushed over and gave him a hug.

"You're looking very good, Mrs. Willis."

"Thank you. I'm feeling good." She smiled. "Would you care for a cup of coffee or something?"

"No thank you. I must be on my way. I have lots of things I have to take care of. And I must apologize for interrupting your family time."

"Not at all. We're delighted to see you again."

As they walked toward the front door, Phil said, "I'll meet you at the courthouse."

"Yes. Eight-thirty on the dot," Roland said as they shook hands.

After he shut the front door behind Roland, Kelley looked at Phil. "What was that all about?"

"Tell you later. The kids are probably anxious for that movie and popcorn. I'll pop the corn, while you get the kids. Then, I'm going to have to excuse myself from family night. I have some research to do before I head to court tomorrow morning. Roland asked me to take a case for his twin brother, who's a priest. He was arrested for molesting a boy."

Kelley's eyes widened. "A priest? Molesting a child? How tragic."

"Yes. I'll tell you all about it later. But, looks like it's really going to be a challenge for me and I have to get hoping on it right away. I'll see you upstairs about eleven."

Later, when Phil came up to their room, Kelley was sitting up reading a book. He climbed in bed beside her, reached over and gave her a quick kiss on the cheek. "Better get your beauty rest little lady. I've got a powerful defense to handle and I'll need your help. I have a feeling that your undercover days might be back."

Chapter 14

At eight-thirty Monday morning, Phil and Kelley walked into the courthouse. They placed their briefcases on the scanner belt, walked through security and asked the guard which courtroom the hearing for Father Reagan O'Malley was scheduled to take place in.

They took the escalator upstairs to Courtroom 310 and found Roland O'Malley sitting on a bench outside the doors.

Tension tightening the lines in his face, he jumped to his feet when he saw them walking toward him. "Got here early. Been waiting for you."

Phil smiled politely. "Hope you don't mind. I brought my wife along to the hearing."

"Not at all. We can use all the moral support we can get," he answered nervously.

A sign on the door next to the courtroom, read "Judge Joyce Taylor."

"Do you know anything about this judge," Roland asked apprehensively as he stood next to Phil.

"I've never personally met her, nor have I appeared before her. She's known for moving cases quickly through her schedule—said to be both fair and just."

"Who's the prosecutor in the case?" Kelley asked.

"This is only an arraignment," Phil answered. "That

will be determined if and when the judge decides to take the case to trial. Today, the judge will just ask for a plea, and then if the state proves they have enough evidence to go to trial, she'll set bail and a trial date. And that's when I'll really go to work."

The double doors to the courtroom opened and an officer ushered them into the room. He led Phil to one of the two long tables placed in front of the judge's bench. Kelley and Roland took their seats in a row behind the table.

A short while later, two police officers escorted Father Reagan into the room from a side door. He was dressed in a plain gray suit, with an open necked white shirt.

Phil stood up as the officers led him to the defense table.

Father Reagan looked at his brother, who smiled at him with a penetrating intensity and gave him a thumbs up.

Father Reagan walked over to Phil, who was now standing with his hand outstretched toward the priest.

"Mr. Willis?"

"Yes. Glad to meet you Father Reagan."

"My brother speaks highly of you. Thank you for taking my case."

From her seat, Kelley looked at Father Reagan, then at his brother. She was astonished at the similarities and the differences in the appearance of the twins.

While both men, had the same dark auburn curly hair, Roland was several inches taller and about thirty pounds heavier than his brother. Both of them had a ruddy complexion that was common to those born of Irish descent.

Phil and Kelley learned that the twins had been raised by devout middle class Catholic parents in the suburbs of Boston. Their mother was a school teacher and their father was a plumber.

Both men, in their late thirties, were intelligent, educated and well liked. Both had a fiery Irish spirit that matched their hair. Living at home, the boys had shared a bedroom and become each other's best friend. In high school, they became Boston's tennis double champions. In college, they choose to room together.

Upon graduation, Roland went on to get a master's degree in Hospital Administration, while Reagan entered the seminary. Now, well into their respective careers, both had found positions in the same city, Syracuse.

Roland worked at the local hospital, while Reagan had assumed the position as Assistant Pastor at St. Johns Parish and taught at its elementary school. Throughout the years, the two had remained very close.

Phil motioned for the priest to have a seat beside him and whispered, "I'll guide you from here."

While waiting for Judge Taylor to enter the chamber, Phil talked the case over with the priest and advised him as to what would occur at the hearing. "Hold your head up high. Let everyone know that you're innocent."

"That will be easy, because I am," Father Reagan responded with fervor.

"Good. Just follow my lead."

The priest held himself steady and lifted his chin. "Yes Sir."

The morning news had a headline in the second section of the paper with a picture of Father Reagan and a short article about his arrest. The name of the boy involved was not mentioned because he was a minor. But at this point, the newspaper article seemed to imply the priest's guilt.

A loud voice bellowed out. "All rise. This court is in session. The Honorable Judge Joyce Taylor presiding."

The Judge entered the room from behind the bench, took her seat and looked around the courtroom. "Please read the first case."

After the clerk read the charge, the judge looked down at the priest. "Reagan O'Malley you have been charged with molesting a minor. How do you plea?"

Phil reached over and gripped Father Reagan's shoulder firmly. "Not guilty," he whispered.

Father Reagan spoke up loudly and in a confident voice. "Not guilty."

"Not guilty," she repeated.

"Yes, your Honor. Not guilty."

Phil raised his hand.

"Yes Counselor?" Her eyes widened.

"Attorney Phil Willis, your Honor. I will represent Father Reagan O'Malley in this case. Father O'Malley has never been arrested before. He has no record. We hope that you will give him a break on the bail and release him into the custody of his brother, Roland O'Malley, administrator of a local hospital." A tiny fire lit his eyes. "Believe me, Father Reagan is no flight risk."

The judge's eyebrows lifted slightly. "Counselor, the charges against your client are extremely serious."

"Yes, your honor. But we believe the charges are false and we plan to prove it."

Judge Taylor rifled through some papers, thought for a few moments, slammed her gavel on the desk and said, "After reviewing the evidence, I have decided that bail is set at fifty thousand dollars. Trial will began one month from now. Father O'Malley will not leave the city and will stay with his brother." She slammed the gavel once again. "Next case."

Relief surged through Phil as he jumped to his feet and led Kelley and Roland out of the courtroom.

Father O'Malley was escorted out of the court room by the deputies and led back to the jail. There, he picked up his personal belongings and waited for the bondsman that Phil had contacted earlier, to post his bail.

The others exited through a side door of the courthouse in order to avoid any waiting news media. Phil explained that he would address the media later, after he had time to carefully craft his statement.

"I plan to state that, 'While it may not be an easy task, we will use all our resources to prove Father Reagan innocent of all charges'."

Phil, Kelley and Roland waited for Father Reagan inside the front entrance of the jail. About ten minutes later, he appeared. "Thanks for all your help, Mr. Willis."

"Father, we need to sit down and talk about your defense," Phil said.

"Yes. You're in charge."

"Good. Let's see if we can find an empty conference room, nearby."

Once seated, Phil said, "Okay, Father, here's the agenda. You'll stay with your brother until it's time for the trial. We have just a few weeks to prepare. I'm planning to ask another attorney to help me with the case. Her name is Jill Sinclair."

"Oh, is she experienced in this sort of thing?" Roland asked in a stiff tone, as his brow shot up.

"Yes. She's one of the best. Two years ago she defended another priest on similar charges and she got him acquitted."

Roland looked at his brother, forced a faint smile and nodded. "Sounds good to us."

Phil turned to Father Reagan. "When you get back to your brother's house, I want you to write down a detailed description of what happened on the day of the alleged incident. Put down the time you arrived at church, the time the boy arrived, what happened and what time both of you left. Also put down anyone that may have walked in or out of the sacristy at that time. Don't leave anything out. What you think might be the littlest detail may prove important to the case."

He paled as he thought about Phil's instructions. "I'll try to remember everything."

"Good. We'll meet at my office tomorrow and go over

everything."

"I'll do my best Mr. Willis."

"And remember, Father, no interviews with the media. I'll handle that."

Roland leaned forward in his chair. "Phil, I want to thank you again for taking my brother's case. You'll have our full cooperation."

"Good. I'm going to get a full background check on the young kid that accused you. Now Father Reagan, is there anything that you can tell me about him?"

"His name is Juan Moralas. He goes to our school." He looked down as though deciding what it was that he wanted to add. "This was the first time that he served mass with me. I think it might be best to talk to his teachers to find out more about him."

"Okay. Put all that down on your report. I wonder why he served mass with you. Was it just out of the blue?"

The priest mulled that question over for a bit then cleared his throat. "I really can't answer that."

"Well, here's my card. Call me at any time of the day, if you can think of something pertinent to the situation. If not, I'll see you tomorrow at my office. "

Leaving the courthouse, Phil said to Kelley, "By the way, I put an ad in this morning's paper for a legal secretary. I've decided that I need to keep you available so you can to do some undercover work on this case."

"That won't break my heart. You know I just love snooping around. Just like old times. Huh?"

Back at the office, Phil sat at his desk to review the court documents on the case. The door opened and a tall young man, in his late twenties, and with a worn briefcase under his arm, entered. "Good day, Mr. Willis. I'm Walter Cossins and I'm here in answer to your advertisement in the paper for a legal secretary."

With a look of distracted preoccupation, Phil, glanced up. "Glad you came in Walter. Please have a seat."

He dropped his briefcase on the floor and sat down in the chair across from Phil. "Please call me, Wally. Everyone does."

Phil didn't bother to hide his smile. "I've never had a male apply for the job. You have a resume?"

"Yes." Wally reached down, opened his briefcase and pulled out a folder.

"Well, leave it with me. I'll look it over. Come back tomorrow when I have more time and we'll talk."

"I'll work hard Mr. Willis. I'm very thorough and dependable." Wally dropped the folder on the desk in front of him.

"Are you familiar with transcribing dictation?" Phil asked carefully as he watched for his reaction.

Easing himself forward in the chair, Wally replied with self assurance, "Yes. And I know my way in and out of a courtroom too."

His self confidence triggered Phil's attention. He looked briefly through the resume. "Let's take a few minutes to talk right now and if I decide that you can fit into my operation; maybe, we can start you today. I have a big case that I'm working on now."

"I would really appreciate that. You won't be disappointed if you hire me. What about salary?"

Phil wrote a figure down on a piece of paper and slipped it across the desk.

He looked at it briefly. "Looks good."

"Okay. Come with me." Phil led Wally to a desk in a back room. "I'll give you an application to fill out and then we can have an interview."

A short while later, Wally returned. "Here's my resume and application."

Phil eyes widened. "I see that you worked at Krest Law Firm for about five years?"

"Yes. Mr. Krest, the older gentleman in the firm, retired. His son took over and hired his wife as the new secretary. I was given two week's severance pay."

Phil looked down at the resume once again. "You're going to night school?"

"Yes. I hope to eventually get my law degree. "

Phil rubbed at the stubble on his chin and thought for a few minutes. "Looks like you have a lot of experience. I like your resume and the salary that you indicated you would accept. Can you start today?"

Relief shot through Wally. "I sure can." He relaxed and leaned back in his chair.

"First of all, I want to tell you that I have a very important case regarding a Father Reagan O'Malley coming up shortly. I need you to set up a file on it: names, dates, and times. Here's the info I have on it now. Use today as the starting date for the file and I'll feed you more information, as I acquire it. I'll dictate what I have on the case to this point. Now, you can go to the desk in the front office and set up a file for it."

Wally jumped to his feet and started to head toward the front office.

"I like your enthusiasm," Phil shouted after him.

He thought carefully as he formulated his plans for the case. He decided he would ask Kelley to go out to the school tomorrow and interview Terry Adams, the principal as well as the Moralas boy's teachers.

He relaxed, and put his feet on his desk as he mused about her. Kelley's going to love helping me out on this case. Her investigative juices will be flowing and she'll love being back in action again. I hope it will help soothe the loss she still feels about the miscarriage.

Chapter 15

The next morning Kelley and Phil drove together to his office. He glanced over at her and said, "I'm hoping that you can put your skills to work on this case. I need to discover why the kid lied about Father Reagan."

Kelley's head bobbed up and down. "Finding that out for you is my job. As soon as I drop you off. I'll head over to the school and interview some of the people."

They walked into the office and spotted Wally Cossins already seated at his desk.

"Morning." He jumped up and gracefully took Kelley's hand in his. "You must be Mrs. Willis. I've heard so much about you."

"And you are Wally, Phil's new secretary. I've heard you're studying for your law degree. Welcome to the team. I just hope you can keep up with my husband." She chuckled.

"I'm certainly going to try."

He pulled a manila folder from his desk drawer. "I have something here for you Mrs. Willis. When Mr. Willis told me that you were going out to St. John's school today to interview some people, I ran a background check on the school. This is a complete list of the staff and a print out of its location. Also a record of all its eighth grade students, which is the grade the Morales kid is in."

Impressed with Wally's efficiency, Kelley grinned, took the folder and looked quickly through the papers inside.

"Also, to break the ice, I thought that you might like to know that the principal is from Chicago." Wally rambled on. "I did a little investigative work myself at my last job and I know how difficult it can be to break the ice with some people."

"Thanks. You're very thorough," Kelley said.

Wally swiveled around in his chair and reached into a pile of papers on the back table. "And lastly, here is a rundown on the kid that accused Father Reagan."

Kelley glanced at the paper briefly, placed it on top of the folder and put everything into her briefcase. She gave Wally a warm smile. "You know Wally, I think we're going to get along extremely well."

"Now, Mr. Willis, If you have a few more minutes, I'll show you how I updated the file on Father Reagan's case."

"In due time Wally. Right now, let's all go into my office and talk over our design of attack."

He sat down, leaned back in his chair and clasped his hands behind his head. "Here's the plan. Kelley, I want you to head to the school now. Keep Wally and me informed of your progress. And, Wally, if anything more comes to mind about the case, please feel free to call Kelley at any time."

She chuckled and beamed at him. "Well, I believe that you've given me enough ammunition to get started. Unless, you have something more you want to go over with me, I'll call the school and get an appointment with the principal. Then, I'll be on my way."

Phil gave her an affirmative nod. "And, while you're gone, I'll contact Jill Sinclair to see if she can advise me on how I should handle this case."

"Now, I'll be off." Kelley said, heading eagerly toward the door. Looking back over her shoulder, she added, "I hope that you'll feel at home here, Wally."

"And Wally, don't hesitate to purchase some donuts from time to time. Take the money from the office expense account," Phil added, grinning.

Kelley pulled into the school parking lot, opened her briefcase, removed the folder, took out the papers that Wally had prepared for her and looked them over carefully. She could see he had done a thorough job.

Kelley noticed that some of the children were exiting the school and heading to the playground. She picked up her briefcase and walked inside the school where she encountered a little girl standing in the hallway. "Excuse me, where's the principal's office?"

"That's Mrs. Adams. At the end of the hall," the girl answered very politely.

Kelley entered the office marked 'Principal' and saw two young girls seated behind a long low counter. One of the girls looked up, flipped her hair back out of her eyes and asked, "May I help you?"

"Yes. I'm Mrs. Willis and I have a ten o'clock appointment with Mrs. Adams."

"Be right back," the girl said, as she stood up, knocked briefly on the door behind her and entered the office.

When she returned, she motioned for Kelley to follow.

The tall, slender, and well dressed middle-aged woman behind the desk, stood up when she saw Kelley enter.

"Mrs. Willis. My secretary said you called and made an appointment. Thank you for calling ahead. Please have a seat. But before we start I must tell you that I think I have an idea why you're here," she added warily.

"Oh?"

"I've read in the paper that Phillip Willis is the attorney defending Father O'Malley in the case that involves one of my students."

Kelley cleared her somewhat dry throat. "That's true."

"I have to inform you that I've been principal here for three years. All of my eighth graders graduated last year and all of them are scheduled to do so this year. I'm very pleased with my academic record and this school."

Kelley regarded her soberly and managed a smile. "I'm sure you're very proud of that accomplishment."

"This school has a history of dealing with troubled students," Mrs. Adams said as her nostrils flared. "It's a small parochial school, located on the south side of Syracuse, and in a poor section of the city. The majority of our students come from single family homes. Others are being raised by their grandparents, as the parents are either in jail or unable to care for their children for some reason."

Chewing on that thought, Kelley replied simply, "That sounds like it could be quite a challenge for you."

"Yes. But I've brought a sense of pride back to the school and have gotten most of the parents and grandparents enthusiastically involved in our activities. A lot of the troublesome outside influences have been eliminated."

"That's all very impressive. But I've come here specifically to hear what you can tell me about Juan Morales." Kelley slid back in her chair and smiled pleasantly.

Mrs. Adams placed her elbows on the top of her desk. "I do have to admit that Juan was extremely difficult to get next to. He's very small in stature and he was teased and bullied before I got here. Fortunately, I was able to stop that. Now he seems to be making an effort to become a fine young man."

"Do you have any idea why he would accuse Father Reagan of such a terrible thing?"

Mrs. Adams chewed on that for a while. "No. I know Father Reagan well and have the highest regard for him. I am not a Catholic myself. Never the less, I do attend morning mass with our students and interact with Father Reagan daily. I must tell you, I believe that your husband has taken on a monumental task. This is probably a case of—who does one believe. And in the end, no one will really win."

Kelley forced a false little laugh and replied politely, "We realize that. But, I hope that you will have no objections to my looking around the school?"

"Not at all. As long as you do it discreetly. Try not to disturb my school too much. Now, Mrs. Willis, I'm late for a meeting. So, if you will excuse me?" With a shrug, she dismissed Kelley.

Kelley stood and extended her hand. "Just one more question. Do you know of any gangs that are active around here?"

"Not that I'm aware of. At least not in this school."

"By the way, Mrs. Adams, I checked you out on the Internet. I noticed that you originally lived in Chicago. In fact we both went to the same high school there. Do you ever get back for a class reunion?"

"Maybe next year," she replied dismissing her.

Kelley started for the door. "Thanks for your time."

"Please be sure to use some diplomacy if you happen to question any of my students or staff."

Kelley's eyes deepened and she replied with icy indignation, "I will."

After she looked around the school briefly, Kelley walked back to her car. A nun approached her. "Are you a visitor here?"

"Yes Sister."

"Well, this parking area is for staff only." A little annoyed, she pointed across the lot. "The visitor parking is over there."

Kelley smiled. "Thank you. I'll remember that in the future." Then after a brief pause, she asked, "Oh by the way Sister, do you know Juan Morales?"

The nun nervously shook her head. "I can't talk to you now. I'm late for class."

Kelley entered her car and got a phone call from Wally, "Mrs. Willis, I'm sending you a photo of Juan Morales on your phone. And I have his address for you. I thought you might want to interview his neighbors," he said with some satisfaction.

After receiving the information Kelley answered, "Hey Wally, ask my husband if he can pick the kids up from day care tonight. And tell him that I'll be late for dinner."

"I'm on it, Mrs. Willis."

"Please, call me Kelley."

Chapter 16

That evening, the grandfather clock in the hallway chimed six times as Kelley entered the front door and shouted, "I'm looking for my family!"

"In the kitchen, Kell."

She kicked off her shoes and walked into the kitchen, where Phil was standing at the granite island, tearing lettuce into a large salad bowl. She strolled to the opposite side and gave him a kiss on the cheek.

"Have a good day?" he asked as he wiped his hands on the apron tied around his waist.

"Yes. So much to tell you. But first, give me an update on the Willis household. Where are the kids?" She slid onto a bar stool.

"I fed them, they're in Alan's room playing games."

He reached down, grabbed a piece of tomato and popped it into her mouth. "Why don't you run upstairs and say hi to them. Take a shower, put on something comfortable and meet me in the family room for supper in front of the fireplace."

She grabbed a couple pieces of green pepper and munching on them headed up the steps to Alan's room.

The children, engrossed in their games, looked up when she entered. Seeing that they were more interested in the games than her, Kelley gave them each a kiss.

"Daddy or I will come in later and tuck you in."

She went into the master bathroom, stripped off her clothes, drew herself a nice hot bath and stepped into the whirlpool tub. After several minutes, her stomach started to growl with hunger. "Oh what should I listen to, my aching body or my hungry tummy?"

She put her head back against the tub and closed her eyes. A short while later, Phil entered, , leaned over and kissed her on the forehead. "Supper's ready."

"Just need another five minutes," she said with a lazy half smile.

She climbed out of the tub, dried herself off, slipped into a pair of pink silk lounging pajamas and headed downstairs.

Phil, now dressed in pajamas and a robe, was sitting on the leather sofa in front of the fireplace. On the coffee table were two wooden salad bowls heaped with fresh salads and topped with dressing. Next to them on a tray, was a bottle of chilled wine and a couple of glasses.

"Let the feast begin," he said as Kelley sat down beside him

She curled up in the corner of the sofa and he handed her a bowl of salad. "Oh my goodness, you even put blue cheese dressing on mine."

"Yes. I have to keep my undercover investigator happy and content. So let's just sit back and enjoy the rest of the evening."

When they finished their salads, Phil pushed himself up and stretched to relieve the kink in his back. He carried the empty salad bowls to the kitchen and returned with a couple of plates filled with hot food. "I made some chicken cordon bleu especially for you. I know that's one of your favorites. Also made a side order of broccoli and some garlic toast."

She looked at the food in amazement. "You're getting to be one great chef, Phil." Her gaze slid up to his and then to the wine. "And I see that you have one of the wines that Marco Rossi sent us from his vineyard in Sicily. Are we celebrating something special?"

"No. Just thought the moment was right. When we're finished with our meal, let's talk about your day," he added, refilling their wine glass.

Kelley took a couple of bites of her food. "Delicious. Where did you get the recipe?"

"I emailed your old partner, James Fleming. Told him I wanted to surprise you and he emailed it back. He's quite the gourmet chef too, you know."

Kelley nodded and savored each bite.

When she was almost finished, Phil asked, "You like?"

She released an appreciative breath. "I like."

After finishing the main course, Phil took the plates into the kitchen, while Kelley stifled a yawn and settled back in her seat. She could feel herself starting to really unwind. She took a sip of her wine and sighed contentedly as Phil returned to the room.

He sat down beside her, smothering a grin. "Okay, now that I've fed you, tell me how your day went."

"Well, I had a brief but good visit with the principal of St. John's Academy." Then rolling her eyes, she added, "And I promised her to be discreet when and if I interviewed any of the teachers or students."

Phil waited patiently, giving her time to continue.

"She also mentioned that Juan Morales was small and didn't seem to have too many friends. Said he had been teased and bullied before she took over as principal, but that she had stopped it. Looks like she runs a pretty tight ship."

Phil shifted in his seat, moved closer. "Maybe Juan accused Father Reagan just to get attention."

"Might be. Wally sent me a picture of the kid over the phone so I would know what he looked like. Gave me his home address too. I waited outside of school, until the kids came out."

A slow smile crept up Phil's cheeks. "And?"

"And, I spotted Juan as he left school. I followed him slowly in my car, but he darted down an alley and I lost him. So I just drove to his house, a modest one story stucco bungalow. I sat outside and waited to see if he would come home. After about a half hour, I walked over to a house across the street and introduced myself to the old lady who was working outside in her front yard. She said she lived in the neighborhood for years and is a widow."

"Did she give you any information about the Morales kid?"

"Some. I didn't tell her why I was asking. I let her believe that I was some kind of social worker. She said Juan and his mother have lived there for about ten years. Just the two of them. The mother keeps to herself. She said the kids on the block would tease and bully Juan all the time. He would curse at them and run inside the house." She settled back and took another sip of the wine. Raising her glass, she said, "Delicious. Just delicious."

"Did she tell you anything else?"

"Yes. She pointed out a vacant house at the end of the block where some of the kids hang out. She said she heard that a couple of the neighborhood kids, eighth graders, had gotten arrested lately. Then, all of a sudden, she clammed up and said 'good-bye.' She went in the house and shut the door."

Phil grew quiet and thoughtful as his mind registered what she had just said. "Maybe if you go to the police station tomorrow you could get some information about those kids being arrested."

Kelley's face broke into a wide grin. "I was hoping you'd suggest that Counselor."

"But good work, Kell. Just keep on digging for me. All

of this might come in handy at the trial."

After they finished their wine, Phil said, "Why, don't you go upstairs, tuck the kids in and wait for me. I'll throw the dishes in the dishwasher and close up."

The next morning, Kelley dropped the kids off at school and went downtown to the Syracuse police station. She told the police officer that she was from the law office of Phil Willis, who was representing Father Reagan O'Malley and wished to speak to a detective about the case. A short time later, she was ushered into Detective Sam Mason's office.

Seated behind a desk, he looked up from his work as entered the room. "Mrs. Willis. I remember you. You lived next door to that Toth guy that was murdered."

"You have a good memory."

"And what can I do for you this morning?"

"I have a few questions about the juvenile arrests that were made recently in Juan Morales's neighborhood. Hope you can supply the answers."

He eased himself away from his desk and leaned back in his chair. "I'll give you what I can."

"Mind if I sit down?" Kelley asked.

He waved his hand toward a chair in front of his desk.

Kelley flopped into it. "But, first I wanted to tell you that I've already done some undercover work on the case. My husband, Father Reagan's attorney, is convinced that he's innocent and intends to prove it."

Detective Mason's brows shot up and he smiled. "He's not the only one that feels that way. My mother told me this morning that she personally knows Father Reagan and that she doesn't believe he would be capable of molesting a child. Maybe, if we put our heads together, Mrs. Willis, we can discover what's really going on with this kid."

Kelley tried not to let her surprise at that statement show. "I went to the school yesterday and talked to the principal. She said before she came to the school, Juan Morales had been constantly bullied by the other students because he was so small. But she stopped that. While I didn't get the opportunity to interview any of the other students or teachers, I did try to follow Juan home yesterday after school. Lost track of him though."

Mason held up his hand as a prickle of alarm danced along his skin. "Let me stop you right there. I think that it might be best if you leave the serious investigating to the police."

"Let me finish." A shadow fell across Kelley's face as she shifted her body in her seat. "I talked to a neighbor who said that some of the neighborhood kids have been gathering at a vacant house down the street."

"We knew about it. But when my men checked into it, they found that homeless guys have been living there."

"The neighbor said that a couple of the local kids were arrested lately. Is that true?"

"Yes." Mason shrugged indifferently. "One was picked up for writing graffiti on a nearby apartment complex wall and another one stole a few items from the hardware store around the corner."

"Have you heard of any gang activity in that neighborhood?" Kelley looked intently at him.

"There was a rumor about that. Involves mostly older kids from the nearby high school."

She gave him a doubtful look. "Do you think they could be recruiting some of these middle school boys into the gang? Maybe talking them into doing some wild things to get into the gang. Like an initiation?"

"Boy, that's really reaching." Wariness flickered across his face. "But, I'll follow it up. The kid that got arrested for stealing from the hardware store has moved to another town. His parents were really upset with him."

"Do you have the boy's new address?" Kelley asked, now determined to pursue the issue. "If it's okay with you, I would like to go talk with him and his parents. He might have an idea as to why Juan has accused Father Reagan of this hideous crime."

"I can't see any harm in you just talking to the kid. Sit tight. I'm not supposed to do this, but, let me check my computer and see if I have his new address."

He swiveled around in his chair, and looked through his computer files for a moment. "Yes. Here it is. Bobby Garrett. Lives in West Brutus now." He wrote the name and address on a piece of paper and handed it to Kelley.

Forcing a false little laugh, she tried to make light of her jitters. "Thanks. Time is running short. The trial is set to begin soon."

"Good luck, Mrs. Willis. Let me know if I can be of any further help."

Inside her car, Kelley phoned the office. "Hi Wally. Kelley here. I'll be in a small town, named West Brutus, this afternoon. I learned that one of the kids from St. John's school moved there and I want to interview him. I think he might shed some light on our case."

"I wanted to tell you that I set up a cork board for Mr. Willis with all the participants and facts in the case. Should be easier for both of you to keep track of the chain of events."

"My God, Wally, you do a lot more than just man the phone and type up reports."

"Just earning my keep," he said with a confident chuckle. "Oh, your husband said to remind you that your in-laws are picking up the kids and that you're having dinner with them tonight at their house."

"Nice. If you talk to Phil, remind him that the folks

need to take ID with them to show when they pick the kids up. Safety first is the school's motto."

"Got it covered."

"Catch you later, Wally."

Driving toward West Brutus, Kelley followed the directions the GPS issued. I think I'm almost there. She glanced down at the note beside her with the Garrett address. Yes. That's the house. No name on the mail box though.

Kelley parked her car in front of the two-story house and walked up. The screen door was wide open, but the inside door was closed. She tapped softly. A tall, thin man opened it.

"I'm looking for Bobby Garrett."

"The name is Moses Zink. Soon I'll be the kid's new stepfather. And who the hell are you?"

"Kelley Willis," she replied with a firm confident tone.

"And why do you need to see Bobby?"

She took a step forward and flashed him a warm smile. "May I come in and have a seat?"

"You're not selling something are you?" He stiffened.

"No Sir. I just need to ask Bobby a few questions about his activities at the school he attended in Syracuse."

"You mean St. John's?"

"Yes. I won't take up much of his time."

Moses stepped back for Kelley to come inside. As she strolled into the living room, she could not help but notice how small and humble the room appeared. It was filled with shabby furniture, a dirty rug and was sorely in need of some fresh paint.

She walked toward the worn sofa that was placed behind a coffee table covered with magazines and empty soda and beer cans and gingerly sat down.

Moses hung his head in embarrassment as he noticed Kelley's wariness. "We're moving soon," he said sheepishly.

Kelley looked up and saw a gray, straggly haired woman, who appeared to be in her early fifties walking down from the upstairs.

The woman's eyes widened as she noticed Kelley. She turned to Moses. "And who is this?"

Moses shrugged his shoulders. "Said her name was Kelley Willis. She wants to talk to Bobby."

She walked over to Kelley. "I'm Bobby's mother, Connie. What can I do for you?"

Kelley stood up and extended her hand. "My husband is the attorney for Father Reagan O'Malley. As you've probably heard, he was charged with molesting one of the boys who attended St. John's where your son used to go."

Connie wiped her hands off on her apron, but did not shake hands with Kelley. Instead, she folded her arms in front of her in a defensive action. "We've nothing to say about that. We moved out of Syracuse so my boy and I could start a new life with Mr. Zink."

Kelley sat back down, reached into her briefcase and pulled out a note pad. "I have just a few questions for Bobby. It will only take a few minutes and it may help greatly with Father Reagan's defense."

Connie's gaze narrowed as she thought for a few minutes. Then, she sighed and looked at Moses. "Well, Father Reagan was always very good to Bobby. Maybe, it wouldn't hurt if he just answered a couple questions."

She turned toward the kitchen. "I'll get him. He's home for lunch. Has to get back to school soon." She called out, "Bobby, come in here please."

With a sandwich in one hand and a can of soda in the other, Bobby walked slowly into the room. "Yeah. What is it, Ma?"

Connie waved her hand toward Kelley. "Son, this is Mrs. Willis. Her husband is the lawyer for Father Reagan and she wants to ask you a couple questions."

Looking somewhat apprehensive, Bobby plopped down on the sofa beside Kelley as Connie and Moses sat down in near-by chairs.

With a deliberate confident movement, Kelley leaned forward and spoke in a low calm voice. "Bobby, I would like to ask you a few questions about your activities while you attended St. John's and if you knew Juan Morales."

He swallowed and shot a questioning glance at his mother. "What you think Mom?"

Connie nodded her head. "I can't see any harm in answering some questions for this lady. Moses and I will stay with you. By the way, Mrs. Willis, I prefer you don't tape this conversation. Once my son's answered your questions, I suggest you don't contact him again," she croaked angrily. "He wants to put his past behind him and just start anew."

Kelley picked up her pen and placed her note pad on her lap in front of her. "I understand. I'll just take a few notes as we chat, Bobby."

He sat on the edge of his seat as Kelley proceeded. "First of all, did you know Juan Morales?"

"Yes."

"Were you friends with him?"

He hesitated. "No. Not really."

"Didn't you both belong to the same gang?"

He cast a quick glance from the corner of his eye at his mother, who said, "You don't have to answer that Bobby."

For just a moment, he wavered. Then, he firmly shook his head and whispered, "It was just a club. You know kids just hanging out together."

"Who ran the club?" Kelley asked as her cell phone chimed and vibrated. She looked down at it. "Excuse me. I need to take this call."

She talked for a few moments, hung up and turned her attention once again to Bobby. "That was Detective Mason. You know the police officer that arrested you for stealing."

"I pleaded guilty. Served my probation," he answered defiantly.

"I know. He told me that. Also said they just raided the abandoned house you kids used as your club house. They arrested some kid there smoking pot. So I guess the old gang is still hanging out together there."

Bobby just sat there in silence, then he looked at his mother for guidance.

Connie got up abruptly. Her brow shot up and her eyes flashed. "Mrs. Willis, I want you to know that in my heart I believe that Father O'Malley is innocent of the charges brought against him. But my boy was not at the school when the incident happened and so he doesn't want to get involved."

"I understand Mrs. Garrett, but I would just like to ask Bobby a couple more questions about the club, if that's okay."

Connie shot an icy glance at Moses. He shrugged his shoulders. "Can't be any harm in that," he said. "Bobby, answer the ladies questions about the club."

Kelley leaned forward. "Did you and the other boys have to do anything special to get accepted into the club?"

"Yes. We were supposed to do something real daredevil like. They dared me to steal and a couple of kids broke into a school and smashed some stuff. A couple of kids bought drugs from a neighborhood guy and took them. One kid wrote graffiti on a school bus."

Kelley took a deep breath. "Can you give me names of some of the other boys who belonged to the club?"

"No. I can't rat on my friends."

"Do you think then, that it might be possible someone dared Juan to make up a lie about Father O'Malley in order to get into the club?"

"Ask him." Bobby rolled his head to the side, fixing

her with an irritated glare. "Anything's possible. All of us were ready to do whatever it took to get admitted into that club. We wanted to be one of the gang."

Kelley took down a few more notes, then closed up her notebook and put it and her pen inside her briefcase. She took out a business card, and handed it to Connie. "I want to thank both you and your son for your cooperation. I hope this information will be helpful to my husband as he gets ready to go to trial with Father Reagan."

She stood up, laid her hand on Bobby's arm and said, "Thank you. It was very brave of you to speak with me."

After shaking hands with both Connie and Moses, she made a quick exit.

Kelley realized that Phil would have to be prepared to handle the trial without the assistance of the boys who belonged to the gang. He had to concentrate on proving that Juan Morales had a motive to lie about being molested by Father Reagan.

Chapter 17

The next few days passed quickly for Kelley and Phil as they spent most of their time preparing for Father Reagan's trial, which was to start on Monday morning. As usual, the Sunday evening before was devoted to their family. After watching the movie "Aladdin" with the children, they retired to bed early. Phil wanted to be rested and alert for the big event the next morning.

The trial was scheduled to begin sharply at nine in Judge Ann Taylor's courtroom. She was known for not only starting her trials promptly but for running a very tight schedule.

Phil was pleased that this judge had been assigned to the trial, since she had a positive reputation and he knew that she would see that his client got a fair trial.

At seven-thirty on Monday morning, all members of the Willis family were dressed, fed and ready to head out the door.

"We don't need a packed lunch today," Alan said. "Miss Beasley is bringing in Chef Ray to make us healthy food."

"It's going to be pizza," Ashley chimed in.

Phil tilted his head to hide his smile, "Pizza, huh?"

"Vegetable pizza," Alan said.

"Sounds healthy to me," Kelley said. "I'll take the kids to school and meet you at the courthouse later." She gave him a quick kiss good-bye.

Phil had spent days preparing for the trial. He was disappointed that his adviser, Jill Sinclair, was scheduled to take her mother to a doctor's appointment early this morning and would be late arriving at court.

When she got to the courtroom, Kelley saw the large clock above the doors read eight-thirty and the doors were still closed. She looked up and down the hall and noticed news media and spectators waiting to enter the courtroom, but no sign of Phil. "Now where is that husband of mine?"

She sat down on a nearby bench as her cell phone vibrated. It was Wally. "Is Mr. Willis there? I've been trying to reach him."

It was now somewhat noisy in the hallway as two police officers tried to get the spectators to line up in an orderly fashion prior to entering the courtroom.

"Hard to hear you, Wally." She walked to the windows at the end of the hall to put a distance between her and the noise. "No. Phil isn't here. He left home after me and I expected him to be here by now. But, no sign of him. Why? What's up?"

"A Mrs. Garrett came here to see him. Said her son decided to give Mr. Willis the names and addresses of a couple of the kids who were involved in the local gang. I took down all the information that she had."

"Good work, Wally. I'll tell Phil what you have."

A clock outside in a nearby bell tower rang out nine times as the courtroom doors finally opened and the clerk emerged. "Sorry. There will be a half hour delay before the court session starts. The night crew didn't clean the room thoroughly last night and we had to call them in to finish up this morning."

By the time he opened the doors, forty-five minutes later, the waiting crowd was very irritated. They rushed into the courtroom.

Kelley took a seat directly behind the defense table, where Phil and Father Reagan were to sit. But so far, no sign of either of them. Roland O'Malley entered the courtroom and took a seat beside her. He seemed to be brimming with anticipation as he greeted her.

On the opposite side of the aisle was a long wooden table. A tall, broad-shouldered man, who appeared to be in his early forties, with brown hair thinning on the top walked up to the table, and threw his briefcase on top.

Behind him was his assistant, carrying a large box. She placed the box on the table, opened it and took out stacks of papers. Kelley realized this was the prosecutor and his aide. They were here to try the case of Juan Morales and the State of New York against Father Reagan O'Malley.

Kelley looked around the courtroom as everyone took their seats. However, there was no sign of Juan Morales or his mother.

"What's going on?" Kelley thought. "Where the hell is everyone?"

The bailiff and the court reporter entered the room from a side door. The bailiff announced, "All cell phones and pagers must be silenced before we call the court to order."

Then, in a loud voice, he called out, "All rise. This court is in session. The Honorable Judge Ann Taylor presiding."

The judge entered and took her seat behind the bench. "Please be seated. Bailiff, please escort the jurors into the courtroom."

Talking noisily among themselves, the crowd slowly sat back down.

The Judge pounded her gavel. "Quiet please."

She looked down at the prosecutor and his aide. "Nice to see you again, Mr. Hawks. But, where is the young man in this case? "

Dwayne Hawks sighed, pushed the thinning hair out of his eyes and stood up. "Don't know, your Honor. My associate went to his house to pick him up earlier. But, called and said that Juan wasn't there. Neither was his mother. Right now, I have no idea where they are."

"You have a problem then, Mr. Hawks."

"Yes, your Honor. I realize that."

She looked over at the defense table, which was empty. "And where is the defendant and his attorney?" she snapped, now getting thoroughly annoyed.

Kelley stood up and waved her hand.

The Judge's brow shut up and her eyes flashed. "And just who are you?"

Kelley took a deep breath and said with as much self assurance as she could muster, "I'm Kelley Willis, the wife of the defendant's attorney, Phillip Willis."

"Unless my eyes deceive me I believe that both your husband and the defendant, Father O'Malley, seem to be missing." The Judge glared down at her. "I hope that your husband has a good reason to explain why he is either absent or late. At the moment, he's off to a bad start in my court room. And that's not wise."

From beside her, Kelley heard Roland whisper, "My God, Kelley, where are they?"

Judge Taylor looked around the courtroom and banged her gavel on the bench. "Ladies and gentlemen, I've heard hundreds of cases in this courtroom; but, this beats all. Mrs. Willis you are standing at the table where your husband should be, with his client, Father O'Malley. Mr. Hawks, you also have no client present. And, if I look to my left, I see our jurors seated and ready to listen to the case. At this point, it looks like I will have to make a major decision. So, my ruling at the present time is…"

Suddenly, the doors to the courtroom were thrown open, and Phil ran to the front of the room. His voice shook as he announced loudly, "Your Honor, Phillip Willis, attorney for the defense is present." He slid into a seat behind the defense table.

Walking into the courtroom behind him was Detective Mason and Father Reagan.

Judge Taylor stared at them coldly. "You and the defendant are a little late Counselor. The court does not take this lightly."

Mason sat down next to Kelley and Roland, while the priest took a seat beside Phil.

Phil slammed his briefcase down on the defense table. Swallowing his excitement, he said, "Please your Honor let me explain. I've got a logical explanation as to why we're late."

"As you probably already know, Mr. Willis, I run a tight ship. But before you speak, take a moment to compose yourself. Then give me your explanation. And it better be good."

She glanced around the room at the spectators, who were now whispering among themselves, and banged the gavel loudly once again. "Order in the courtroom."

She stared down at Phil intently and added sternly, "Now Mr. Willis. You are going to present the court with a reasonable explanation as to what is occurring."

"Yes, your Honor. But first, I would like to tell the prosecutor, Mr. Hawks, where Juan Morales is at, since he's not present in court today."

"On with it, Mr. Willis."

Phil stood up, took a deep breath and continued. "Your Honor, just as I was getting ready to leave my home this morning, I received a call from Juan's mother. She said she was calling from the emergency room of Syracuse General Hospital, where the paramedics had just taken her son. She had found Juan unconscious, with an open bottle of sleeping pills beside his bed. It appears that he tried to commit suicide."

A stunned Dwayne Hawks gave Phil a disbelieving look, the courtroom spectators gasped in surprise. Kelley whispered, "Oh, no." She grabbed Roland O'Malley's arm.

Judge Taylor's eyes narrowed. "And where was the defendant, Father Reagan?"

"He was at the hospital too," Phil continued. "You see Mrs. Morales asked me to bring the priest to the hospital. With her son in a life threatening situation, she wanted him to be with her and to give her boy the last sacraments. I realize your Honor, that Father Reagan is under house arrest and that I was supposed to bring him directly to court. However, under this unusual situation, I called Detective Mason and asked him to accompany Father Reagan and myself to the hospital to see Juan."

"And how is the boy doing?" The Judge sat back in her chair, dwelling upon this sudden change in the case.

"They pumped out his stomach. Right now, he is resting comfortably. I believe Detective Mason has a statement he would like to present to the court at this time."

"Stand up Detective," the judge ordered. "Would you please enlighten the court?"

With a folder in his hand, Mason came forward and stood beside Phil. "I believe, your Honor, that my information should close this case once and for all."

He removed a paper from the folder. "I have in my hand, a sworn and signed statement from Juan Morales. He dictated it to me in the emergency room after he resumed consciousness. He signed it in the presence of two nurses who served as witnesses."

The prosecutor shot to his feet. "Your Honor, I protest. This is a major deviance from standard court procedure."

Judge Taylor slammed her gavel. "Overruled," she announced. "Please continue, Detective."

Mason cleared his throat. "In this statement, the young man swears that the Father Reagan did not molest him in any way. He made up this lie as part of his initiation into a local gang. He also gave me some information on the gang."

He waved his folder in the air. "May I approach the bench?"

"Hand your folder to the bailiff." The Judge sat back in her chair, now somewhat weary.

Mason handed the folder to the bailiff, who in return, took it up to the Judge. She read through the papers for a few minutes. "Mr. Willis and Mr. Hawks, please approach the bench."

She talked quietly with them, handed Hawks the folder and ordered the men to return to their seats. As the audience started to buzz like a beehive, the Judge gave them a withering glance and slammed her gavel again. "Order in the courtroom. Or, I'll clear it."

Prosecutor Hawks returned to his table, looked through the papers briefly and shook his head as though to clear it. "May I speak your Honor?"

She nodded. "Yes. Mr. Hawks."

"If it pleases the court, your Honor, after briefly assessing the new evidence that Detective Mason has brought to court, the State of New York wishes to drop all charges against the accused."

The Judge looked at the priest. "Mr. O'Malley, excuse me, Father O'Malley. Detective Mason has presented the court with evidence attesting to your innocence in this case. And the prosecutor has just asked me to dismiss all charges against you."

The priest put his hands to his face and wiped away the tears that were rolling down his checks as the Judge continued. "I find that all charges against Father Reagan O'Malley are dismissed. You are free to leave the courtroom. This case is closed."

The audience jumped to their feet and cheered as the Judge rose from her seat and left the courtroom.

Hawks walked over to Phil and shook his hand. "Nice job, Willis. If you ever decide to work on this side of the law, we're always looking for good people." Then he grasped the priest's hands. "I'll see you in church on Sunday, Father."

Roland ran around to his brother's side and embraced him. Grabbing Phil's hand, he said in a thick voice that didn't sound like his own, "Great job. Why don't you and Kelley have supper with us tonight to celebrate?"

"We'll take a rain check on that," Phil answered. "I want to go back to the office and call the Bishop and give him the good news, so he can re-instate your brother."

"Thank you," Father Reagan said. "I'm anxious to get back to my congregation. These past couple of weeks have been hell on earth for me."

The tremor in his voice wrenched Kelley's heart. She gave him a brief hug. "We'll look forward to seeing you at mass this week."

He clasped her hands in his and whispered, "You and your husband will be in my prayers for years to come."

Leaving the courtroom and starting toward the escalators a voice called out. "Mr. Willis, wait."

Turning around, they saw the Judge walking towards them. She came up to Phil and shook his hand. "Nice job, Counselor. You reminded me once again that there are a lot of good people in this city. Hope we meet again soon."

Kelley and Phil strolled toward their car. "Let's make a stop at the office," he said. "I'll call the Bishop and fill him in on the situation. After that, I'm going to call a news conference to set the record straight about Father Regan."

Chapter 18

After the charges against Father Reagan were dismissed, the priest resumed his normal duties at St. Johns Church and Kelley and Phil returned to their everyday lives.

Months later, Phil received a phone call from Father Reagan telling him that he had accepted a position working at Vatican City. He thanked Phil once again for what he had done and invited them to spend some time with him if they came to Rome in the future.

Their lives changed dramatically in the next few years. Kelley's mother, Ann, who had continued to live in Chicago, was rushed to the hospital. Kelley flew there to be with her. Within a few days, pneumonia and heart failure took their toll and she passed away.

Phil and the children flew in to Chicago to join Kelley and Ann's companion, Veronica Miley, for the funeral. After a quiet ceremony, Ann was buried beside Kelley's father.

Kelley's Nanna Kate was too ill to fly over from Ireland for the services, but she sent a huge bouquet of flowers and started a trust fund in Ann's name for the Willis children.

After Ann's death, Veronica moved to California, where

she eventually married a retired naval officer, but kept in touch with the Willis's and sent them a lovely Christmas card every year.

Phil had enrolled at Syracuse University and studied tax law. Kelley also took courses on taxes so that she could assist him in this new branch of his law practice. Within a few short months, he had developed a nice tax client base and his business was flourishing.

They seemed to have an ideal life. No longer were they involved in undercover work. Phil had stopped working on criminal cases and his practice was mostly centered on tax cases in addition to simple everyday legal work.

They worked together daily and spent their evenings and weekends with their growing children. Ashley was now in the seventh grade and Alan was in the eighth. Sunday evenings, which were still family nights, continued to bond the family.

This particular Saturday afternoon was no ordinary day, as the annual school talent show was scheduled for that evening. Ashley, who was scheduled to participate, was busy practicing her act.

She was singing and dancing to, "The Sun Will Come Out Tomorrow" in the family room. Kelley watched her go through her song and dance, and could see that she was not too enthusiastic.

Kelley looked out from the kitchen, where she was putting the lunch dishes in the dishwasher. "That little red dress and that auburn wig look just lovely on you, Dear."

Ashley stopped in the middle of the routine and gritted her teeth in dissatisfaction, "It's boring, Mom. Some kid does this number every year."

"Don't worry, Honey. You'll be just fine."

Phil walked by heading out the back door. "I have a

couple of things to take care of at the office. I'll meet you at the school. The program starts at two, correct?"

Kelley wiped her hands on a dish towel. "That's right. And please pick up Mrs. Trot's tax form while you're at the office. You can drop it off to her afterwards."

Kelley, Ashley and Alan walked into the school auditorium, about a half hour before the program was due to start. The hall was filling up with students, their parents and family. Everyone appeared to be anxious to see the nine student finalists who had been previously selected to participate in the last round of the contest.

Kelley and Alan took a seat in the second row with the other contestant's parents.

"Ashley sit here with us and hold a seat for your Dad," Kelley instructed.

Ashley dropped the back pack that contained her dress and wig on the floor and sat down with a dejected look. She didn't even bother to talk with her friends.

Phil entered the auditorium from a side door next to the stage and spied his family. After he walked over, Ashley lifted her head and whispered to him. "Daddy, can I change my number? I want to do the one that you helped me with earlier."

He hesitated before answering. "Don't you think it's a little late to change?"

"I'm eighth in the program." She stiffened and leaned forward. "Maybe it's not too late."

"I'm certain you'll do fine," Phil whispered, as the school's musical director walked onto the stage and made his opening announcement.

After the first young participant played a piece on the piano, the director announced that the second performer, Sandy Lockwood, was going to change her number to 'The Sun Will Come Out Tomorrow,' from "Annie."

Kelley sat there, stunned, as this was the very song that Ashley had been practicing. The wheels in her mind spun like the cylinders on a press. This was a tragic state of affairs for her daughter now.

Ashley grabbed her father by the arm. "That's it Daddy. I'm sunk. I'm not going to do the same song as her," she muttered. "I've got to change to something else."

Her desperation ate at Phil's heart. He thought for a few moments, then smiled and whispered back.

Releasing a deep breath, Ashley broke into a big grin. "Yes. Yes, Daddy. We can do it."

The two of them slipped out of their seats.

"Where are Ashley and Dad going?" Alan asked his mother, as he swiveled around in his seat to watch them leave the room.

"Beats me."

After a few more contestants performed, the musical director returned to the stage. "Ladies and gentlemen, we have another change in our program. Ashley Willis and her father will entertain us with a number from the musical 'Annie.' They will be dancing and singing to 'I Don't Need Anything But You'."

Ashley and Phil stepped out, both wearing straw hats and carrying canes. As they sang "Yesterday Was Plain Awful" and "Nothing Can Ever Divide Us", they did a lively tap dance routine together.

Kelley and Alan sat forward in their seats, amazed. Alan whispered, "Say, they're really good Mom. I mean, look at Dad go."

"I didn't know that he could tap dance," Kelley's mouth dropped open in disbelief. As the act continued, her shoulders relaxed. She hated to admit it, but her husband was good. In fact, they both were really good.

After their number, Ashley and Phil were called back onto the stage to take several bows.

When Phil returned to his seat, Kelley asked, "My God,

Willis, when did you and Ashley whip up that routine?"

"Our little secret, my Dear. Our little secret."

Kelley smiled. It was incidents like this that brought about a tight bond in the Willis family.

At the final judging, Ashley, and a young lady who had played a number on the harp, were tied for first place. Both were called on stage and given a ribbon.

After Ashley returned to the family, Phil asked, "And what is my reward for helping you young lady?"

"You can take me to Disney World this summer, Daddy." She winked, brushing her hair out of her eyes.

"Deal. But now, I need to head back to the office. I forgot to bring Mrs. Trot's income tax form with me. I want to drop it off to her on the way home. So why don't you follow me back to the office with the kids, Kell? Then we can go out to eat."

While they were in Phil's office, Alan heard the sound of a car pulling up outside. He walked over to the window and peaked out through the blinds. "Hey, Dad, there's a big black limo outside."

Hearing a brisk knock on the door, Kelley opened it and saw two very large men wearing black trench coats standing outside. "May I help you?"

One of the men took off his hat and tipped it to her. "Excuse us madam. My name is Gino Basilio. I realize that Mr. Willis's office is closed today, but if he is in, may I have a few moments of his time?"

Kelley stepped back to let the men enter. "Sure. Follow me."

She led the men to Phil's office. "This is Mr. Basilio and he wishes to talk to you."

Gino, with the other man behind him, strolled in. "Just five minutes of your time, Sir. Please hear me out."

Phil gave her a quizzical glance and shrugged his shoulders. "Kell, take the kids out to the front. I'll be just a few minutes."

Kelley motioned for the kids to follow her as Phil looked at Gino Basilio. "Now, what is it that you wish to talk to me about?" His eyes widened with curiosity.

A short silence. Then, Gino replied, "I gotta job for you that I hope you won't refuse. First let me introduce my body guard, assistant and driver, Max."

Chapter 19

After they shook hands, Phil asked, "And exactly what is it you wish to talk to me about?"

Gino stiffened and frowned. "May we have a seat before I discuss my situation?"

"Of course." Phil pulled out chairs in front of his desk for them and walked around to the back of the desk where he flopped in his swivel chair, sat back and waited patiently for an answer.

Gino seemed to be choosing his words carefully. "I would like to hire you to do my taxes. My neighbor tells me that you have done his taxes and that he was quite pleased with your work."

He took a folder from his assistant and laid it on Phil's desk. "I was hoping you could look over my current year's taxes and that we could start working together next week."

A ragged sigh slipped through Phil as he studied the papers. Then, he leaned over and pulled his calendar out from a desk drawer. "At first glance, I can see that your tax situation appears to be quite complicated, but I think that I can fit you into my schedule."

Gino reared back in his chair and shot him a challenging look. "The firm that I have used previously has gotten me all fouled up with the Internal Revenue Service. I need you to straighten out my past several years taxes with them and then to do both my business and personal taxes correctly in the future. You could work out of my office, which is located above my restaurant. There you'll have quick access to my past years' records. I was told that your wife helps you prepare tax returns and that speeds the process along."

"That's true. She's now my associate."

"Maybe, you can give me a rough estimate of how long it will take you and what you'll charge. Give me that figure when we meet next week." Gino looked at him with a sharp assessment.

"You'll find that I never overbill my clients Mr. Basilio. And I'm confident that you'll be satisfied with my services."

"I like what I've heard Mr. Willis," Gino replied. "And here's my card. It's of upmost important to have my taxes done correctly so I can sleep nights. I'll leave you now. You do know who I am, don't you?" He narrowed his eyes.

"I recognized the name. Also noticed on your papers that you own the Del Posto Restaurant. My wife and I have eaten there once or twice. Five star."

"Glad to hear that." A big smile broke out on Gino's face. "We pride ourselves on both excellent cuisine and service. So, thank you for the kind words. And because, we're going to be working together in the future, I would be honored if you and your wife would be my guests as my family celebrates my wife's grandmother's one hundredth birthday. It's going to be held at the restaurant Saturday night."

Phil was momentarily surprised at the invitation. Then, he looked down as though deciding what it was he wanted to say and finally responded. "I'm certain that my wife would enjoy that tremendously, Sir. And it will help us to get to know each other better."

"You see, Mr. Willis, my wife, Eleni is Greek and I'm

Italian, so the restaurant features both types of food. Greek and Italian together make a great combination both for a marriage and for a restaurant.

Anyway, here is the formal invitation. I know that it's short notice, but I would be pleased if you both could attend. I'd like you to meet some of the other people who will be there. And please, call me Gino in the future."

He stood up, reached across the desk and shook Phil's hand. His assistant did the same.

After the men left, Phil looked through the papers that Gino Basilio had left him. He realized that the man's taxes were quite complex and that they would require a tremendous amount of his time. Looking at his calendar once again, he decided that he had to clear some of his other appointments so that he would have time to work with Gino.

He closed up the folder, sat back in his chair, crossed his arms over his chest in a no nonsense pose and pondered the situation, as Kelley and the children entered his office.

"So, what's up Phil?"

"New client. Looks like it could be a complicated job. And time consuming. Oh, and by the way, make a call to your hairdresser. See if she can fit you in Saturday morning."

He handed her the invitation. "We're going to a party that night at Mr. Basilio's restaurant, The Del Posto."

"Whoa," she said, her eyes popping open. "I just love that place. And I see from the invite that it's formal. Have to get my long evening dress out. I'll call right now for an appointment."

She dialed the number. "Thanks Cindy, you're a pal."

Glancing at Phil, she gave a thumbs up gesture. "It's all set. I got her to squeeze me in late in the morning."

"Good. And we'll call my folks and see if they can keep the kids overnight. We'll make a night of it." And as if reading her mind, he added, "And I'll have to see if I can still fit into my tuxedo."

"How old is your tuxedo, Daddy? Ashley asked.

"It doesn't matter how old the tux is, little girl," he answered. "It's just that your old dad has started to put on a couple of pounds."

Kelley responded with a grin. "Nonsense. You're still the handsome and trim fellow that you always were."

"Thank you for the kind words." He turned serious once again. "It's time for me to drop Mrs. Trot's tax forms off. After that, on to supper, kids." Phil took them by the arms and pushed them toward the door.

"Where are we going Dad?" Alan asked.

"Why Ci Ci's for pizza of course. I'll meet you there."

The following Saturday night, Kelley and Phil dropped Ashley and Alan off at his parents' house and headed toward Del Posto's Restaurant.

"I saw a review on this restaurant in last month's issue of 'Syracuse's Fine Dining Magazine'," Kelley said, her voice quivering with excitement. "They had a five page color photo spread. Said that it was one of the finest restaurants in the area. One of the most expensive too."

"Well, in that case, I'm glad that I'm not paying for this dinner."

"I think it's been about a year since we ate there. And that was lunch."

Phil pulled into the parking lot and saw cars lined up in front of theirs, waiting for one of the young valets to park them. As they waited for one to come for their car, Kelley glanced over at Phil. "See your tux did fit after all. And, did I tell you how handsome you look in it?"

He reached over and squeezed her hand. "You look like prom night in that green satin strapless gown. And you fill it out beautifully."

She fought back a smile. "Starting Monday, I go back to the gym. It was all that I could do to zip it up."

Getting out of the car, Phil opened the back door, removed a wooden box from the floor, picked up a small gift wrapped box from the seat and handed it to Kelley. Tucking their packages under their arms, they headed toward the stately-red brick building.

Kelley stopped at the entrance to admire the flower boxes on the sidewalk. "I just love these flowers. So colorful." She bent over to touch the overflowing arrangements of red and white geraniums intermixed with ferns.

Phil took her by the arm and gently guided her inside where the tuxedoed maitre d' snapped to attention and greeted them. "We're so happy that you could join us this evening. Your invitation, Sir?"

Phil handed him the invitation as Kelley looked around the elegant restaurant with its old world charm. The dark paneled walls and wrought iron light fixtures pinned tightly to the ceiling added to the intimate appearance. She knew the restaurant boasted of an award winning wine cellar with thirteen hundred bottles.

The maitre d' bowed courteously. "Please follow me."

He led them into a secluded drawing room where servers immediately passed in front of them with trays of hors d' oeuvres and glasses of champagne, while a pianist in the corner lulled the guests with music.

Phil took two glasses of champagne and handed one to Kelley. Noticing Gino standing in the far corner of the room, he took Kelley gently by the arm and led her over. Gino bowed slightly as Kelley was introduced. She could not help but notice how distinguished the short stocky man with slightly graying hair looked. He was dressed in an Armani tuxedo that appeared to have been custom fitted.

"Please enjoy the appetizers," Gino said. "Our menu tonight jumps back and forth with a selection of both

Greek and Italian foods in accordance with both my heritage and that of my wife."

He waved over one of the waiters who had a tray in his hands. "Please try these Greek seared deep sea scallops topped with honey sugar."

Kelley took a small plate from the waiter and placed two of the hot scallops on it. She took a slow and careful bite as a small, slender woman, dressed in a two-piece white silk pantsuit, embellished with white and gray sequins, walked up to Gino.

He put his arm casually around the woman and drew her to his side. "This is my wife, Eleni Callis Basilio. Even though we have been married for over twenty-five years, she still insists on carrying her Greek name of Callis. Everyone said that a marriage between a beautiful Greek lady and an arrogant Italian would not work. But, we proved them wrong."

He gave her a gentle squeeze. "And this is Phil Willis, my new tax attorney and his lovely wife, Kelley."

Eleni greeted them graciously, extending her hand, then whispered to her husband, "I think my parents and my grandmother are starting to get a little tired. Perhaps we should lead our guests into the dining room soon."

"A good idea. While my wife's grandmother's mind is very good, her feet bother her and she cannot stand for long periods of time."

Eleni and Gino led their guests into a private dining room where round tables had been set with crisp gray linen tablecloths, peach colored napkins and elegant gold embellished china. Centerpieces of peach and white flowers with large hurricane lamps containing burning candles gave the room a romantic look.

The maitre d' led Kelley and Phil to a table near the back of the room. After they were seated, they introduced themselves to the other guests at the table.

Kelley watched as the room filled up, then tilted her

head to the side and whispered to Phil, "It looks like this gathering consists of all the leaders and shakers of Syracuse. Look there's the mayor and his wife."

Glancing around the room, Phil's eyes widened with disbelief. "Oh my God, there's the chief of police. And over there, the Attorney General of New York."

When everyone was seated and the crowd quieted down, Gino stood up and tapped a knife on a wine glass. "Good evening. A special thanks to all of you who so graciously agreed to join my family as we celebrate Dione Callis's one hundredth birthday."

Taking the portable microphone a waiter had handed him, he walked around the room, stopping at various tables, greeting his guests by name and introducing them to the others in the room. When he got to Kelley and Phil's table, he stopped and announced, "And here are our newest friends, Phil and Kelley Willis."

Phil stood up, shook his hand and acknowledged the introduction. "We are honored to be here, Sir."

Gino swiveled around and glared at the maitre d', who was standing in back of him. With a frown on his face and his hand over the mike, he snarled, "Why are my special friends seated in the back of the room?"

The maitre d' offered no explanation. He shook his head and shrugged his shoulders.

"Please Mr. and Mrs. Willis, accept my apology for this oversight," Gino whispered. "You must join my family at the head table."

Phil nodded his head and bent over to pick up the packages he had placed under the table. Somewhat embarrassed, Kelley and Phil followed Gino to the long head table at the front of the room. He led them to seats at the end of the table.

Gino took the mike once again. "Now, we will start our dinner which will consist of selections of hearty Greek and Italian foods, all served with a touch of class."

The waiters exhibited impressive professionalism as they filled the wine glasses and served the first Italian course of large calamari, stuffed with mild, salty cheeses and grilled to create a particularly heady combination of flavors and textures. This was accompanied by the first Greek course which was as assortment plate with stuffed grape leaves, spanakopita, hummus and Greek olives.

After the first course, Gino stood up and raised his wine glass. "And now everyone will please raise their glass and join me in wishing Grandma Dione a very happy birthday. After we enjoy our main entrees, we will celebrate with some festive desserts in her honor."

With large trays held high over their heads, the waiters entered the room with the entrée. The Italian entrées were a choice of delicate spinach stuffed ravioli in a mild red sauce and an impressive gnocchi in creamy blue cheese sauce. The Greek entrees offered were a rack of lamb with porcini-parmesan risotto and a braised leg of duck with candied almonds and greens.

Kelley wiped her mouth with her napkin as she finished and turned to the woman seated beside her. "This takes me back to the days when I lived near Dolphin Springs, Florida. I used to eat Greek food all the time. I didn't realize how much I missed it."

While the waiters were clearing the tables of the empty dishes, Gino walked up to Kelley and Phil with a glass of wine in his hand. "I would like to introduce you to my wife's parents, her grandmother, Dione Callis, and my two lovely daughters."

They got up and followed him to the middle of the table where he stood next to a tiny, white-haired, perfectly coiffured lady, dressed in a lilac colored two-piece lace evening gown. "This is my wife's grandmother and our guest of honor, Dione Callis. These lovely people are my wife's parents, Chris and Erika Callis. And the beautiful young ladies sitting beside them are my daughters,

Alexia and Chara."

Phil bent over Dione, gently kissed her hand and congratulated her on her birthday. Kelley gave her a kiss on each cheek as she whispered good evening in Greek, "Kalo Apogeyma."

After they spoke briefly to the rest of the family, Phil said to Gino, "You are to be congratulated. You have a lovely family."

Gino smiled and bowed. "Thank you. I think so."

Kelley and Phil returned to their seats as the waiters wheeled in a cart. It held an immense three-tiered birthday cake, covered with pink and lilac roses and topped with one hundred flaming candles.

They lifted the cake from the cart and placed it in front of the guest of honor. Gino stood up and blew into the microphone to get the attention of the crowd. "Ladies and gentlemen. Please join me in singing 'Happy Birthday' to this very special lady."

He helped Dione to her feet and motioned for her to lean over to blow out the candles. After several attempts, and with the help of her two great-grand-daughters, the candles were finally extinguished.

The waiters lifted the cake back onto the cart and wheeled it to the back of the room, where they cut it and placed slices on individual dessert plates. While one of the waiters passed through the crowd with a cart loaded with the birthday cake, two other waiters followed with two additional carts. One was covered with an assortment of baklava and other Greek pastries, the second contained tiramisu, Italian cookies and ices.

The guests enjoyed the desserts, served with coffee and tea, the waiters cleared the tables and brought around after-dinner liquors for everyone. Gino and his wife strolled from table to table thanking their guests for attending. Most of them were used to dining at five-star restaurants, but they complimented them on one of the finest meals that they had ever eaten.

While the piano music played softly in the background, the guests stood up, spoke briefly with the guest of honor and talked in small groups. About nine-thirty, the music stopped and the guests started to leave.

Gino helped Mrs. Callis up from her seat and placed her in the wheelchair that the maitre d' had brought in. "Eleni and the girls will see you home, Grand Momma," he said as Kelley and Phil walked up.

"I have a gift for you Mrs. Callis," Kelley said, placing a beautifully wrapped package with a large white bow on top, in her lap.

"Oh, I thought that no one was supposed to bring me gifts," Mrs. Callis said, her voice was full of surprise.

Kelley smiled down at her. "After I visited Sicily several years ago, a dear friend of mine sent me several beautiful scarves from an exclusive shop in Milan. I saved them for very special occasions. And this is such an occasion."

Turning toward Alexia, Kelley suggested, "Why don't you open this for your great-grandma?"

Alexia tore the paper off the box, lifted the lid slightly and placed the box on Mrs. Callis' lap.

The elderly lady opened it and slowly pulled out an exquisite silver and lilac silk scarf. "Oh, it is beautiful and it goes well with my dress," she said with appreciation. "Put it around my shoulders, Alexia. I will wear it outside since the air is probably chilly now."

She took Kelley's hands in hers and kissed them. "Thank you my dear. This has been a lovely party, but I'm just a little sad that my grandson, Jason, could not attend. I miss him so." She waved her hand at her daughter, Eleni. "Now, it is time for me to go home."

As Eleni and her daughters escorted Mrs. Callis from the room, Phil tapped Gino on the shoulder. "And I have a gift for you, to thank you for including my wife and myself in this wonderful occasion."

He handed Gino the wooden box.

Gino placed it on the table and opened it. As he peered inside, a look of delight exploded across his face. "It's a bottle of Rossi wine. And a rare one at that. How did you get it?"

Phil grinned. "We had occasion to visit the Rossi Vineyards in Sicily several years ago. And Marco Rossi sends me a few special bottles every year. Are you on his mailing list?"

A very impressed Gino shook his head. "No. He only sells wines to an exclusive group."

"Well, let me email him and ask him to add your restaurant to his group."

Gino shot him a challenging glance. "You can do that?"

"Of course. He is a very close friend of mine."

Gino put his arm around Phil's shoulders. "Before you and the wife leave, let me show you where you'll be working when you come on Monday."

The restaurant was now only about half full as he led them through the professional stainless steel kitchen to a stairway that led upstairs to his private office on the second floor.

Chapter 20

The following Monday morning, shortly before nine, Kelley and Phil entered the Del Posto restaurant through the back door. He carried a heavy briefcase, loaded with the tax records Gino had given him, a couple of calculators and his laptop. Kelley carried a small green insulated bag and her laptop as they walked up the one flight of steps to Gino's office. Phil tried to open the door. Discovering that it was locked, he set his briefcase down and knocked several times.

The door was opened by a tall, stately middle-aged woman, with short black hair, wearing a gray pantsuit.

She smiled. "Mr. and Mrs. Willis, I presume?"

"That's us," Phil said.

"You're right on time. I'm Marci Holland, Mr. Basilio's secretary and bookkeeper."

Phil picked up his briefcase with one hand and shook hands with Marci with the other. "I'm Phil and this is Kelley."

"Where do you want us to work?" Kelley asked.

"Follow me." She led them down the hallway. "Let me give you a brief tour. The big office is Mr. Basilio's. Mine is across from his."

Walking further down the hall, she pointed to a door. "You'll use the back room, across the hall is a small kitchenette. It has a refrigerator, coffee pot and micro-wave. You're welcome to bring in food from outside. The dining room downstairs doesn't open until four and Gino prefers that we not order any food from there. That door at the end of the hall is to the restroom."

Kelley held up the small thermos bag she had tucked under her arm. "We didn't know what to expect, so we brought our lunch."

They entered the room that had been assigned to them. Phil put his briefcase on one of the two long tables in the back of the room while Kelley took her laptop from the case.

Marci gestured toward a computer on the desk. "That computer has the tax records for the last two years only. That's when we finally had a specialized accounting sys-tem set up for us. Prior to that, the taxes are all on paper and are in those file cabinets. They go back to the last ten years."

"Thank you. We'll take it from here," Phil said as he pulled out a chair for Kelley to sit down.

Marci took a step backwards. "Well, I'll let you two get started. Call me if you need anything. I'll be at your disposal."

"I'll look through last year's taxes. We'll use them as a guide for this year." Phil sat down in front of the com-puter and turned it on. "You dig out the new tax forms and line up the bookkeeping records for this year."

For the next hour they were completely absorbed in their work and barely heard the soft knock on the door. Marci opened it and stuck her head inside. "I forgot to tell you, Mr. Willis, that I also handle the payroll for the res-taurant. I usually meet with the restaurant manager on Wednesday about three to get the checks ready for Friday morning distribution."

Phil looked up from his work as she continued. "I as-sume you met most of Mr. Basilio's family at the party the other night except for his brother-in-law, Jason, who lives in Florida."

Kelley looked at Phil with a half-grimace. "Grandma Callis did mention something about Jason being absent. She was upset because he didn't attend the party."

Phil nodded. "Yes, she seemed to feel bad about that."

Marci turned to leave the room, paused and whirled around. "Oh, and Gino called. Said he was attending a luncheon. He'll be in later this afternoon."

After Marci shut the door, Kelley lowered her head and whispered. "I think that Jason is the black sheep of the family. I heard one of Gino's daughters ask where he was the other night and Mrs. Basilio shushed her up in a hurry."

They returned to their work. Sometime later, Phil glanced up at the clock. "Time for lunch."

They walked into the kitchenette and saw Marci sitting at one of the two small tables with her lunch and the newspaper spread out in front of her. "Just made some fresh coffee. Help yourself."

Kelley flopped into a chair beside her and opened her lunch bag, pulled out two foil wrapped sandwiches and a bag of potato chips. Phil went to the coffee maker, poured two cups, added creamer, stirred them, and brought them over to the table and sat down.

Marci swallowed a bit of her sandwich and leaned in closer to Kelley. "So tell me how the birthday party was the other night? None of the hired help were invited of course, but I did get a gander at the menu and the cost for the party. Looks like it was quite a shindig."

"It was really superb. We were surprised that Gino asked us," Kelley answered.

While they ate, Kelley described the party to Marci, who listened with great interest.

"I'm sorry I missed it. But to tell, you the truth, I haven't been in much of a party mood lately. I recently lost my partner. She and I were close."

Not knowing how to respond to this personal information, Kelley and Phil stared at each other. Kelley muttered in reply, "We're so sorry for your loss."

"Thank you," Marci's voice shook. "Time to get back
to work."

She stood up, wadded up the wrapper from her sandwich and threw it in the trash bin, walked over to the
sink, rinsed out her cup and left the room.

"Seems like everyone has a burden to carry doesn't
it," Kelley whispered to Phil. "Guess, we don't know how
lucky we are."

Friday morning Phil and Kelley were still at work in the
office. He was sitting at the desk, working on the computer, while she was standing at the back table, putting
some papers in order.

Phil leaned back and looked at her with a confident
smile. "I think that we're well on our way to getting Gino's tax records completed. We should be done with our
end of it by next week. Then, it's just a matter of reviewing everything with him, getting the papers signed and
sending them in."

Kelley continued with her work. "It's kind of nice that
Gino hasn't been in here constantly checking on us."

"But the fact is that he may not be too happy with
this year's return from the looks of things." Phil released
a groan of dismay. "Right now, it looks like he might owe
the government a heap of money. I've got to scrounge
through all these records again and make sure that he
takes advantage of every deduction he's allowed."

The door to the office was thrown open and a nervous
looking Gino walked in. "Good morning. I just talked to
Marci. She said you're nearing the end of your work. You
expect to be finished by next week?"

Hearing the concern in his voice, Phil looked up. "That's right. Would you like a quick update?"

"Later." Gino paced back and forth in front of the desk. "Right now, I have a big favor to ask of you both."

"What's that?" Phil asked.

Gino sat down on one of the chairs and waved for Kelley to come around and sit down beside him.

"You don't know this. But I always run a background check on every one I employ. I did one on both of you before I contacted you."

Stunned, Kelley's mouth fell open. "And?"

"And, I learned that you lived near the west coast of Florida for a considerable amount of time and therefore, are familiar with the area."

"That's true," Kelley replied, as a shadow fell across her face. "And what else did you discover?"

Gino's eyes met hers. "That both of you were private investigators, and you Kelley worked as an undercover agent for the State."

Kelley gave a sharp retort. "Just to set the record straight, Mr. Basilio, that was over fifteen years ago."

Phil leaned forward and added with a slight frown crossing his brow, "Right now, I'm just a simple tax attorney. And my wife helps me in my business. Does it bother you that we did that kind of work before?"

"On the contrary. It pleases me very much." Gino threw his hand up in the air. "You have the kind of experience that could be of tremendous help to me in the situation I find myself presently in."

"And just what is that?" Kelley bit down on her lip.

"Before I explain it to you, I have to ask if you could both re-arrange your schedules and fly down to Florida with me for about three days."

Kelley and Phil stared at each other in surprise. Finally, Kelley answered, "We have two children and that complicates things for us."

"I know," Gino nodded and his voice deepened. "But, I also know that your parents live nearby and occasionally care for them. I will, of course, cover all your expenses, and compensate you well for your time and trouble. I can even manage to pay your folks for watching the children."

Phil thought for a few minutes. "My parents love to have the children. So that won't be necessary. What do you say Kelley? Are you ready for three days of fun and sun in Florida?"

Gino shook his head. "I doubt if it will be fun and sun, but I would appreciate it if you could accompany me. And, I will consider it a great personal favor."

Kelley mulled the situation over for a few minutes; then, nodded. "Okay. Three days. I'll bring comfortable clothes, but I won't plan on the fun and sun part."

"What are the plans, Gino?" Phil asked.

"We're going down to visit my brother-in-law, Jason Callis. I'll explain everything to you on the way down tomorrow. Take the rest of the day off. But bill me for your time. And plan on billing me for double time while we're in Florida."

"By the way, where in Florida are we headed?" Kelley asked.

"Your old stomping grounds, Dolphin Springs."

Chapter 21

The next morning, Kelley, Phil, Gino and his body guard, Max, boarded a Cessna 210 at a private airport just outside of Syracuse.

"One of my friends owns this sweet little lady. Lent it to me for our trip. I've got a license and have been flying for years. Max is also licensed and experienced; he could take over in case of an emergency. So don't worry," Gino said reassuringly to Kelley as she looked warily at the small six seat, high performance, single engine plane.

She had brought only a carry-on bag, since Phil had reminded her that they were only staying a few days and that the weight on the plane could be restricted. With good weather and no stops, Gino said they should arrive at the small Clearwater, Florida, Airport in less than five hours.

Kelley thought the trip south in the small plane was very exhilarating, and was thrilled that they flew low enough so she could enjoy the change of scenery along the way.

After a smooth landing, they exited the plane and entered the air-conditioned terminal. "I have a rental SUV reserved for us," Gino said.

"Why don't you add my name to the rental agreement," Phil suggested. "That way I can do the driving. I know my way around Dolphin Springs, since Kelley and I used to live here."

Max retrieved the luggage and he, Gino and Kelley went out to the curb to wait for Phil to pull up with the rental. Max threw the luggage in the back and they climbed in.

"Where in town are we going?" Phil asked as he turned north to Dolphin Springs.

"My brother's house and not a minute to lose," Gino said. "When I talked to my sister-in-law, Sofia, last night, she said that Jason was frantic, talking out of his head; afraid that he was going to do something drastic."

When they reached the center of the town, Phil asked Gino, "Where now?"

"Turn left. Big pink house. Backs up to the bayou."

The vehicle pulled up to an impressive three-story pink stucco house with a circular driveway. The house had a wrap around balcony that overlooked the bayou, and further down, in the far distance, the Gulf of Mexico. A set of circular steps led up from the driveway to the double glass entrance doors on the second level.

Kelley gazed around the neighborhood, noting that this section of the quaint old town appeared to have been built in the last few years and contained some of the largest and most impressive homes.

They exited the vehicle and the doors to the house opened. A tall, slender and elegantly dressed woman, who appeared to be in her late forties, stepped out.

She rushed down the steps and threw her arms around Gino. "I'm so glad you're here. Jason is so disturbed, I'm afraid he is going to do something drastic."

Gino put his arms around her shoulders, trying to calm her. "That's why we're here, Sofia. To help both of you. Now, let's go inside."

Jason Callis and his sister, Eleni Callis Basilio were born in Dolphin Springs where their grandparents, Dione and Dimetra Callis owned and operated Callis's Greek Restaurant. When Grandpa Callis died, Jason and Eleni's parents, Chris and Erika, took over the restaurant and ran it successfully for several years. After retiring, they decided to move to Syracuse, together with Grandma Dione and live near Eleni and Gino.

Jason and Sofia had bought out the other's interest in the restaurant and remained in Dolphin Springs. Jason managed the restaurant and Sofia continued with her job as a teacher at the local high school.

After retiring, Sofia spent most of her time doing charity work for the church. Over the years, the childless couple had grown somewhat apart.

In the years since Jason had assumed its management, the restaurant had gone slowly into decline. Desperate for cash to keep it afloat, he had borrowed heavily from local people. Eventually, he turned to gambling at a Tampa casino to try to repay his debts. Within the past few weeks, Jason had reached the end of the road with his finances and was ready to file for bankruptcy.

Inside the house, Gino turned toward Kelley and Phil. "This is my attorney, and tax man, Phil Willis ,and this is his wife, Kelley. They came with me to help Jason sort out his finances."

Sofia shook hands, barely able to hide her nervousness. "Thank you so much. I really appreciate it. I'm certain that my husband will too."

She looked at Gino and wrung her hands. "You must do something to help Jason."

Gino glared at her, now getting somewhat impatient. "And speaking of your husband. Where is he?"

"Oh, he left about an hour ago. He didn't sleep at all last night. Just paced around the house."

"Please Sofia, try to catch your breath and tell us

where Jason is now."

She stopped up short and thought for a moment. "I think he might be at the restaurant. Yes, maybe the restaurant."

"Well, we better head over there and talk to Jason, right away," Gino said, starting for the door. "I'll call you after we talk to him, Sofia, and let you know what's going on. In the meantime, try to calm yourself. Maybe, go into the kitchen and bake some baklava for my friends here."

Kelley took Sofia's hands in hers. "That's a wonderful idea. We used to live near here and we haven't had good baklava in years."

Sofia watched as the four headed out the front door and to the SUV.

Climbing into the driver's seat, Phil turned on the ignition. "I know just where the restaurant is. It's not far. We should be there in a jiffy."

In less than ten minutes, they were at the restaurant. Phil pulled into the parking lot and parked beside a white Toyota Camry.

"That's the kind of car Sofia said Jason was driving," Gino said.

They jumped out and rushed to the front of the building, where they found a large sign that read 'Closed.' Gino reached out and pounded loudly on the door several times. A voice on the other side yelled, "Can't you read? We're closed. Go away."

"We're here to see Jason. I'm his brother-in-law."

The voice shouted back, "Not here."

Gino pounded on the door once again and yelled, "I said that I'm his brother-in-law. Where the hell is he?"

The door slowly opened and an old man, dressed in torn overalls and wearing a dirty apron, shuffled forward a few steps. "Like I said, he's not here."

"His car is parked right outside," Gino snapped.

"Maybe he went for a walk. He was very troubled. Yes,

I think that he went to St. Nicholas Church. Probably went to pray. Never saw him like this before. Almost crazy with worry."

"I know where that is, about three blocks from here," Phil said.

Gino whirled around and headed for the SUV with the others racing behind him

Phil wheeled the vehicle through the small Greek enclave. Many of its three thousand Greek-America residents traced their roots back to the Greek Islands in the Aegean Sea.

On Epiphany every January, visitors headed for the bayou to watch Greek youths dive for a cross thrown by the visiting bishop. Tourists came throughout the year to fill bags with gift-shop sponges and eat Greek specialties.

Phil pulled up on a side street next to the large yellow brick and white trim Cathedral. To the left of the church was a courtyard with a flag pole that had the blue and white Greek flag, the flag of the United States and the flag of the Greek Orthodox diocese flying.

At the sight of it once again, Kelley immediately remembered how she had always loved the beautiful Cathedral with the round dome, topped with a cross and a tall bell tower.

With the others following close behind him, Gino opened the door and entered the vestibule where Kelley recognized the famous Icon of St. Nicholas. Kept in an elaborately carved glass enclosure, it was the most precious item in the Cathedral. On December 1, 1970, a cleaning woman had discovered drops of moisture around the eyes of St. Nicholas. Later, a church priest became an eye witness to this phenomenon and since that time hundreds of Orthodox Greeks from around the world came to view the Icon.

Max threw open the double doors leading to the main

part of the church and they slowly entered. Except for the shadows cast by a few lighted candles, it was very dark.

They moved down the aisle where Gino spotted what appeared to be Jason, seated on the bottom step that led up to the altar. Next to him, dressed in black garments and wearing a white clerical collar, was a priest.

Gino walked slowly up to the men as Kelley, Phil and Max slid into the front pew.

"Jason, it's me, Gino. I'm here to help you." He sat down on the step beside him and put his arm around his shoulders.

Jason slowly lifted his head and Gino could see the tears running down his cheeks.

"Gino, thank God you are here. Father Carino just told me to have faith; that help was on the way. And suddenly, you are here. It's a miracle."

Gino reached across Jason and shook the priest's hand. "Father Carino, I'm Gino Basilio, Jason's brother-in-law.

"Father Michael Carino. Pastor of St. Nicholas's. Glad to meet you," the priest answered. "It was good of you to come. Jason needs help."

"Thank you for comforting Jason. I'm here with my friends to give him a hand." Gino stood up and helped both Jason and the priest to their feet. He led them over to the pew where the others were seated.

"This is Phil Willis, my attorney and tax man. And this is his wife, Kelley. And this is Max, my assistant." Gino's voice was low and hoarse-strained as he introduced them to Jason and the priest. "They've accompanied me here to help you, Jason. Why don't we go back to your house and sort things out."

"No one can help me, everything has gone wrong," Jason said, with a tremor in his voice.

"Now listen, I didn't take the time and expense to fly here and not help you. I've even brought my tax expert to help you sort out your finances," Gino said firmly.

"But, what I need is money," Jason whimpered.

"First of all, let's get you home. Your wife is sick with worry."

"You'll help me?"

"Yes. I give you my word," Gino replied.

Jason looked sadly at Phil and Kelley. "And you good people will help me?"

"That's why we're here," Phil said with confidence in his voice

"Yes. These people are all here to help you, my son." Father Carino said reassuringly. "Now, why don't you do as they suggest. Go back to your home and work things out." He took Jason by the arm and led him back down the aisle to the door.

Starting to leave, Phil noticed Jason's jacket laying on the step of the altar. He walked over, picked it up, and was in the process of putting it under his arm when he felt a bulge in the pocket. Reaching in, he pulled out a small automatic. Wow, best we keep this thing, he thought. He slipped it into Kelley's hands and whispered, "Put this in your purse."

She looked down and whispered back, "Maybe we got here just in time."

As she followed the others down the carpeted aisle to the exit, Kelley admired the light that came in the beautiful stained glass windows and reflected off the simple white walls with gold trim. She had always thought that this was one of the most beautiful churches that she had ever seen. Thank goodness it had not been a scene of tragedy today.

Leaving the church, Jason hugged Father Carino and thanked him for being such a comfort to him.

"Go in peace, my son. I am confident that the Lord will help you through your troubles."

After they got back in the vehicle, Gino called Sofia

and told her they had found Jason and that he was okay. He said they were all on their way back to the house and suggested that she prepare a small luncheon since he and his guests had not eaten since early that morning.

"Back to the house?" Phil asked as he drove away from the church.

"Yes," Gino answered. Turning around to look at his brother-in-law, who was in the back seat, he added, "You owe your wife a big apology Jason. She's been through Hell worrying about you."

Jason nodded sadly in agreement. "Wait, my car's at the restaurant. Please, I need my car. Let's go get it."

Phil whipped the SUV around; made a sudden turn and headed back to the restaurant. When they arrived, Jason got out. "I need to talk to a couple of my workers before we head for the house. Gino, why don't you and your friends come inside for a few minutes?"

The others got out and followed Jason as he unlocked the front door and led them inside.

Kelley was immediately impressed with the ambiance of the bright and spacious restaurant. It was tastefully decorated with white and blue sea paintings on the walls. The tables were covered in white linen and the leather on the chairs matched the blue of the pictures. Ceiling to floor windows on one side of the room overlooked the bayou, where several boats were docked nearby.

A large glass fish tank was stationed just inside the entrance and Kelley concluded that this was where the restaurant had kept their supply of fresh lobsters.

A sign next to the front door, listed the various authentic Greek dishes which were featured, Horiatiki-Tsipoura and others. The sign also said the fish dishes were guaranteed to be fresh daily.

"I can't understand why this restaurant was failing," she whispered to Phil. "It used to be fantastic and it still looks great."

He shrugged his shoulders. "Sounds like Jason wasn't managing it too well for some reason."

Kelley looked at Jason, smiled and said, "This is one classy place."

He frowned. "Yes. It used to be a Five-Star restaurant. But, I ruined it. When business slowed down a little, I listened to some bad advice. Started offering a menu with American, Italian and Mexican dishes. We weren't used to preparing those and they weren't very good. In fact, a write up in the local paper last year gave us a bad review. After that, business went downhill rapidly."

"Couldn't you have just changed the menu back to the old Greek dishes?" Phil asked.

Jason shook his head. "I tried. As you can see by this sign, I tried. But it was too late. By then, I had started to borrow money to keep afloat. Then, I gambled to try to pay off my debts. I just got deeper and deeper into an endless pit. Now, I don't know how I'm going to pay off my creditors."

"Well, all that's going to change now that my tax man and I are here to help you," Gino said with sincere sympathy in his voice.

"Yes. We'll figure out a way to get you back on your feet," Phil added.

Jason shook his head. "I sure hope so. I need all the help I can get." He walked into the back of the restaurant and asked his four remaining employees, who were cleaning up the kitchen, to join him up front.

"I'm sorry, I have to let you go as of today. I'm not sure the restaurant will re-open; but, I promise you that I'll pay you up until this very day." He nodded toward Phil. "This gentleman has agreed to help me through this situation."

Not surprised, the men hung their heads at the news. One walked over to Jason and shook his hand.

"We certainly hope it works out for you."

Kelley leaned over and whispered to Phil. "Boy, do you have your work cut out for you."

"Got no choice, but to help these people."

Chapter 22

A short while later, the SUV with Phil, Kelley and Max inside, pulled up in front of the Callis house. Jason and Gino had followed them in Jason's car. They climbed out of the vehicles and entered the home

Hearing the door open, Sofia ran to the front hall, wiping her hands on her apron. She threw her arms around Jason. "Thank God, you're okay my Dear. I have been praying to the Lord Jesus about you all morning."

He gave her a kiss and patted her on the back. "I'm sorry to have worried you so."

Kelley lifted her head and sniffed the air. "What is that wonderful smell?"

Sofia smiled. "When I get nervous, I bake. I made some homemade Greek bread for the luncheon sandwiches. I also have fresh coffee and dessert. Let's go eat."

She took Kelley by the arm and lead her to the kitchen. "You must all be starving." The thought of hot coffee, sandwiches and homemade baklava perked Kelley up.

On the large oak dining table were several large platters piled high with sandwiches made of the fresh Greek bread and laden with slices of turkey, cheese, lettuce and tomatoes. In the center was a huge bowl filled with Greek salad topped with black olives.

Sofia went over to the counter and returned with a

large carafe of hot coffee and filled everyone's cups.

"My wife, she can cook. Right?" Jason said, looking at her with great pride.

Except for the exchange of the usual pleasantries, they ate in almost silence. Phil sat back in his chair and sighed contentedly. "This bread is delicious."

Jason smiled proudly. "That's what everyone says. I have always told Sofia she should open her own bakery."

When they finished their salad and sandwiches, Kelley jumped up and helped Sofia clear the table. While Kelley refilled the coffee cups, Sofia brought a large silver platter to the table piled high with diamond shaped baklava, dripping in honey.

Gino pushed his chair away from the table and stood up. "Now that everyone has eaten, it's time for Phil to take a look at your troubles, Jason."

"We need to start by going over your assets and your liabilities," Phil added.

"Please come with me into the library. I have my ledgers in there," Jason answered.

Phil and Gino followed him and sat down. As Jason gave him the figures, Phil listed the assets in one column—the house, the restaurant, insurance policies, etc. There was no money in the bank accounts. Then, in an opposite column, Phil listed the debts. He immediately assessed that the liabilities far outweighed the assets.

While Jason called out his debts, Gino looked on silently, with a look of complete disgust as he learned what a deep hole Jason had put himself in.

"At least this gives us a picture of how we can start to get you back on your feet," Phil said.

Phil continued to pour over the books for the rest of the afternoon. Finally, he said, "I believe we're making a little headway through this mess; but, I think that we've covered enough for today."

The men returned to the kitchen where the others

were seated at the table, talking.

Jason looked at Sofia. "We need some supper now, my good woman."

She got up, walked over to her husband and hugged him. "You don't look like the man who left the house early this morning."

He grinned weakly. "I'm not. I've come to realize I have family and friends to help me."

Phil placed his papers on the table as he and Jason sat down. Sofia put a casserole in the oven and set the table with dishes for supper.

Gino leaned forward and stared at Phil. "Well, Counselor, what do you suggest at this point?'

Phil thought for several minutes. Then sighed and looked directly at Jason. "First, I think you should call this Stamos guy that you owe all the money to for your gambling debts. See if he would be available to meet with us. Say about ten tomorrow morning."

"But, where will I get enough money to pay him off? Jason asked.

"We'll discuss that in due time. But first, tell me about this Stamos fellow."

"Not really much to tell. Thaddius is a local businessman that I've known a long time. When I needed cash to put into the business, I borrowed from him. Then, I went to his casino to try to win it back. At first, I did win. Then I lost. The more I gambled, the greater was my obligation to him."

Phil looked down at one of the papers he had placed on the table. Pushing it toward Jason, he asked, "Is this the figure that you owe Stamos?"

Jason bowed his head and answered humbly. "Yes."

"Well, call him after we eat and see if you can set up a meeting with him in the morning. Right now, I think we should wrap this up for the day. Let's all get some sleep. Tomorrow, you'll be making some major decisions. I think you'll need to plan on selling both this house and the restaurant, in order to work your way out of this jam. I suggest that you call a Realtor, and see if you can get an appointment for tomorrow after we talk to Mr. Stamos."

Sofia looked startled. "Will that really be necessary?"

"I think so," Phil replied firmly. "You're going to need all the money that you can get out of this house and the business to pay off Jason's debts."

Gino glared at Jason and Sofia. "And then, you'll need to down size and cut back on your living expenses in the future. After that, you should have a little piece of mind. Sofia, I didn't make any hotel reservations. I know you have a couple of extra rooms. So, why don't you put Max and I up in one of them and put the Willis's in the other one. That way we can get right back on this, early in the morning."

She looked a little startled, but nodded her agreement quickly. "Of course."

After supper, she led Kelley and Phil upstairs to a guest room. The exhausted travelers hit the bed early and were soon sound asleep.

The next morning, Kelley woke as Phil gently nudged her shoulder. "Are you awake?"

"I am now. I can smell fresh coffee and homemade pastries. I must be in Heaven."

"Yes, probably homemade bread again," Phil exclaimed, almost drooling. "You don't need an alarm clock in this house if your nose works okay."

They both jumped out of bed and put on the white fluffy robes Sofia had placed on a nearby chair for them.

"Let's head downstairs and get some of those goodies," Phil said.

They entered the kitchen and spied Jason, Sofia and

Gino dancing around the kitchen, and singing at the top of their lungs. When they saw Kelley and Phil, they grabbed their hands and spun them around, dancing in a circle together.

"Join us in our happy Greek song," Sofia said.

"What is it called?" Kelley asked as she blushed with the heat and excitement of the moment.

"It is called 'Agapi Kai Alithia'," Jason replied. "It means 'Love and Truth.' And that is what my house is filled with this morning, thanks to you."

Kelley and Phil could only hum the tune as the three sang. After a few minutes, Jason and Sofia bowed to each other and to their guests. "Now time to pour our guests some coffee," Jason said, "and serve them your, 'Tsoureki'-sweet Easter bread."

Kelley could see that Jason was not the same man she had observed crying in the Greek Cathedral yesterday. A new spirit had energized him.

Gino took a seat at the table and gestured for Kelley and Phil to join him. They were busy munching on the sweet bread and sipping their coffee when Max entered the kitchen.

He walked over to Gino, leaned over and whispered in his ear. Gino whispered something in return, and then stood up. "I must leave you all. Max just learned that I'm needed back home in Syracuse. There has been a small fire in the kitchen of my restaurant. My wife has called and asked that we return to deal with the clean up and the insurance adjuster."

"But, I thought that you were going to stay and see us through this," Sofia said, now suddenly alarmed.

"I don't think you'll need me any longer. I'm leaving Mr. Willis here to help you take care of things. "

Looking at Phil, he added, "Max has already packed our bags and I'll have him take us to the airport. You can stay in communication with me by phone and let me know how things are progressing here."

Gino stood up and hugged his brother and sister-in-law and reassured them that everything would be all right. "Phil, walk with me out to the car."

Max loaded the bags and jumped into the driver's seat. Gino shook Phil's hand and said, "I know I can count on you to take good care of my family here. Stay until you feel my brother-in-law's business is settled satisfactorily. You'll have to book a flight back to Syracuse, but make it first class. I'll take care of all your expenses of course. When you return, we'll finish our business there."

Phil glanced down at his watch. It was almost nine o'clock and the difficult part of the day stretched before him. He knew he had to talk Sofia and Jason into selling both their luxurious home and their beloved business.

It was about nine forty-five when Phil and Jason sat down on the brown leather sofa in the library to await the arrival of Thaddeus Stamos, who was scheduled for ten. Later, Grace Haney, a Realtor, was due.

Spread out in front of them on the coffee table were the papers that Phil had prepared outlining his proposal to relieve the Callis's of their financial burdens.

"This will be an important day for you, my friend," Phil said as he glanced at the worried looking Jason. "Just keep your confidence up. You certainly don't appear to be as defeated as you were yesterday."

"I'm ready for the challenge today. It's funny how money or the lack of it can turn your world around. I just wanted Sofia to have beautiful things."

Sofia entered the room. "Did I hear someone mention my name?"

Jason jumped to his feet and gave her a kiss. "You certainly did. You'll stick by me if we have to sell the house and restaurant, won't you?"

"I never wanted a lot of fancy things. You and I are a team, Jason. And a damn good one." She lifted her head as she heard a knock on the front door.

Phil glanced at his watch. "That should be Stamos."

She went to the door and returned with a tall, slender man, who appeared to be in his late sixties, following her. He was wearing a brown turtle neck shirt, beige slacks and a brown blazer. "Thaddeus is here," she announced. "I'm going to the kitchen now to keep Kelley company. I'll bring in some refreshments later."

Jason jumped to his feet and rushed to shake Stamos's hand. "Thaddeus, this is my counselor and tax consultant, Phil Willis."

The men did not shake hands; instead they took a few moments to eye each other up and down. "Glad to meet you, Mr. Stamos," Phil finally said.

"From the look on your face, Mr. Willis, I get the impression that you expected me to look somewhat different. I'm a businessman."

"Good. I hope that we can iron out some of Mr. Callis's financial problems," he replied. Then, changing the subject, he added, "I see you found the place okay."

"Hell man. My wife and I grew up in this town. In fact, we were married in the local Cathedral. We've been living in Tampa for the past twenty years though."

Suddenly Phil noticed a woman standing behind Mr. Stamos. "And this is?"

"My secretary," Stamos answered. "Brought her along in case she's needed to take notes or help witness some papers. Now let's get down to business." He glared at Jason. "I hope you're prepared to give me my money."

Phil took Stamos by the arm and guided him toward a seat. "Let's all sit down. I want to explain to you how you will be fully repaid."

Stamos reluctantly sat on the sofa and his secretary sat down beside him. "No funny business, Willis. I just want my money and we're done here."

Phil tried to slow down the conversation by rationalizing. "First of all Sir, I heard you say that you grew up here in Dolphin Springs; so, you must have known Sofia and Jason."

"No. I meet Jason when he came into my Tampa Casino to gamble. At first, he won a little. Then, he started to lose and lose some more. Unfortunately, gambling is rarely a winning game. The odds are always in favor of the house and Jason kept getting deeper and deeper into debt with me."

Phil, who had taken a seat beside Jason, tried to appease Stamos. "My wife and I worked in this area for quite some time, years ago, so we understand how everyone loves Dolphin Springs. Surely, you can understand why Sofia and Jason would like to come to a favorable conclusion to their problems and continue living in this community."

Stamos nodded. "Yes. I can understand that. What do you propose?"

"Jason and Sofia are planning to sell both their home and their restaurant so they can take their equity out of them to repay you."

Stamos' head shot up and his nostrils flared in anger. "You call that a restaurant! He's run it into the ground! Hell, he even served Italian and Mexican food in a Greek restaurant. No wonder the people stopped going there. It was Greek and part of the established business community for years before he miss-managed it."

Phil sighed and leaned forward. "Sir that is why Jason is selling it. Not only to repay his debts but to give someone else the opportunity to bring it back to its glory days of being a Five-Star Greek restaurant."

Stamos' body snapped forward in his chair. "Now, that's the first good news that I've heard."

"Jason and Sofia are meeting with their Realtor to arrange the sale of this magnificent home. We're certain that it will sell in no time and they'll get their equity out of it. All the Callis's need is a little more time and you'll have your money."

Jason jumped to his feet. "I'll pay you back every cent that I owe you Thaddeus. I give you my word."

Before Stamos could answer, the doorbell chimed. Jason stood up, excused himself and went to answer it. Within seconds, he came back into the library with a heavy-set, gray-haired woman behind him.

After he introduced the Realtor to Phil and Stamos, she turned to Jason, "I understand you want to sell your house as soon as possible. Is that true?"

He lowered his head and sadly replied, "Sofia and I have agreed that it would be best if we sell both the house and the restaurant and simplify our lives."

"Good. I can give you a quick appraisal of the house. My firm also sells commercial real estate. I'm confident that we can find a buyer for the restaurant. Of course, we'll have to do a thorough inventory of all the assets."

Phil pulled up a chair for Grace to sit down, walked over to the coffee table and pulled a couple sheets of paper from a pile. "We have already inventoried the restaurant. I'm sure you will find this accurate."

Grace looked at the paper briefly, and nodded in agreement as Sofia, with Kelley behind her, walked into the room pushing a cart laden with a carafe of coffee, dishes and a plate of the almond butter cookies,' Kourabiethes', she had made earlier.

"I thought that all of you could use some refreshments," Sofia said.

Stamos stood up, grabbed some cookies and put them on a plate. "I wish my wife could bake like this."

After everyone drank their coffee and enjoyed the sweets, Phil approached Stamos. "Well, Sir, do you think   you can give Jason some time to get your money to you?"

He sighed, thought for a few moments, and then answered. "I'm not an unreasonable man and I realize that these folks are in a real jam. I can give them some time. But not too long."

He stood up and gestured for his secretary to do the same. "Now, we have to be on our way. I have other commitments today. "

Jason jumped up. He and Phil followed Stamos to the door. Jason thanked him and the two shook hands. Stamos said, "I think we can conclude this business with just a handshake at this point. But, I want you to know, you've got one smart friend in Willis. Listen to him."

"I intend too," Jason answered with humility as he smiled at Phil.

"One more thing Mr. Stamos," Phil said, placing his hand gently on his arm. "Have you ever thought of buying a restaurant? With all of your experience, running a casino and other businesses it should be a natural."

Stamos stared at him. "A restaurant. Me, own a restaurant?"

Then, a light seemed to come on slowly in his head and was reflected in his eyes. "Yes. I can see it now. Stamos's Five-Star Greek Restaurant. You know, that's not as far-fetched as it might sound."

"And there's one available, right in downtown Dolphin Springs. Lots of local Greek customers there too," Phil added smiling. "Just think about it."

Stamos rubbed his chin. "You know Willis. You might be on to something here."

"By the way Sir, my wife and I plan to take Jason and Sofia out to dinner tonight. Maybe your wife and you would like to join us?"

"Where at?"

"In Dolphin Springs of course. A little café, Mythos Greek Café."

"I know the place. We'll be glad to join you. If I plan to open a restaurant of my own, I'll have to check out the competition. Right?"

"Good. I'll make reservations for six," Phil said, looking pleased with himself.

As Stamos walked down the steps to his car, Phil could hear him muttering. "Stamos Greek Restaurant. That sounds pretty good."

Phil accompanied Sofia and Jason as Grace Haney made a thorough appraisal of the house. After, Sofia and Jason signed a few papers arranging for the sale.

Phil handed Mr. Stamos' business card to Grace. "Why don't you give Stamos a call about the sale of the restaurant," he suggested.

After Grace left, Kelley and Phil were alone in the library with Sofia and Jason.

"More coffee?" Sofia asked.

"No. Thank you. I'm sure that I'm going to put on weight with all these Greek sweets," Kelley answered.

"Same here," Phil said. Then, he paused for a moment. "You know. I've been thinking that this Stamos guy is a pretty decent sort."

"Of course," Sofia said. "He was born and raised in Dolphin Springs. Everyone from here is family."

Chapter 23

In the next few months, new challenges arrived for Kelley and Phil. After he completed Gino's tax return and saved him thousands of dollars, the word had gotten out in the community that Phil was a very competent tax lawyer and his business increased tremendously.

Jason and Sofia had gone to New York in time to spend three days visiting with his grandmother, Dione, before she passed away peacefully in her sleep. The visit with his grandmother and sister gave Jason the opportunity to mend his relationship with them.

After he returned to Dolphin Springs, he sold the restaurant to Thaddius Stamos. Stamos remodeled the restaurant and reopened it. Within a short time it not only became a favorite with the locals, but was soon very popular again with the tourists.

Jason and Sofia sold their large home on the bayou and planned to start a newer and simpler life. A young couple had purchased a small bakery on the edge of town and hired Sofia to show them how to make Greek bread and pastries. The bakery was a big success.

After Gino donated a large sum to the Cathedral in Jason and Sofia's name for their new roof; the town's people accepted them once again and welcomed them back into the church community. The Callis's even chaired a dinner and auction, to help raise funds for the renovation of the inside of the Cathedral.

Meanwhile in Syracuse, Gino had accepted an offer from a large restaurant chain in New York City to purchase his restaurant. He and his wife planned to retire to Sicily and enroll their daughters in an elite college in Europe.

As their former clients were busy rearranging their lives, Kelley and Phil continued to work diligently handling complex tax cases. They decided that a future vacation would be to Sicily, visiting Eleni and Gino.

"I'll be ready for a real vacation soon," Kelley said.

The next five years flew by swiftly. Phil's parents, Kaitlin and Dexter McLane, sold their home in Syracuse and moved to a condominium in Florida, where they were content to enjoy the warm sunny Florida days after enduring years of the cold New York winters. Dexter was pleased that his expert investments had provided the pair with a large portfolio that would serve them well in their retirement years.

The Willis children, Ashley and Alan, were both doing remarkably well. Alan, now over six feet tall with sandy brown hair was the image of his father. He and his best friend had been accepted in the New York Military Academy just outside of Syracuse. Ashley, five foot six, with curly auburn hair, had applied to and had been accepted at Xavier, an all girls' preparatory school. She had recently told her parents that she planned to attend law school after graduation from college.

Alan, on the other hand, seemed to have no interest in following in his father's footsteps His school had placed him on the rifle team and he hoped that would eventually lead to his career choice—law enforcement either in or out of the military.

Phil had been an outstanding father and husband. Their marriage was rock solid and the only thing that Kelley worried about was Phil's recent rush to the emergency room with a kidney stone. It was so big, the doctors had to admit him overnight and crush the stone with sonic waves.

However, as the years passed, Phil became quite bored with the tax business.

Occasionally, Phil's name had come up in local politics when his friends urged him to run for an office. He always answered, "Not at this time."

On Saturday evenings, the family would spend their time watching a movie and eating popcorn together, as they had done when the children were younger. Later, Phil would pull out college brochures and discuss the different choices available to the kids.

One Saturday evening, Kelley suggested to Phil, "Maybe we should watch a racy video together after the kids go to their rooms."

"You know Kell, I don't need a racy video. Just looking at you excites me."

"But look at us, Phil. We are almost middle-aged."

He grinned. "You know I've been thinking a lot about our future lately."

"I'm surprised that you had time to think of anything other than taxes."

Reducing his grin to a resigned smile, he said, "You're right. Nothing, but taxes, taxes and more taxes."

"Not too exciting is it, Mr. Willis?"

As they sat staring at each other, not uttering a word and contemplating their dull everyday lives, the phone rang.

Kelley answered. "Hello. Hello? You're who?" Sure, he's in." Her face lit up as she handed the phone to Phil. "It's for you dear. You'll never guess who it is."

Chapter 24

"Boy, are you in for a surprise," Kelley said, as she handed him the phone.

"Hi, Phil. It's Gayle Tanner. Remember me from your old law firm?"

There was a short stretch of silence as his mouth fell open in surprise. "Of course. You were just a newly hired law clerk at your dad's law firm and still going to law school when I worked there. But that's been ages ago."

"Glad you remembered me."

He lifted his head, blinking as if he was not sure what to say. Then replied, "I couldn't forget someone as pretty and smart as you. What's going on with you these days?" Phil asked as he plopped down in his easy chair.

"I have something important that I want to talk over with you. I'm at the Final Verdict Bar and Grill. I was hoping that you hadn't eaten yet and could join me for a bite. Great fish and chips here. And of course, bring Kelley."

Phil paused for a moment and looked at Kelley who was standing nearby. "Hold on for a minute Gayle."

He put his hand over the mouth piece and whispered, "It's one of my old law friends, Gayle Tanner. She's inviting us out for fish and chips. Did we eat yet?"

Kelley grinned and drew a sharp breath. "You would

certainly remember if we did. Let's take her up on her offer. It'll do us good. It'll only take me a few minutes to freshen up."

"When a woman is being taken out to dinner, it takes more than a few minutes to get ready," he replied, smiling at her.

"Just talked to Kelley," Phil said into the phone. "Give us about twenty minutes and we'll be right over."

"Sure. Can't wait to see my favorite couple."

Phil and Kelley hurried upstairs and dressed casually in jeans and pull-overs. The restaurant was close by, so they decided to walk. Strolling along, they talked about the years when Phil had worked with Gayle.

"Miss those days, Hon?" she asked.

He swallowed and shook his head. "Well. I'm not sure."

They entered the dimly lighted bar and heard a voice call out, "Hey Willis. Phil. It's Bobby. I used to wait on you when you were in Sarasota. I moved back to Syracuse last year."

Phil looked quickly around the room. Then, recognizing the bartender, he walked over. "Bobby. Sure, I remember you. It's been quite a while."

They shook hands. Phil inclined his head slightly toward Kelley. "You remember Kelley of course. She's now my wife and we have two teen-age kids."

Bobby shifted his gaze to her, then ran around the bar and hugged her. "My God, you look fabulous. Have you got time to sit down and talk?"

"Not right now. Meeting someone," she replied.

Bobby trailed his fingers along Kelley's arm. "See me before you leave guys. I'll need some updates."

Over the sound of the other patrons talking and laughing, they heard another voice call out. "Hey, Kelley and Phil. Over here."

Looking up, they spied Gayle and pushed their way through the crowd and started to walk toward the booth.

Bobby called out, "Hey Willis. Don't forget to come back."

Without breaking his stride, Phil waved his hand over his shoulder in acknowledgement.

"Well, look at you," he said to her, as she stood up. "You're all grown up."

Gail lifted her hand to her hair, pushing a stray tendril back behind her ear. "And look at you Mr. Willis. You're getting gray around the temples. And I love those tinted glasses. Yes, you do look the part of a prominent attorney."

She shifted her gaze from him to Kelley and gave her a brief hug. "And you look like the perfect attorney's wife," she said, smiling. "Sit please."

They slid into the seat across from Gayle as the waitress approached them. "What can I get you folks? And, by the way, the drinks are on Bobby."

"I'm treating my friends to some of your delicious fish and chips," Gayle replied. She looked at Kelley and Phil. "How about a beer to go with that?"

They made no comments, just nodded. The waitress wrote down the orders and walked away.

"Now, tell me what you wanted to talk about, Gail," Phil said.

"In due time. First of all, I want to tell you I've been following your career lately. Dad was very sorry to see you leave the firm. But, it appears that you both have been doing extremely well since."

"We've only been doing taxes lately. It's not that exciting," Phil glanced up, his gaze holding hers. "But, thanks for the good words. From all that I've heard from the local law community, you've been doing quite well, too. Winning that well publicized case for Judy Vernon has done a lot for your profile."

"It was great to win that case for Judy. She's one of my dearest friends and I spent a lot of time on it. Divorce cases aren't fun."

"I wouldn't know about that," Phil replied, reaching for Kelley's hand. "But, tell me how your dad's doing."

"You probably read in the papers that Dad retired from the law firm. He and Mom are living in a gated retirement community in Ft. Myers; playing golf and more golf. Mom even joined a bridge club."

"My parents are in Sarasota, not far from Ft. Myers. I guess all the retired folks are heading to Florida."

"Give me your parents address before we leave here," Gail said. "Maybe the old retirees can get together."

The waitress returned to the table with a pitcher of draft beer. "Your food will be out in a few minutes folks. Busy night."

"How about adding a few extra pieces of fish for my friend," Gayle said. "He's still a growing boy even though he's got teenage kids."

"Sure. No problem," the waitress said walking away.

"Speaking of kids," Kelley said. "I've got a few pictures with me if you would care to see them."

"That's a must."

Kelley pulled some photos from her wallet and slipped them across the table to Gayle, who studied them.

"I can't believe you have children who are practically grown."

Gayle and Phil exchanged stories about their experiences in court, while Kelley listened with great interest.

After the fish dinners arrived, they chatted very little as they quietly ate.

"Good, huh?" Gayle asked, as she waved the waitress over for more beer.

"Enough beer for me," Kelley said, cupping her hand over her glass.

"Me too," Phil added.

They sat back in the booth, finishing their food, when a tall young man in his late twenties approached them. "Hi Gayle. Good to see you again."

"Hi Daniel. Good to see you too. You remember Phil Willis, don't you? And this is his wife, Kelley.'

Phil stood up and shook hands with the man. "Oh, yeah. You clerked at Tanner and Tanner too."

"Say, Gayle, I'm having a party in the back room for my brother who's going off to college. Why don't and your friends join us?"

Gayle looked at Phil, who in turn, looked at Kelley and shrugged his shoulders. He was anxious to hear the real reason why Gail had invited them out tonight. But she did not seem to be in any hurry to elaborate at this point. So, he just said, "Sure. Why not. We're not in any rush to get home."

Gayle waved the waitress over. "Here's my credit card. We'll be in the back room after you run it."

"If you'll excuse me," Kelley said, "Think I'll visit the ladies room. You go on ahead. I'll be there in a minute."

Gayle and Phil followed Daniel into the back meeting room which was filled with men and women, laughing and talking loudly. Most of them appeared to be dressed in dark professional suits. Looking around the room, Phil quickly recognized several people that he knew and was soon engaged in conversation with them.

Returning from the ladies room, Kelley was taken by surprise at the crowd. She did not immediately see Gayle and Phil, so she slipped into a chair near the door. She looked around and spotted Phil. He was busily shaking hands, laughing and talking. In fact, Kelley thought it had been a long time since she had seen him so animated and out-going.

A tall, red-haired young woman, in her early thirties, slipped into the seat beside Kelley. "Hi, I'm Joy Foreman. I don't think we've met," she said extending her hand.

"I'm Kelley Willis." She swung her head around and gestured toward Phil. "That's my husband, over there.

We're with Gayle Tanner."

"Oh, yes. I know Gayle. I see that you don't have a drink. Want a beer?"

"No thanks. As a matter of fact, I was thinking of sneaking out of here soon and heading for home." She gave a half smile and said, "It looks like my husband has a lot of catching up to do and with his old pals and might be planning to gab for a long time."

"I was thinking of leaving myself," Joy said. "Do you need a ride?"

Kelley shook her head. "I'm within walking distance. But, thanks for the offer."

She excused herself, walked over to Phil and tapped him on the arm. "I think I'm ready to walk home."

"Sure you don't want to stay?"

With a shrug, she dismissed the idea. "No. I'm tired. You stay as long as you want and enjoy yourself."

The idea gave him pause before he answered. "No. I'll just say good-bye to Gayle and head for home with you. You shouldn't walk alone." His expression was contrite and he walked toward Gayle, who was now seated alone at a table in the back of the room.

He sat down beside her. "Say Gayle, you never did tell me what you wanted to talk to me about and Kelley and I are getting ready to leave now."

"Oh, yes. I've taken on a high profile civil case that I was hoping you would consider second chairing with me. My wealthy client is suing a Gypsy couple for stealing a good part of her fortune. The case is very complex and may take up a lot of your time, so you might want to give it some consideration before you agree to join me."

Phil leaned forward in his chair, his adrenalin soaring. "Sounds very enticing. And, I think that I am might be up for a challenging case. My docket has been very dull lately."

"Why don't we plan on getting together at my office

tomorrow morning? We'll discuss it in detail."

"I've been working with Kelley lately on all my cases," he said after a few moments pause. "And she's an extremely good investigator."

"That's good to hear. I'm certain we'll have a lot of work that she can help us with."

"Thanks. I'll see you then." Phil got up and returned to Kelley.

On their way out, they stopped to tell Bobby good night and said that they would be back at a later date to talk with him.

Phil strolled into the library, turned on his computer and read his email. He then put a reminder to himself in the calendar of his phone. "Meet Gayle Tanner tomorrow morning in her office." He turned off the lights and headed upstairs.

Kelley looked up, with one eye open, when he entered the bedroom. "Guess what Gayle wants me to do?"

She sighed and sat straight up with a sense of apprehension. "Okay, tell me."

"She wants me to second-chair on a case she's working on. It sounds like something I can't turn down. Tell you all about it after I talk to her tomorrow."

Chapter 25

Later the next morning, Kelley's cell rang incessantly. "Morning Kelley, this is your happy attorney, Phil."

"Oh, yes, I remember you. You're the fellow that I was looking for this morning when I woke up. All I found was a note on the bed stand, saying you were off for an early morning run. And now, its mid morning, and I still hadn't seen nor heard from you. I was just starting to get a little concerned. Where are you?"

"After my run, my long legs decided to continue on to Gayle Tanner's office for my nine o'clock appointment with her. I'm just ready to leave her office now. What are you up to?"

"Just the usual errands. After I got the kids off to school, I took two of your suits, your sports coat and four of your white shirts over to the cleaners. Mr. Wong gave me the four hour deal. He also told me to thank you for your great work on his taxes. After that, I stopped on the way home and had the oil changed on the car. So, what's up with you and Gayle?"

"We talked about the case she wants me to help on."

Kelley could hear from the excitement in the tone of his voice that something was different about him this morning.

"So, tell me about it."

"First of all, we need to finish all the tax cases that we've got pending and not take any new ones on. I have to clear my docket for this upcoming trial."

Kelley froze, and her breath lodged in her throat as she fought a sudden wave of apprehension. Then, trying to appear calm, she asked, "What kind of a case is it?"

"It's a civil case."

Kelley was momentarily stunned. "I can't believe you want to give up your lucrative tax business."

"I didn't say anything about giving it up. Just want to take a break from it for a while. I'll only be second chair at the trial."

Some of her tension ebbed away in that reassurance. But still her voice wavered. "That's good. But, right now, my head is spinning."

Phil was so keyed up that he didn't even hear the momentary discomfort in Kelley's voice.

"Gayle and I will need your assistance in some of the investigation. I'll clean up my schedule of pending clients this afternoon and then look out—the old Willis is back.

"Gayle already has the case moving along. It all hangs on proving that Mrs. Cliff was duped out of her life savings. The counsel for the defendants, Mr. and Mrs. Burjan, is Miller Franks. He's one tough lawyer and has a track record for winning. He could be difficult to beat."

"Sounds like you're all fired up over this case, Phil."

"I sure am. We're both scheduled to meet with Gayle tomorrow morning to get our strategy planned. I just wanted to give you a call and let you know I'm on my way home now. What's on your agenda for the rest of today?"

"You remember my days as a housekeeper at the hotel in Miami years ago. Well, I'm still a housekeeper. Cleaning and more cleaning."

"Let's plan on a quiet evening at home tonight, so we can get up early tomorrow. I'm anxious to get started on the case, since I believe it will be a tough one."

Kelley realized that Phil's mind was now zeroed in on the new set of circumstances. "Oh, by the way Phil, you might plan on heading to the mall this afternoon and get yourself a new pair of shoes. If you're going to appear in court, you need to look spiffy."

"Will do, see you soon Hon."

The next morning, they headed to Gayle's office where they sat down with her to discuss the case of "Edith Cliff versus Shreif and Luna Burjan."

She explained that after the death of her husband, her client, Edith Cliff, had been befriended by the Gypsy couple. They had convinced Edith that her deceased husband, Howard, talking through séances, was instructing her to give them her car, jewelry and large sums of money.

After summarizing the case, Gayle told them she had discovered two other women in the community who had also been swindled out of much of their savings by the Burjans.

"Maybe, we can contact these women and get them to testify in this case," Phil suggested. "Let's send Kelley to talk to them. She has a way of persuading people to cooperate."

Their conversation was suddenly interrupted by Gayle's legal assistant, who knocked briefly, then poked her head around the doorway. "Gayle, there was a message for you from the court clerk. Said they had a fire in the electrical room at the courthouse over the weekend. Smoke filled the entire building. It'll be closed while they clean up the mess. The judges have delayed all pending cases for a week."

Gayle fought back a smile. "Looks like this is a break for our team. Gives us another week to prepare for our opening statement and to gather more evidence. Now, let's sit down and go over our strategy."

Phil grinned, eager to get started.

After talking over the case for a couple of hours, Kelley leaned forward in her chair and pulled out a sheet of newspaper from her briefcase. "Say. I've got an idea. I cut this article out of this morning's paper. Phil told me a couple of Gypsies were involved in this. So when I read that Ringling Brothers circus is going to be in New York next week at Madison Square Garden, I got an idea of how to proceed with the investigation. Our old friends, the Flying Wilders are featured in the show. And Flo, the Gypsy fortune teller, is going to be there. Maybe, she could give us some information on how the modern Gypsies think and work their schemes."

"That's a great suggestion," Phil said. Then, turning to Gayle, he added, "Years ago, Kelley and I spent a week with circus people in Sarasota Florida. We trained with them and they taught us a lot."

Gayle sifted to a more comfortable position in her chair, and considered Kelley's proposal. "You know that sounds like a terrific idea. When can you leave for the city?"

Kelley's head snapped up. "The article gives a number to call for tickets. Why don't I call there and see if I can get the circus manager's number? Let me make a call to him now and find out where the circus people are staying."

Gayle handed the phone to Kelley. After identifying who she was and stating why she was calling, Kelley finally reached the manager. She talked briefly to him and then hung up the phone.

"Some of the folks are staying in rooms at the Belvedere Hotel, at 48th Street and 8th Avenue. That's not too far from Madison Square Garden. And that's where Flo will be."

"If you leave here, early tomorrow morning, you can

be in the city in less than five hours," Phil said.

Now fired up, Gayle added, "Plan on it, Kelley. Of course, the firm will take care of all your expenses. So keep track of them."

Kelley giggled. "Well, I might have to treat Flo to lunch and it may be more than a Nathan's hot dog. As I remember, she loved to eat."

"And speaking of eating, why don't I have some lunch brought in for us from the deli around the corner?" Gayle suggested. "That way, we can continue plotting our action. What would you two like to eat?"

"I'll have a BLT," Phil said, "And I think Kelley would like her favorite—a Reuben."

At the mention of a Reuben sandwich, Kelley indicated her agreement with a quick nod of her head.

Gayle smiled, "What would you like to drink?"

"A couple of Diet Pepsi's for us." Phil sat back in his chair, "I'm really getting anxious to head to the court room once again."

Chapter 26

Only days remained until the civil case of Edith Cliff versus Luna and Shreif Burjan was scheduled to begin. Phil and Gayle planned to spend every moment in Gayle's office preparing their strategy for the trial.

Meanwhile, Kelley had left Syracuse at six in the morning for the drive to New York City and the Belvedere Hotel in downtown Manhattan. Passing Madison Square Garden, on her way to the hotel, she spied a gigantic red and white banner hanging from the building, announcing that the Ringling Brothers Circus, featuring the Flying Wilders would be performing there later in the week.

She pulled into the twenty-four hour parking garage at 48th Street and 8th Avenue next to the Belvedere. The parking attendant, who appeared to be about six feet tall and weighed over three hundred pounds, slowly climbed out of the booth and asked, "How long, lady?"

"I'm not sure. Maybe a couple of hours." She scowled as she noticed from the posted sign that the parking fees in downtown Manhattan were exceptionally expensive.

Kelley stepped out of the car as the attendant lumbered up to her. "Leave the keys in the car. My name is Jake. I'm on till midnight. I'll park your car and have the keys in the courtesy booth."

"Thank you Jake. I'm Kelley and I shouldn't be too long."

Looking like a gentle giant, he smiled down at her and said soothingly, "Don't worry Ms. Kelley; your car is in good hands."

"Thanks. I'm visiting my friend, Flo, one of the circus people staying at the Belvedere."

Jake's face broke into a big grin, showing gold capped front teeth, "Why didn't you say so? I'm a friend of Flo's."

"You know Flo, the fortune teller?"

"Yeah. Me and her go way back." He took his baseball cap off and wiped the sweat from his brow. "Lived near her in the Bronx for years. Say, tell her that I said 'hi'. And by the way, the parking is free for Flo and her friends."

"Thanks. And I'll say lots of nice things about you." She winked at him. She opened the back door of the car, pulled out her briefcase and headed out of the parking garage.

Entering the hotel, Kelley approached the reception desk and asked the clerk, "What rooms are the circus people staying in?"

"You should be able to catch most of them in the dining room now. They came down late for the buffet breakfast."

"Which way is the dining room?"

The clerk pointed across the lobby. "Take a left at the elevators."

The hostess looked up from the tickets that she was reviewing as Kelley entered the dining room. "We're still serving brunch. It's $19.95 for hotel guests."

Smiling, Kelley stepped closer. "Oh. I'm not a guest. I'm just here to visit Tony Wilder and his circus friends. I was told that most of them were in here eating."

"Yes. They're seated in the back room. Follow me."

Kelley followed her into the secluded dining area and

looked across the room. Tony spied her, jumped up, ran across the room and threw his arms around her. "I can't believe it, Kelley Ryan, my favorite pupil."

Kelley put her briefcase down on the floor and gave him a squeeze. "Haven't done any tightrope walking lately. But, you forget Tony, I'm now Kelley Willis."

"Oh, yes. I remember now. But it's been years. And you're just as lovely as ever. Come, join us for a bite." He led her to the back of the room where they were seated in several booths.

"Look everyone," Tony shouted, unable to hide his enthusiasm. "Look who's here, our dear friend, Kelley."

They all stopped eating momentarily, looked up and waved at her.

"Join us for some breakfast," Tony said, as he took her briefcase and put it on the seat where he had been sitting.

"Don't mind if I do. I just had a coffee and Danish before I left Syracuse. And it's been a long drive."

Kelley walked up to the buffet line and waited for the chef to make her an omelet. After adding toast and fresh fruit to her plate, she sat down across from Tony.

He reached across the table and took her hands in his. "Tell me what brings you into town."

"I read in the newspaper that you and the crew were doing a show at the Garden. So I came into the city specifically to see all of you. Why are you here doing this show Tony? I thought you retired a few years ago."

"I did. But, I got a call that the new tightrope walkers and performers that the circus was bringing in from Europe got detained. Something to do with their passports. So I got some of the old gang together and took the gig." His gaze locked with hers across the table. "Of course, we're all a bit older, but we've been keeping in shape over the years and doing a few performances here and there. I don't know if you read about my nephew, Nik Wallenda. He works on his own now and is advertised as the world's greatest tightrope walker. He's paid top dollar for his daring stunts. "

"Oh, yes. I did see something in the Syracuse newspaper about him," Kelley replied.

"In a few weeks, he's going to walk over Niagara Falls. We're really proud of him. And the circus world needed a fresh new face."

Tony finished his plate of food, leaned back in his chair and started to reminisce. Kelley's heart tightened as he told her that in the years since his wife had passed away he had lost some his zest for the circus life. This booking with Ringling Brothers would be his last.

"Since this is the last time out on the road for most of us, we're doing it up right and staying at this fancy hotel." He tried to erase any trace of regret from his face. "Came up here with Flo and a couple of the old timers. You remember Flo, don't you?"

She glanced up at him, a teasing grin curving her lips. "Yes. Of course, I do. Is she here?"

"She slept in late this morning. Said she'd be down shortly." He lifted his coffee cup and took a small sip. "But first, Kelley, tell me about you and your family."

Now it was her turn to update Tony on the past few years. Her eyes lit up with pride and she pulled a packet of photos from her purse. As she showed Tony each picture, she accompanied it with a related story. "So, you see, Tony, I've never been so happy. But tell me your plans after you retire."

He sat back in his chair. "Going to sell the ranch in Sarasota and move to a condo. I plan to write my memoirs about the circus and my life as a tightrope walker. It'll be filled with photos too."

He looked up, spotted Flo walking into the restaurant and waved to her. "Flo, over here. Come over here. Look who's here to visit us."

Flo half turned, her eyes wide, and she hurried over to the table. Kelley jumped to her feet and threw her arms around the short, heavy-set woman in an enthusiastic embrace. Gray hair had now blended in with Flo's wild red hair and gave her a softer and more mellowed appearance. Kelley grabbed Flo's hand and whirled her around. "Flo, you look marvelous."

Flo took a step backwards and snorted. "It's kind of you to say that Kelley. But, I've gained a few pounds and my age is starting to catch up with me. A lot slower getting around than I used to be. But you look just wonderful, Sweetie."

"Grab a plate and join us Flo," Tony urged. "In fact, Kelley, I think it's time you fill another plate too. After all, the food is on Ringling Brothers."

Kelley laughed, "This will be enough food to cover breakfast, lunch and dinner."

She put her arm around Flo's ample waist as they walked up to the buffet table. "By the way, what's with you and the parking attendant at the garage next door?"

Flo giggled, "You know me. These blue eyes can still attract the boys, like bees to honey." Then, sighing, she added, "No seriously, I've known him for years."

After they finished eating, Tony stood up. "Well. I'll leave you ladies. I've got a few calls to make. While, I'm in New York, I'm going to try to find someone who might be interested in my tales of the wild circus life."

Kelley shifted her gaze to Flo. "Let's go to your room, Flo. I came to the city especially to talk to you. Need you to tell me everything you know about modern day Gypsies and their life. My husband, Phil, I guess you remember Phil Willis, he worked with us at the Wilder Ranch years ago. Well, we're married now and have a couple kids."

"Yes. I remember that adorable man. He was really cute. He got so embarrassed when I teased him." Flo's eyes lit up and a mischievous grin came across her face.

"Well, he's a lawyer now, assisting in a case against a Gypsy couple. He needs all the information he can gather about modern day Gypsies."

Flo stood up, helped Kelley to her feet and then took her by the arm. "Well, let's go up to my room, Sweetie, I'll give you the low down on what I know."

Kelley grabbed her briefcase and purse and accompanied Flo upstairs to her room where they sat down at the table in front of a large window overlooking the nearby hotels and buildings of New York.

"You don't mind if I turn on my tape recorder do you?" Kelley asked as she unzipped her briefcase, took her recorder out and placed it on the table. "It's easier than trying to take notes or attempting to remember everything you tell me."

"No problem. Let's get going."

Flo told Kelley how most of the present day Gypsies in the United States were second and third generation. Their parents and grandparents had emigrated from numerous European countries including Romania, Italy and Russia. Scores of them had originally settled in New York City, where they lived in poorer neighborhoods.

"Lots of today's Gypsies are what you'd call street-educated," Flo said, as she lifted her shoulders. "They do whatever is necessary to bring money home. Some of them who live in Virginia and the southern states are called travelers—going on the road to repair roofs and black-top driveways. Others live in the cities; make their living by operating in small gangs to steal from grocery or department stores. A few of them live off of fortune-telling. This has been the Gypsy way of life for many generations and it's all that many of them know. While they speak the national language when in public, most of them still speak their own Gypsy tongues at home."

"That's really interesting," Kelley said.

"I even have a small dictionary of the language if you want to use it to translate their words."

"Thanks. I'll take it. It might be helpful to Phil and the lawyer he's working with."

Flo folded her hands across her chest and leaned back in the chair. "Now-a-days a number of the Gypsies have found inventive ways to make a very comfortable living. Some of them live near each other in large gated communities, up and down the East coast. And believe me, these are no penny-ante thieves, they're big timers, known to bilk families out of their life savings."

"That's exactly what happened in the case Phil is working on."

"Some Gypsies have such a first-rate line of bull they have their victims believing they can foretell their future," Flo said. "And those poor suckers are willing to pay big money to hear what they want to hear."

For the next hour, Flo talked, while Kelley recorded the conversation. Finally, feeling she had accumulated a lot of information that Phil and Gayle could review, she glanced nervously at her watch. "It's getting late Flo, think I better get going. It's quite a drive back to Syracuse and I don't like to travel after dark. Thanks for all your info. You've been an immense help."

"Anytime girl. And here's the dictionary with the Gypsy language. Feel free to keep it. I don't need it anymore. My home address and phone number are inside. And, tell that gorgeous husband of yours to feel free to give me a call if he has any questions or wants me to testify at the trial. I would love to tease him again."

"I can't thank you enough, Flo. You've been a big help."

Kelley put her recorder in her briefcase, stood up and cupped Flo's hands in hers.

Flo gripped Kelley's hands tightly. Releasing them, she reached down in her pocket and pulled out some tickets. "And by the way. Here's six 'Annie Oakley's' to the circus from Tony."

Kelley let out a little chuckle. "Thanks. I remember that 'Annie Oakley' is circus slang for passes. And, I'm so glad that your friend Jake said I could park free today."

"And speaking of Jake, tell him I'll see him about eight tonight," Flo replied with a twinkle in her eyes.

Kelley picked up her brief case from the table, and heard a couple of quick raps on the door.

Flo walked over and looked through the peep hole. "Oh, it's Tony." She threw the door open.

Tony strolled into the room, walked over to Kelley and put his arm around her shoulder. "Glad I caught you before you left. Just wanted to say how good it was to see you once again."

Smiling, Kelley gave him kiss on the cheek and thanked him for the circus passes.

"Hope you and the family can make it."

Kelley kissed him again and stroked a finger along his cheek. "We'll try. Phil and I have many fond memories of you."

"Same here. If you can't make it to the performance, maybe you and your family can come to Sarasota sometime."

"It's a date."

After bidding a final farewell to her two friends, Kelley returned to the parking lot. She found Jake sitting on a tall stool inside the courtesy booth and asked for her car.

"I'll get it for you, Ms. Kelley. By the way, you owe me forty bucks. I noticed that your gas tank was almost empty, so I took it down the street to the gas station, and filled it. I knew you'd have trouble finding a cheap place in the city."

Her mouth fell open in surprise. "Gee. That was nice of you. But, I don't have that much cash on me. Will you take a personal check?"

"Sure. Any friend of Flo's is a friend of mine."

"Oh. And by the way, Flo says eight tonight." She winked at him.

Kelley zipped out of the parking garage, anxious to get home.

Driving along, Kelley contemplated what lay ahead for Phil and the trial, and she realized that the rest of the week would be very busy.

Chapter 27

"All rise. This court is in session. The Honorable Judge Marilyn Hilton presiding," the bailiff announced. "This is Case No. 28070, Mrs. Edith Cliff versus Luna and Shreif Burjan. Mrs. Cliff is suing the codefendants for one million dollars which she says they extorted from her in cash and jewelry."

The Judge looked at the defendants who were sitting next to their attorney, Miller Franks. "And how do you plead to the charges, Mr. and Mrs. Burjan?"

In response, they said something out loud that no one in the court room could understand.

The Judge snapped, "In English, please."

Miller Franks whispered something in Shreif's ear. In return, Shreif stood up, drew himself erect and with a determined set to his chin, pronounced loudly, "Not guilty." His wife rose to her feet. "Not guilty," she said almost inaudibly.

The Judge smiled politely at the couple. "That's more like it. Please direct your clients to respond to all the questions in English in the future, Counselor. Not everyone is familiar with the Romani language."

Judge Hilton had been a judge for over fifteen years and there was talk in the legal community that she might soon be appointed by the governor to the State

Supreme Court. It was well known from everyone who
had ever appeared in her courtroom, that she ran a very
tight ship.

Phil knew it would take all of Gayle's and his legal
expertise to convince the six member jury and the two
alternates that this Gypsy couple was guilty of fraud and
of bilking Mrs. Cliff out of her financial assets.

Gayle confidently approached the podium for her
opening statement. "The Burjans have claimed to confer
with gods, spirits and even Michael the Archangel to talk
with Edith Cliff's deceased husband and to offer Edith
comfort and support in return for money and jewelry.
They used 'magician's tricks' to win over Mrs. Cliff and
demanded large sums of money."

In his response, the Burjan's attorney said, "As the
case progresses you will see that Luna and Shreif Burjan are innocent. The Burjans believe that their Gypsy
heritage gave them the ability to converse with the dead,
to heal people psychically and that their business was
legitimate. They state that Edith Cliff voluntarily gave
them gifts and money for helping her through difficult
times."

After the attorneys made their opening statements,
the Judge sighed, "We are ready to proceed. Ms. Tanner
and Mr. Willis will you please call your first witness."

Phil stood up, exhaled nosily and with a withering
look at Miller Franks announced, "We call Ruth Higgins."

A heavy-set woman, who appeared to be in her late
sixties, slowly walked to the front of the courtroom and
entered the witness box, raised her right hand and was
sworn in.

Phil pursed his lips as he approached his first witness. "Your name for the record, please."

"Ruth Ann Higgins."

Phil smiled at her in a reassuring manner as he started his questioning. "And how long have you been em-

ployed as a housekeeper for Mrs. Cliff?"

She took a deep breath. "Twelve years. But I wasn't a housekeeper. I was her companion and confident. She has a housekeeper who comes in twice a week."

Phil glanced over at the Judge and noticed that she was already looking at her watch. He frowned at her behavior and continued. "Then, I assume that you knew Mrs. Cliff's deceased husband, Howard?"

"Yes. But not very well." She eased herself forward in her chair. "You see he didn't live in the house with Mrs. Cliff. He lived with their daughter. Mr. and Mrs. Cliff did not seem to get on well together. The mister could be very arrogant and the two argued a lot when they lived together."

"Did Mr. Cliff like the fact that you seemed close to his wife?"

With a rigid back, Mrs. Higgins thought about that for a moment. She seemed to be trying to hold her tongue a bit as she finally answered, "I don't think that he really cared what she did as long as he didn't have to bother with her."

Phil took a step backwards, his eyes narrowing. "So would you say he was somewhat indifferent to his wife."

"Yes."

Phil folded his arms and looked at her stonily. "And how did Mrs. Cliff feel about his apparent coldness toward her?"

"It hurt her deeply." Mrs. Higgins shifted uncomfortably in her seat. "You see, even though he was cold toward everyone, including her, she loved him dearly."

"And how did she react after his sudden death?"

She hesitated and fought an apparent tide of emotion. "The poor dear was very upset. I think she always thought he would change and draw closer to her as they grew older. When he died suddenly from a heart attack, she realized that would never happen. She just seemed to lose it after he passed away." Her expression grew strained and she wiped a tear from her eye. "She shut herself in her room for over a week. Wouldn't speak to me or her daughter. Said she wanted to join him in the here-after."

Phil stepped over to the table, withdrew a tissue from a box, returned to the witness stand and handed it to Mrs. Higgins.

"And after a week or so did something happen that drew Mrs. Cliff out of her distressed state?"

She stiffened and sat upright in her chair. "Yes. She was visited by Mrs. Luna Burjan."

"And did Mrs. Cliff tell you why Luna Burjan had come to see her?"

Now annoyed, Mrs. Higgins wiped her eyes. "Edith said Luna Burjan told her Mr. Cliff had contacted her from the here-after and instructed her to visit Mrs. Cliff."

"And how do you think that Luna Burjan knew that Mr. Cliff had died?"

Her chin hiked higher and she rolled her eyes. "Why everyone knew about him dying. There was a long article in the newspaper about his death and the fact that he had been a very wealthy and prosperous investment banker."

Phil stepped close to her, trapping her in his steady gaze. "And after that did Edith Cliff continue to confide in you?"

She looked down and nervously fingered the tissue in her hands. "No Sir. After that her friend and confidant was Luna Burjan. She said the Gypsy lady was helping her talk to Mr. Cliff."

As his careful and gentle questioning of Mrs. Higgins progressed, Kelley watched with great admiration.

Phil returned to the desk, picked up a manila folder and walked back to the witness stand. "Mrs. Higgins, do you know anything about Mrs. Cliff's finances?"

"No. But she always said she didn't need to worry about money." Her eyes flashed. "She said Mr. Cliff had an immense portfolio."

Phil stood silent as he carefully considered what his next question would be. After a few moments, Judge Hilton looked impatiently down at him. "Please Counselor. Let's get on with it."

Dragging his focus back, Phil slammed the folder down on the witness stand and whirled around. "Mrs. Higgins do you see Luna Burjan in the courtroom?"

She kept her voice calm and cool as she pointed toward the heavily made up and well dressed woman seated at the defense table. "Yes. That's her over there. She drives Mr. Cliff's blue Mercedes."

Phil opened his mouth and then shut it again. Finally, he chuckled. "Oh, did she buy the car from Mrs. Cliff after her husband's death?"

"No Sir. Mrs. Cliff gave it to her. She said she didn't drive and her daughter had a nice car. I thought she would sell it, but instead she just gave it to that horrible woman."

Attorney Franks banged his fist on the table. "Your Honor. I object. Mrs. Higgins just stated that she knew nothing of Mrs. Cliff's finances."

"Objection overruled. The witness can testify as to what Mrs. Cliff told her."

Pleased, Phil shot her a grateful glance. "Thank you, your Honor. I have only a few more questions for the witness."

The Judge's brows rose in exasperation. "Get on with it, Mr. Willis."

Phil inclined his head in assent and walked up to Mrs. Higgins. "Did you ever actually see Edith Cliff give any money to Mr. or Mrs. Burjan?"

She leaned forward, wringing her hands together. "No. But after Mrs. Burjan called on her a few times, I went to Mrs. Cliff's bedroom and noticed that a large box of jewelry was missing."

"Did you ask Mrs. Cliff what had happened to it?" Phil asked, looking pleased at her response.

"Yes. She said that she gave it to Mrs. Burjan for all that she had done for her. And she told me to mind my own business."

"And how did Mrs. Cliff act after the visits from the defendant?"

Mrs. Higgins looked at Edith Cliff who was seated beside Gayle Tanner and was now holding her head in her hands.

She took a deep breath, swallowed, and replied. "Mrs. Cliff looked more and more despondent after each of Mrs. Burjan's visits. Like something terrible was going to happen to her. When I asked her what was wrong, she just hung her head and wouldn't talk to me. Like I told you before, once she started to get visits from the Burjans, she wouldn't tell me anything. It was like we had never been friends. I think those people put a curse on Edith or brainwashed her."

Attorney Franks jumped to his feet, seething with anger. "Objection, your Honor. Mrs. Higgins has no way of knowing Edith Cliff's state of mind."

The Judge sent Phil a bland look. "Objection sustained. The jury will ignore that last comment."

"No more questions your Honor," Phil said as he turned and strolled back to the table where Gayle and Edith Cliff were seated.

The Judge looked at the defense table. "Mr. Franks. Cross-examine?"

He picked up several papers from the table in front of him, stood up and walked over to the witness box. Leaning on the stand, his voice was steady as he asked, "Mrs. Higgins, you don't live with Mrs. Cliff anymore do you?"

"No Sir." She looked up at him and swallowed over the

discomfort that had lodged in her throat.

"And isn't it true that she dismissed you? Said you couldn't be trusted."

Ruth Higgins sat up straight with indignation, the color draining from her face. "Yes, she did fire me, but that's not the reason she let me go."

Franks took a step closer to her and said loudly, "You wanted her money yourself."

"That's not true. Those terrible people turned her against me." She pointed her finger at the Burjans.

Franks sneered and turned away. "I have no more questions for this witness."

The Judge looked at Phil. "Any rebuttal Counselor?"

Phil remained in his seat and calmly looked at Ruth Higgins. "Mrs. Higgins, if Edith Cliff let you go, why aren't you angry with her? Why are you here testifying on her behalf today?"

She lifted her head and said proudly. "Because we have been friends for years, I still love her like a sister."

"No more questions, your Honor," Phil announced with a steady voice.

The Judge rapped her gavel. "We'll take a lunch break now. Be back promptly at one thirty."

Everyone stood as the Judge left the courtroom.

Phil put his arm around Edith as she stood up. "When the jury hears from Gayle and our next witness, they'll really take notice. Gayle's going to call your banker, who'll share information about your finances before and after your relationship with the Burjans. That narrative should really help to nail those two."

Chapter 28

"That seemed to go very well. You did a great job, Phil," Gayle said while they were eating lunch with Edith in the downstairs courthouse cafeteria.

"One of our scheduled witnesses, Flo Mancini, a fortune teller friend of mine should shed a lot of light on how you were bilked out of your savings," Phil said reassuringly to Edith as he took a bite out of his sandwich. Turning to Gayle, he added, "But first, it's your turn girl to go after the Burjans."

"And boy, am I ready." A gleam of anticipation brightened Gayle's eyes. "When I finish with the bank manager, the jury will see the shady way the defendants worked."

After they finished their lunch, Gayle said, "Time to head back, Counselor. Now, you'll see why I love working on criminal cases with lots of action. I just can't believe that you worked on dull tax cases for so long."

Phil's lips curled into a small grimace, and he gave no answer.

With everyone seated once again in the courtroom, the trial continued.

"Please call your next witness, Ms. Tanner," the Judge instructed leaning back in her chair, keeping her expression carefully bland.

Dressed in a tailored burgundy colored business suit,

with matching suede high heels and a tailored white silk blouse, Gayle looked the part of a very successful attorney as she stepped forward. "I call Mrs. Vivian Fox to the stand."

Vivian Fox walked slowly to the stand. A graying middle-aged woman with smile lines, she fit the image of a typical bank manager. She wore a plain dark brown suit. The large glasses that framed her round face did little to soften her blunt hair cut with straight bangs. She stepped forward with a sense of dignified confidence.

After Vivian gave her name and was sworn in, Gayle moved closer and asked, "Mrs. Fox will you please give us a brief description of your job and your relationship with Mrs. Cliff?"

"I manage the Union Trust Bank in downtown Syracuse and Mrs. Cliff is one of our regular customers. I am accustomed to seeing her in the bank about once a week now that Mr. Cliff is deceased."

"Did you see her in the bank much while Mr. Cliff was living?"

Mrs. Fox sat upright. "Oh no. He used to come in two or three times a week to switch his monies around. He handled all the family finances, told me he and his wife lived apart. Said he lived downtown with his daughter in an apartment not far from the bank. He also mentioned that Mrs. Cliff resided in the family home with a housekeeper and a companion on the outskirts of the city."

A half smile teased Gayle's lips. "And would you say that Mr. Cliff was a very good businessman?"

The question seemed to give Mrs. Fox pause and she deliberated for a short time before answering. "He was a very astute businessman. Very sharp and extremely outgoing. He seemed to know where every cent of his money was and he watched the stock market closely. Talked about his portfolio all the time. He was so proud of the new top of the line Mercedes that he had purchased. He said it had all the bells and whistles."

"And how long have you known Mrs. Cliff?"

"It wasn't until after Mr. Cliff pasted away that I got to know her." A muscle twitched in her jaw. "I met her when she came into the bank with her daughter."

"Did she seem to have a grasp of her finances then?"

"Oh no." The bank manager smiled with a hint of satisfaction. "Both she and the daughter seemed amazed at how large Mr. Cliff's investment portfolio was. And I later learned that in addition to the stock portfolio and the expensive house, he also had a large life insurance policy with the missus as the beneficiary."

Gayle walked over to the table and picked up a folder. With it in hand, she returned to the witness box.

She placed the folder on top of the witness stand and looked through it briefly. "Yes. I can see from this report that Mrs. Cliff's husband had left her with the satisfaction of never having to worry about her financial freedom. Did you offer to help her with the large portfolio that Mr. Cliff had left her?"

Mrs. Fox sighed, glanced toward Edith Cliff and replied sadly, "Yes, I did, but, she refused my assistance. I saw her daughter try to help her too. But she sharply rebuffed her. I heard her tell her daughter that she could get by on her own."

"After that did Mrs. Cliff continue to come into the bank with her daughter?" Gayle asked.

"Only once or twice. After that she came in with another lady, someone I didn't know."

Gayle snapped the portfolio shut, her eyes gleaming with expectation. "And is that lady present in the courtroom today."

Mrs. Fox narrowed her eyes. "Yes."

"And would you point that lady out to the jury?"

A flash of anger crossed Mrs. Fox's face. She inhaled sharply as she leaned forward and pointed her finger directly at Luna Burjan. "It was her, Mrs. Burjan."

"Do you have direct knowledge of any of the large monetary transactions that Mrs. Cliff made?" Gayle's lips curved into a smile.

"Yes. Several times. One of my staff would approach me about his or her concern over the large amounts of cash that Mrs. Cliff was withdrawing from her account."

Muttering an expletive, Miller Franks gained his feet in an instant. "Objection your Honor. The witness has no way of knowing if Mrs. Burjan instructed Mrs. Cliff to withdraw money."

The Judge narrowed her eyes and nodded briefly. "Objection sustained. The jury will ignore that last statement."

Gayle pondered the situation for a few minutes, decided to allow the matter to rest there and turned her questions in another direction. "And, Mrs. Fox, did you have an occasion when you went directly to Mrs. Cliff's house to ask her about a large check that had been recently cashed by Mrs. Burjan?"

"Yes. I did," she replied, as a frown touched her brow.

"Tell us what you observed when you went to Mrs. Cliff's home."

Fixing her attention on her hands, which were folded in front of her, Vivian Fox said, "When I pulled up to Mrs. Cliff's house, I saw the big blue Mercedes that Mr. Cliff had owned. It was being driven away from the house by those people." She pointed to the Burjans.

"And did you talk to Mrs. Cliff about it?"

Vivian cleared her throat, forcing herself to ignore her nervousness and nodded. "Yes. When I went inside, I asked her why those people were driving away in Mr. Cliff's car. She said she gave it to them because her husband told her to. Then I asked how Mr. Cliff could tell her that since he was dead. She said that Mrs. Burjan talked to him in the here-after all the time and instructed her to give the Burjans the car and some money."

"And how did you feel about what you had just heard Mrs. Fox?" Gayle asked, as she stepped closer.

Vivian lowered her head, struggling to control her emotions. "That made a red light go off in my mind. I became very concerned for Mrs. Cliff. I realized then that she needed help."

"And did you experience any further incidents that caused you alarm."

Vivian frowned, clenching and unclenching her hands. "Yes. About a week later Mrs. Cliff came into the bank and wanted to withdraw ten thousand dollars in cash. When I told her that I would have to fill out a report for the government for any withdrawals of ten thousand or more, she said she would take nine thousand instead."

"And did you try to stop her from taking the cash?"

"I did." She wet her lips and sighed. "I told her that I thought that Mr. Cliff had worked hard for his money and that he would be upset that she was withdrawing such a large sum. She replied that it was her money and she could do with it what she wanted."

Appearing to be deep in thought, Gayle walked back and forth in front of the witness stand, then stopped and looked directly at the witness. "Did you watch Mrs. Cliff leave the bank with the cash?'

Vivian grimaced. "Yes. She walked out of the bank and entered the big blue Mercedes."

"And did you notice who was driving the car?"

"Yes. It was that lady over there." She pointed at Luna Burjan. "She was driving the car."

Gayle leaned forward and put her arms on the edge of the witness stand. "One last question Mrs. Fox. Have you talked with Mrs. Cliff lately, and how does her mental health appear to you at this point?"

Holding back her tears, Vivian answered. "She's not

well. Not well at all."

Miller Franks spoke up loudly. "I object to this line of questioning. Mrs. Fox is not a physician and is not qualified to make a judgment as to Mrs. Cliff's mental health."

"Objection sustained. The jury will disregard that statement," the Judge said.

Gayle spun around and flashed a defiant look at Franks. "I'm finished with this witness, your Honor."

Judge Hilton peered over her glasses. "Mr. Franks, do you have any questions for this witness?"

With his pulse accelerating, Franks got to his feet and walked over to the witness box. "Mrs. Fox, isn't the real reason you are upset with Mrs. Cliff is because she withdrew all her funds from your bank and you lost a large part of your bank's investment portfolio?"

Vivian narrowed her eyes at him, defiantly. "No. That's not true. I felt bad because Mrs. Cliff needed help with her investments and these people were just conning her out of her money."

"Isn't it a fact Mrs. Fox that you are being transferred out of your branch and to a lesser position because you didn't meet your quotas these past few quarters?"

Vivian sat forward in her chair, anxious to defend herself, when Franks waved his hand at her. "No need to answer that question. No more questions, your Honor."

The Judge leaned toward the witness. "Mrs. Fox, you may step down. Next witness please, Ms. Tanner."

Gayle's eyes lit up as she announced. "We call Lucy Cliff Anderson to the stand."

A tall, slender thirty-something woman, with black hair, walked up to the witness stand and took a seat.

"Please state your name and your relationship to Edith Cliff," the bailiff said.

The woman took a deep breath. "I am Lucy Cliff Anderson, the daughter of Howard and Edith Cliff."

'You are their only child?"

"Yes."

Gayle stepped closer to her and looked her in the eye. "And did you have occasion to help your mother with her finances after the death of your father?"

Lucy swallowed, her throat dry. "Yes. I took her to the bank after my father's funeral and we went over her accounts and her investment portfolio."

"And how much money were we talking about at that time?"

"My father left an estate of over two and a half million. And he willed it all to my mother." Lucy's throat tightened around the words.

"And did you help your mother manage her money after that?"

Seeming slightly wounded, Lucy drew in a deep breath. "Only for a short time. I offered to have my husband help her manage her investments since he is a money manager. But, after she met Mr. and Mrs. Burjan, she would not discuss any money matters with me and she refused to meet with my husband about it. When I asked her how she was doing, she always said just fine. But then, I noticed that little by little she became more and more apprehensive. She said that Mrs. Burjan was helping her speak with my Father in the hereafter and that the two of them were guiding her with her finances."

"And when did you last speak with her about her monies?"

"About two months ago." Unease tightening her muscles, Lucy leaned back in her chair. "Mother said that Mr. and Mrs. Burjan were guiding her investments and she insisted that she didn't need any help from me."

Gayle folded her arms across her chest as she calmly led her witness. "And how was your mother's emotional state?"

"She had become almost paranoid," Lucy replied

loudly with a tremor in her voice. "She mentioned devils and seemed to be losing her mind."

"I object, Mrs. Anderson is no psychiatrist," Miller Franks shouted out.

The Judge looked down at him, "Objection noted, but overruled. She was never presented to be one." She nodded toward Gayle. "Continue," she snapped.

Gayle took a step back and looked directly at the defendants. "And did you have occasion to speak with either Mr. or Mrs. Burjan about your mother?"

"No." Lucy's throat seemed to be tightening around her words. "One day as I was coming up to my mother's house, I saw them leaving. I tried to talk with them, but they just jumped in their car and sped away. Excuse me, they jumped in my father's car and sped away."

Gayle turned back toward her and asked calmly. "And did you ask your mother why they were driving your father's car?"

Lucy looked sadly at her mother, who was now hanging her head. "Yes. She said she gave it to them in payment for the séances that they conducted with my father."

"One more question, Mrs. Anderson. Have you noticed your mother wearing her jewelry lately?"

Lucy could not hide the hatred in her eyes as she glared at the Burjans. "No. As a matter of fact, when I saw Mrs. Burjan, she had on a diamond necklace and diamond earrings that my father had given my mother on two anniversaries. I believe that she's wearing them right now."

Gayle smiled sweetly at Attorney Franks as she said, "No more questions, your Honor."

The Judge looked toward the defense table. "Your turn, Mr. Franks."

Franks approached Lucy. "Only one question, Mrs. Anderson. Do you have any proof that Mr. or Mrs. Burjan forced your mother to give them her automobile and some of her jewelry and cash?"

She sat upright, as her pulse accelerated. Her mouth settled into a flat, angry line. "No Sir. I have no proof that she was forced. I just know that if Mother was in her right mind she wouldn't have done it."

"No more questions." Franks whirled around and returned to his seat.

The Judge looked down at Gayle and Phil. "Any more witnesses?"

Phil stood up as his gaze swept up and down the courtroom. "Yes, your Honor. At this time, I would like to call Florence Mancini to the stand."

Coming from the back of the courtroom, Flo lumbered slowly up to the witness stand and at the instruction of the bailiff, was sworn in.

Phil approached her, "Ms. Mancini would you state your full name, address and profession?"

She stated her name and gave her address, loudly and clearly. Then she added, "I have been a psychic and fortune teller with various circuses for over thirty years. And everyone just calls me, Flo, the Gypsy Fortune Teller." She leaned closer to Phil and battered her lashes at him.

The audience laughed as the Judge pounded her gavel. "All quiet please. Continue Mr. Willis."

"Flo, would you please tell us in a few words what it's like to be a Gypsy?"

Sitting upright, she answered, "There are two ways that most Gypsies live in the States these days. I, like a few others, work in circuses and carnivals, making my living by reading tea leaves, Taro cards and palms. Some read crystal balls, but I personally don't care for them. I give the customers an honest reading—telling them their future, as I see it. I believe I give my customers their money's worth."

His lips curved. "And the other Gypsies?"

"Some do not even try to tell the future, they prefer to obtain money by using various schemes to cheat inexperienced and gullible people. Like those two people over there." She pointed to Mr. and Mrs. Burjan.

Franks jumped to his feet. "Your Honor, I object. This witness is just stating her personal opinion."

"Objection sustained." The judge frowned at Phil. "Please Mr. Willis, instruct your witness to just state the facts."

Phil winched. "Yes your Honor."

He moved a step closer. "Ms. Flo do you know anything about Mr. and Mrs. Burjan?"

"I heard from talking with my various acquaintances that they are Russian Gypsies. Many of them immigrated to the eastern coast and make their so-called living by defrauding innocent people, instead of working for an honest living." She shrugged her shoulders. "Most Gypsies are decent, honorable and hard working people. But, a few like the Burjans, give Gypsies a bad name."

Franks slowly rose to his feet. "Your Honor, how long are we going to listen to this witness?" He paused for a moment and then added, "She doesn't even know these people. What she is stating is nothing but hearsay."

The Judge looked down at Phil and said firmly, "Mr. Franks is correct. Please stop this line of questioning."

"I have just one more question for Ms. Flo." Phil stepped closer to the witness box. "Do you have personal knowledge of anyone else who may have had experiences with Mr. and Mrs. Burjan?"

Flo pursed her lips as she considered the question, and then replied, "Yes Sir. My friends said that there was a couple in Ft. Lauderdale who were also bilked out of money by them."

"I object your Honor," Franks shouted out, slamming his fist down on the table.

"I'm finished with this witness," Phil said, smiling and

backing up.

"Mr. Franks, would you care to cross examine the witness?" the Judge asked.

Franks rose to his feet and strolled up to the witness box. "Just a couple of quick questions, your Honor."

Standing directly in front of Flo, he asked, "And what exactly is your real name, Flo Mancini? Isn't it true that you are here in America illegally? And how many times have you been arrested?"

Before Phil could open his mouth to voice his objection, Flo sprang to her feet and shouted to the courtroom. "My real name is Florence Mancini. I'm an American citizen. And I've never been arrested. Not ever."

Phil slammed the papers that were in his hand down on the table, "Your Honor, I object to this line of questioning."

"Noted," the Judge said as she gave Franks a withering look. "Enough of this badgering of the witness."

She looked at Flo. "Please resume your seat Ms. Mancini."

As she sat back down, Flo responded stiffly. "I am a good woman and I speak the truth."

The Judge looked over at Franks. "Do you have any more questions, Counselor?"

"No your Honor." He raised an apologetic hand, turned on his heels and walked back to his table.

"You are excused Ms. Mancini," the Judge instructed.

Flo got up, walked past the jurors and flashed her diamond rings at the ladies. "I got these by honest work," she muttered to them.

Then, as she brushed past Phil, she whispered, "Good to see you again, my Love."

Gayle leaned over and said to Phil with assurance, "I think we won this round, Counselor."

After conferring briefly with Phil, Gayle stood up. "Your Honor, may we approach the bench?"

Judge Hilton waved for them to approach as Miller Franks jumped up and followed them.

Gayle leaned toward the Judge. "Your Honor, we see no gain in presenting any more witnesses now."

Franks looked confused, "How's that?"

Gayle continued, "Our client, Edith Cliff has suffered enough. I'm prepared to sum up the case."

"Well, I'm not," Franks said, angrily. "I have a witness to call."

"Is your witness ready to testify this afternoon?" The Judge eyed him with curiosity.

"Yes. However, since my opposing attorneys are finished long before I anticipated, I will need some time to get my witness here."

"And who is your witness?" Phil asked.

"Samantha Evers."

Phil turned around, rushed back to the table, opened his briefcase and rummaged through some papers. Carrying a document in his hands, he returned to the bench. "Yes. Mr. Franks did list her name as a witness," he said.

The Judge sighed, pushed herself up from her chair and waved her hand in dismissal. "If everyone is in agreement then, we will adjourn to allow Mr. Franks time to get his witness to the courthouse. We will resume at four-thirty." She hit her gavel on the bench.

Leaving the courtroom, Gayle asked Phil in a jittery voice, "Do we have anything on this Samantha Evers?"

He stopped in mid-stride. "Kelley has been checking her out for the past couple of days."

"Call her. We need all that she's got."

When Phil called Kelley, he learned that she indeed had done her homework.

"I'm on my way to the courthouse now to give you my brief on Ms. Evers. Boy, have I got the lowdown on this broad."

"Well, hurry over. We resume court at four-thirty. Meet

us in the café downstairs at the courthouse as soon as you can. We'll be there going over our notes."

As Phil and Gayle sat having a coffee and a pastry with Edith, she said, "I am so relieved that I don't have to testify in front of Mr. and Mrs. Burjan."

A little disappointed at this statement, Gayle warned, "You realize don't you Edith, that this is your choice. You might help your case by testifying."

"I know, Dear. But the very thought of testifying in front of that terrible couple just frightens me. All I want now is my money back and peace of mind. I intend to sell my house and purchase a small condo. Maybe, I can even talk Ruth into coming back to live with me."

Shortly before three-thirty, Kelley walked into the café and took a seat in the booth. She reached into her briefcase and pulled out a large folder and handed it to Phil. "Here's a three-year history of Ms. Evers."

Phil and Gayle quickly looked through the notes. Gayle's lips parted in surprise as she read the file. "Good girl, Kelley."

Thoroughly pleased, Gayle gave Phil a big grin. "Don't look now but this witness is going to back-fire on Mr. Franks. She's going to help our case not his. As second in command, I want you to drill this woman. And I'll handle the summation. We should be able to wrap this case up soon and hand it over to the jury."

They stood up and gave each other a fist bump.

"Now, let's see some of that 'Willis Justice'," Kelley said, as she helped Edith Cliff to her feet.

Chapter 29

It was now four-thirty and the jury was scheduled to see and hear the witness provided by the defense. At this point, the faces of the jury seemed to give no hint of what their decision would be.

After the court was called to order and all parties were seated, Judge Hilton ordered, "Call your witness, Mr. Franks."

"We call Samantha Evers."

A short, stocky woman, who appeared to be in her late fifties, walked up to the witness stand and was sworn in.

"Please state your name and where you reside," Franks instructed.

"My name is Samantha Evers and I live in Syracuse, New York."

Franks took a step closer to the witness stand. "And Mrs. Evers when and where did you meet the defendants, Mr. and Mrs. Burjan?" He pointed at the couple seated at the table.

"I met them several months ago outside a drug store. I had a flat tire and Mr. Burjan came over and offered to help."

"And did you accept his offer?" Franks leaned a little closer.

"Yes," she looked directly into his eyes. "The sweet man put on the little spare donut tire. He even offered to follow me as I drove to get the regular tire replaced."

"And did you see Mr. and Mrs. Burjan after that?"

She looked down at the Burjans, smiled and shot back. "Yes. They were kind enough to ask me out to dinner with them that evening. It was their treat."

Franks riffled through papers in his hand. "And did they have occasion to help you in any other way later?"

"Yes. When we first met, I mentioned that I had lost my husband to cancer the previous year."

She looked over at the jury and added, "He smoked too much. I guess you would call him a chain smoker. Well, the Burjans were very comforting to me. Mrs. Burjan even gave me several readings. She told me my future would take a turn for the better in the upcoming months."

Franks cleared his throat. "And did she charge for the readings?"

"At first they were free." She hesitated for an instant, and bit down on her lower lip, wishing he hadn't brought up that bothersome issue.

Just for a moment, she let herself dwell on that. Then raising her head, she replied rather sheepishly, "Later, over the course of about a year, I paid her one hundred and fifty dollars for each session that lasted about forty-five minutes. It was worth every penny."

Franks stepped up to the witness box and placed his papers on the ledge as a muscle jerked in his cheek. "Now think carefully, Mrs. Evers. Did the Burjans ever ask you for money or jewelry in addition to what you paid for your séance sessions?"

"Oh, no," she said. "In fact they introduced me to a gentleman who works for an investment firm and got him to agree to help me with my finances."

"And in what way did he help you?" Franks asked with

a confident grin, anticipating her response.

"He moved my monies into an annuity and found a buyer for my house," she informed him with positive nod of her head.

"You're going to sell your house?"

"Yes." She sat forward in her chair; her eyes opening wide with anticipation. "I'm planning on moving to a retirement community in Florida with other people my age. So you see, Luna and Shreif Burjan have become my dear friends—almost my family now."

Franks hesitated for a moment, and then returned to his chair. "No more questions, your Honor." He sat down, confident that his side of the case was proceeding exceedingly well.

The Judge looked at Gayle. "Ms. Tanner, do you wish to cross examine the witness?"

Gayle answered in a quiet voice. "Yes, Mr. Willis will take over at this point."

Phil opened a folder that was on the table in front of him, picked it up and walked with assurance to the witness stand. Placing the folder in front of the witness, he said, "Before I start to question you, Mrs. Evers, I have some information here that you should know about."

She squirmed in her chair and eyed him suspiciously. "Okay. I have nothing to hide."

Phil opened the folder and continued. "Our investigator talked to the car dealership about your incident with the tire. The repair man who fixed your tire said that it looked like someone had taken a knife and deliberately slashed your tire."

Franks looked up with dismay on his face. "Your honor, where is Mr. Willis going with this information?"

"Yes, Mr. Willis. Please make your point," the Judge replied, her voice taking on a stern quality.

Phil nodded, choosing his words with care. "I believe that the defendant, Shreif Burjan deliberately slashed the tire and used the incident to gain Mrs. Evers' confidence."

Franks jumped up, yelling, "I object your honor. Does the Counselor have proof of this allegation?"

Phil strolled back to the table and pulled a video out of his briefcase. "Your honor, I wish to submit into evidence a video taken from the security camera outside of the said store on the day of the incident. It will show Mr. Burjan walking by Mrs. Evers' car and bending down to the rear tire with an object in his hand."

He handed the video to the clerk to admit as evidence.

Clearing his throat, he continued, "And I also have information that the Burjans and their friend, the investment counselor, were working together to bilk Mrs. Evers out of her monies."

Samantha Evers looked crestfallen for a brief moment, then brightened and sat upright in her seat. "Oh no, Mr. Willis, these people are my friends."

"Isn't it true Mrs. Evers, that you authorized the investment counselor to withdraw half a million dollars from your account to purchase the property in Florida?" Phil looked at her, his gaze direct and determined.

"Yes. Yes. But he saved me a hundred thousand on the condo, by jumping in on the deal at the right time," she whispered.

"I must ask you, Mrs. Evers have you ever actually seen this condo?"

Her mouth dropped open, "Well, no. They said they were doing some renovations on it now. Putting a granite counter top and new cupboards in the kitchen. I'm planning to go down and see it when the work is done."

After giving her a sympathetic look, Phil said. "I hate to be the bearer of bad news, my dear, but my investigator found out that the condominium that you supposedly purchased does not exist."

Mrs. Evers stared at him as she fought a sudden wave

of alarm, the full impact of his words sinking in. "There must be some mistake."

Miller Franks heaved himself to his feet and waved his arms in small distraught circles. "Your honor, I protest. Mr. Willis has no proof of this."

Phil withdrew a photograph from his folder, walked over up the Judge and placed the photo on the bench. "Your honor, I request that I be allowed to submit this photograph of the said property in question."

The judge looked briefly at the photo. "Request granted."

Phil picked up the photo, walked over to where Franks was seated and put the photo in front of him. Looking at the attorney with a smug grin, Phil flung his words at him, "As Mr. Franks can plainly see that address is a shopping center, not a condo complex."

Mrs. Evers sucked in a gasp of air and hung her head, not wanting to believe what she had just heard. "Lies. All lies. The Burjans told me the truth."

Phil shook his head, firming his lips into a stubborn line. "I'm sorry to break this shocking news to you. But lady, you've been had."

Then, he turned to the Judge and said quietly, "I'm finished with this witness, your Honor."

"Mr. Franks do you wish a rebuttal?"

He shook his head, the pain showing on his face. "Not at this time."

"You may step down," the Judge said.

Samantha Evers stared down at the Burjans as she walked past them and hurried out of the courtroom.

Judge Hilton announced, "We will stop for the day and will resume at nine tomorrow. Mr. Franks and Ms. Tanner, you will present your summations at that time. Finally, I wish to remind the jury that they are to discuss this case with no one." She slammed her gavel on the bench. "Court is adjourned."

Late that night, Kelley was standing in the doorway of the bedroom, while Phil, dressed only in pajama bottoms, was pacing around the room like a Bengal tiger, rehearsing various summations. He lived, breathed and ate logic and was determined to be ready for the next morning, in case Gayle called on him to assist or relieve her.

She watched as he walked back and forth, rehearsing various speeches. Clearly at a loss of how to help him, she said "Dear, I'm going to sleep in Ashley's room tonight. That way you won't disturb me when you come to bed. Besides, I have a feeling that you'll be sleeping very restlessly tonight."

Phil stopped in his tracks, stifled a groan and inclined his head. "Sure. It could be late when I'm done."

Phil parked his car in the lot around the corner from the courthouse the next morning and spotted Gayle emerging from her car nearby.

"Good morning, partner," she called out as he approached her with his briefcase in hand. "I hope you're prepared. I expect this to be our shining hour."

He turned away to cover his smile. He thought Gayle seemed to be beaming with anticipation.

As he walked beside her, she continued, "I'm so proud of you Phil. You really tore down Mrs. Evers' testimony. I watched the jury shake their heads in disbelief as you told her that the money she gave to the Gypsies and their accomplice was a swindle. The location of the supposed condominium was really a shopping mall. That fact really undermines the credibility of anything else the Burjans have to say."

He fought the urge to laugh. "Yes. Apparently Miller Franks didn't bother to check the facts about Mrs. Evers testimony."

Gayle stopped and looked directly at him, "You know,

that's not like him. He seems to be skipping a few steps lately. I have a feeling that retirement might be his next move after this case."

They approached the door to the courthouse as a taxi cab pulled up to the curb and Edith Cliff and her daughter stepped out.

Phil took Edith by the arm to help her up the courthouse steps. "Good morning, Mrs. Cliff. Let's hope that this case will be over shortly."

His simple words gave Edith some reassurance. She stopped and gave him a grateful look. "I sure hope so. You and Ms. Tanner have been just wonderful. And I'm so thankful I didn't have to take the stand." Struggling for words, she added, "I'm certain I would have been overcome with emotion, would have wound up crying."

"By the way, where is Mrs. Willis this morning?" Edith's daughter asked.

"Oh, she had some errands to do for me. She'll see us later," Phil replied. "Now let's head inside."

Entering the courtroom, Phil noticed that it was filling up with the press and spectators.

He and Gayle were about to take their seats at the table, when a middle-aged man with brown hair and a ruddy complexion walked up. "Hi there, Mr. Willis. Do you remember me?"

Raising a skeptical eyebrow, Phil answered, "Sorry, can't say I do."

"I'm Sergeant Russell Hobbs. I worked undercover with your friend Kelley, while she was in Miami. I moved to Syracuse a couple of years ago and joined the local police force. I'm Officer Hobbs now and assigned to the courthouse for the time being."

Phil hesitated for an instant then replied apologetically. "Say, I do remember you. You trained Kelley when she worked as a housekeeper in that Miami hotel. And by the way, she's my wife now."

Hobbs shook Phil's hand. "Congratulations. That was one terrific job that Kelley and you did helping to capture the guys who stole the Wilson jewelry. How's she doing by the way?"

"I expect her to stop by later. She'll be glad to see you again."

"Well, don't let her get away without talking to me."

Phil opened his briefcase. "No problem. But, if you'll excuse me, I've got to get ready for action." He took his seat next to Gayle as Officer Hobbs walked to the back of the room.

The bailiff entered the room from a side door and called out, "All rise. This court is now in session. The Honorable Marilyn Hilton presiding."

Everyone in the court room rose as the Judge walked in. Phil glanced around the table and noticed his name on a large manila folder sitting nearby.

He reached over, drew it towards him and slowly opened it. He pulled out an 8x11 sheet of paper with large printing on it. He stared at the paper in silence for a few moments, and then exclaimed softly, "What the hell?"

After reading it for a second time, he inhaled deeply and cried out, "Oh, shit!"

The Judge raised a skeptical eyebrow. "Mr. Willis, contain yourself. You're in my courtroom now."

He pulled out his cell phone and dialed Kelley's number. No answer. Panicked and somewhat sick to his stomach, he jumped to his feet and called out. "Your Honor, may I approach the bench? Please!"

Judge Hilton rapped her gavel loudly as the audience responded by whispering to each other. She reproached them. "All quiet in my court room. Mr. Willis this better be very important. Approach the bench."

"What's wrong, Phil?" Gayle asked with sudden alarm, as she jumped up and reached for his arm.

He leaned closer to her, made a helpless gesture and

whispered. "I'll explain later. Please stay here while I talk to the Judge privately."

With a tense look on her face, Gayle let the matter rest and quietly sat back down as Phil hurried up to the Judge. Approaching the stand he could see the indignation darkening Judge Hilton's eyes.

"Your Honor, I just found a manila envelope on our table, addressed to me. I don't know who left it." He struggled for words. "Please read the message."

The Judge read the paper carefully and then looked at Phil in disbelief. "Is this some kind of theatrical trick Mr. Willis?" She shot him a look of rebuke.

"No. I can assure you it isn't." He struggled for breath and forced himself to look directly into the Judge's eyes. "Your Honor, could we please go to your chambers to discuss it?"

Judge Hilton shot a frustrated glance at him, paused for a few minutes, and then announced loudly, "Ladies and gentlemen, there will be a fifteen minutes recess."

She pounded the gavel, and with the paper in her hand, headed toward her chambers with Phil close behind her.

Sitting down at her desk, the Judge stared at Phil in disbelief. "Mr. Willis, this note indicates that someone is holding your wife hostage."

Phil looked at her with pain in his eyes and ran his hand through his hair. Words temporarily failed him. He whispered, "That's what it says."

"Maybe this is just a cruel joke. Can you reach your wife now and see if she's okay?"

Hanging onto his dignity through sheer will power, he replied, "She doesn't answer her phone Judge. And she had it with her this morning. I tried calling her when I first read the note. But I'll try again."

Phil pulled his phone from his pocket and frantically dialed Kelley's phone a second time. Still—no answer.

He looked at the Judge and shook his head.

"I think that we should contact the police immediately, Mr. Willis."

"We can't." Struggling for words, he added, "Read the last line of the note. It says that if I contact the authorities I will never see my wife again." He frantically paced back and forth across the room.

"Please Mr. Willis, sit down. Let's be calm."

"Calm. How can I be calm?" He forced himself to hold back the threatening tears, as his voice wobbled in fear. "The kidnappers want two million dollars ransom for her. Where am I going to get two million dollars?"

The Judge shifted uncomfortably in her chair, dropped her voice, and leaned forward. "I think we should contact the authorities."

He shook his head with determination. "I can't. I won't. I have no idea who left this note. But I know, one thing—I'll do whatever it takes to get my Kelley back safely."

"You don't think that Mr. and Mrs. Burjan could have something to do with this do you?"

"Hell. I don't know what to think. It could be almost anyone. Could you just postpone the summations of the case so that I can take care of this situation first?"

The Judge shrugged uneasily, "Well, whoever is behind this note could certainly hurt your wife."

"All I'm asking of you, Judge Hilton, is some time. They want two million dollars, I need time to raise it."

The Judge mulled the situation over for a moment. "I see no reason why we can't resume the case in a week. That should give you plenty of time to resolve this."

Phil's whole body started to shake as he fought the urge to cry. "And Judge, no one can know about this note until I've had time to take care of things. You must promise me that you won't go to the authorities. It might mean my wife's life."

She leaned forward and said in a subdued voice, "I

must tell you, Counselor, that I feel you are making a big mistake by not contacting the police immediately. But you have my word that I'll remain quiet for the time being. I'll reset the commencement of the trial for a week from today. But you must keep me informed."

"Thanks."

"Here's my private cell phone number." She reached into her desk drawer and drew out a card. "Keep me up to date and call me immediately if I can be of some help. But be careful, Mr. Willis." Her face became grim. "You might be dealing with some very dangerous people.'

Phil's eyes misted over. "I realize that. But, now it's 'Justice for Willis' time."

Chapter 30

After the court reconvened, Judge Hilton announced that due to "unforeseen circumstances" the trial would be postponed for a week and set a new date and time. Then, slamming her gavel, she adjourned the trial and left the courtroom without any further explanation.

Gayle Tanner's eyes widened in confusion and disbelief. Her breathing ceased. Her hands fell to her side. She leaned over and hissed at Phil, "Okay Willis, what the hell is going on?"

"I have a personal problem to take care of. Can't tell you about it right now." His gaze hardened. "But the Judge knows the reason."

She lowered her head, very concerned. "Wait Phil, you just can't leave me hanging without an explanation."

"Sorry Gayle, I'll call you later, I promise." He closed his eyes briefly and stood up.

Phil inhaled deeply, zipped up his briefcase and ran out of the courtroom. His head was pounding in a slow, dull rhythm.

He hurried down the hall toward the down escalator. Officer Hobbs rushed up to him and grabbed his arm. "What's up? I just heard that your case has been delayed."

"I have a personal crisis to take care of," Phil answered, trying not to let his anxieties reflect in his voice.

"Anything I can do to help?"

Phil gave a shake of his head, thought for a few moments, then swallowed very hard. "Yes. Maybe. Did you see anyone go into the courtroom carrying a large manila envelope before I entered?"

"I got here about eight thirty. Opened the courtroom doors and made sure that the cleaning crew had taken care of the room last night." Hobbs chose his words with great care. "But, I can't say that I remember seeing anyone unusual go in there."

Phil stepped closer to him, speaking in a low voice. "Are there surveillance cameras on the outside of the courtroom doors and inside the courtroom?"

Officer Hobbs took his time deciding how to answer that question. Then he turned to the other officer stationed outside of the courtroom. "Hey Cooper, take over here for a few minutes. I've got to use the john."

Turning to Phil, he said in an intense tone, "Follow me, Mr. Willis. We'll take a look at the video from the cameras this morning."

He led Phil to the basement of the courthouse and into a separate room where numerous security camera screens displayed the outside of the courthouse, the halls and inside of the courtrooms.

The officer seated in front of the monitors looked up. Sensing something was wrong, he sat up straight, alarm coursing through him. "Hey, what's up Hobbs? You know this is a restricted area."

Hobbs lifted his chin and motioned toward Phil. "This is my friend, Attorney Willis. He's working on a case upstairs. We need to see video of the entrance doors to court room ten this morning."

The officer didn't hesitate for an instant. "What time?"

"From eight-thirty to about nine-thirty or ten."

"Piece of cake." The officer reached over and replayed

one of the recorded discs. Carefully viewing the monitor, they saw a woman dressed in a housekeeping outfit approach the door to the court room. She had a large brown manila folder under her arm.

"That's odd," Hobbs said, his brows drawing together in concern. "We have only one maintenance man on duty in the courthouse during the day. All the cleaning people come in at night."

"Do you recognize the woman?" Phil asked as he felt a hint of unease.

Hobbs stared more closely at the monitor. "No. She seems to be hiding her face from the cameras. But, I don't think she works here. And, that doesn't look like the uniform that our cleaning people wear."

As they exited the room, Hobbs stopped cold, expelled a disgusted breath, turned to Phil and asked, "Now, Mr. Willis, what's really going on?"

"Call me Phil," he replied.

"Please tell me what's going on." The worried look on Phil's face tore through Hobbs and increased his concern tenfold. "Maybe, I can help."

Phil sat down on one of the chairs in the hallway. With seeming reluctance, he took the manila folder from his briefcase. Handing it to Hobbs, he muttered, "They've got my Kelley. And the note says not to go to the police." He sighed and as desperation crept into his voice, he added, "At this point, I just don't know what to do."

Hobbs read the note a couple of times. "I've done a lot of undercover work in the past. Handled a couple of hostage cases when I worked in Washington. Let me line up a plan to help you." A curious glint entered his eye as he smiled briefly.

Phil's stared at him in silence, then said simply, "I could use some help at this point."

Hobbs handed the note back. "We'll find these guys.

No one is going to hurt my friend Kelley as long as I have a breath in my body. We'll get her back for you safe and sound."

Phil could only nod his relief; too nervous to reply.

"Here's my card, Phil. Has my cell phone number. I'll get back with you in the next couple of hours. "

Phil returned to his house to await further instructions as the note had instructed him to do. After making several calls, trying to raise the ransom money, his fear increased. Carrying a cup of coffee, he restlessly paced back and forth, waiting for the call from the kidnappers. He felt helpless knowing that Kelley was in danger and that he could do nothing to help her at this point. The concern for his wife battered his nerves as solidly as a steady drum.

He attempted to decide what, if anything, he could do next, when he heard the front doorbell chime insistently. He rushed to the door and opened it. Officer Hobbs was standing in front of him, dressed in beige colored pants and a white shirt and a white hat, both with a red "Orkin" logo on them.

Hobbs put his finger to his mouth, indicating that Phil should remain silent. "Mr. Willis, I'm here from Orkin Pest Control. Before I give your lawn its scheduled treatment, I need you to sign a renewal of your contract. May I come in?"

Looking puzzled Phil nodded, "Yes. Come in."

"Good." Hobbs stepped inside, put a finger to his mouth once again, indicating that Phil should be cautious in what he said.

Phil bowed his head in understanding. "Come into the kitchen. I was just about to pour myself another cup of coffee. Would you like some?"

"Yes, thanks," Hobbs answered as he followed him

down the hall.

In the kitchen, Hobbs pulled a note pad from the pocket of his shirt and wrote on it. "Could be audio bugs in the house. They're probably listening to see if you called the authorities."

Aloud, he said, "I'll leave the contract here for you to read and sign. But please accompany me outside, Mr. Willis. I want to show you that you have chiggers in your lawn. We need to eliminate them right away."

Phil opened the door and walked out into the back yard, followed by Hobbs.

Stopping a good distance from the house, Hobbs said, "Should be safe to talk now. Did you hear from the kidnappers?"

Phil nibbled on his lip and took a step backward as anxiety gripped his gut. "No. Not yet. I left my land line clear in case they tried to reach me. I've been on my cell phone trying to raise the money for the ransom. Can't stay out here for long in case they call."

Hobbs asked in a very stiff voice, "I noticed that the ransom note demanded two million. How much can you raise?"

"On my own I should be able to come up with a million. I contacted my stepfather for the other million. He said he should know by tomorrow morning if he can raise it."

"Okay." Hobbs' eyes suddenly flared. "I think I have an idea on how to help you. Meet me at Connor's Gym tomorrow at nine in the morning. By then, I should have formulated my plan to get your lady back."

Walking back to the house, they could hear the phone ringing loudly. Phil dashed inside the kitchen and grabbed it.

"Hello. Hello. Yes, this is Willis," he shouted into it.

A distorted voice asked, "Have you got the money?"

Phil wiped the sweat off his brow and tried to calm

himself. "It's not easy raising that kind of dough on such short notice. I'll know more tomorrow. But first, I want to talk to my wife. I need to know she's okay."

"No way."

"Then, we're not taking this any further. I must know she's all right before I proceed."

Phil stood silently in torment, until a soft voice came over the phone. "Phil, it's me, Kelley."

Phil gave a sigh of relief, before he whispered, "I'll get you back. I promise."

The distorted voice interrupted. "Let's get on with it pal. When are you going to have the money ready?"

"No," Phil answered, incapable of hiding the tremor straining his speech. "I need to know if my wife is alive this minute and that you aren't just playing a recording you made of her earlier. Put her back on the line and have her tell me the date and the time, right now."

"Okay asshole." There was a moment of silence before Phil heard him snap. "Your old man wants to know if you're still alive Sweetie. So tell him the date and time. And be quick about it."

After a slight sob in here voice, Kelley said, "I'm okay, Phil. And my Rolex, don't I wish, says its twelve-thirty on October 15th."

"That's enough," the voice snarled. "Okay, Willis. We're done here. You should have time enough to get the money ready by Friday. I'll call you later to tell you where the exchange will take place. Just do as you're told and you'll get your little lady back in one piece. And remember, no cops."

With a click of the phone the kidnapper had hung up.

Phil blinked in bewilderment as Hobbs put his finger to his mouth once again and started to look around the room.

Phil followed him as he methodically searched the kitchen, family room and library, looking everywhere for audio bugs. After finding one in the kitchen underneath the granite island, two in the family room inside of lamps and one in the library on the underside of the desk, Hobbs ripped them out.

A smile curved across his mouth, as he turned to Phil. "Now, we can talk. I was pretty sure that whoever took Kelley had some experience in this line of work and would think this out ahead of time and plant some audio bugs. They wanted to be sure that you didn't contact the police."

"And they've probably moved Kelley to a new location by now," Phil replied, his voice still shaky.

"I know Kelley is one intelligent lady and as a former investigator she would try to give you some clue as to where she might be or who might have her. Did you get anything from talking to her?" Hobbs asked.

Phil shook his head. Then, he paused and thought for a few minutes. After replaying his phone conversation with Kelley in his mind, he added, "The only thing that seemed odd was that she called out the time and date on her Rolex watch. Kelley doesn't have a Rolex. In fact, she always wears the Bulova watch that I gave her last year for her birthday."

"That's it, Phil." Hobbs eyes widened. "She was giving us a clue. Maybe the kidnapper wears a Rolex. Do you know anyone who always wears a Rolex?"

Phil pondered this idea for a while and then spoke rapidly, "Say, Benny Lotts, who worked undercover for me, always used to flash a lot of fancy jewelry, including a Rolex. But he's in prison. Has been there for some time. Not due to come out for another year."

"Do you know what prison he's in?"

"As far as I know the prison in upstate, New York."

"You mean the Correctional Facility in Malone?" Hobbs asked.

"That's it."

"Say. I know a few people up there. Let me make a call." Hobbs dialed a contact name on his cell phone.

"Warden Dunn, this is Officer Russell Hobbs from Syracuse. We met a couple of months ago at a convention. Yeah, glad you remember me. Say, I need a favor. I want to know the status of one of your prisoners up there, Benny Lotts. Does that name ring a bell?"

Warden Dunn laughed. "Are you psychic? I've got his file in front of me right now. He was released two weeks ago on good behavior. But he can't leave the state without permission. Why the call about him?"

Hobbs looked at Phil and grinned as he continued, "I've got something going on here that I believe he might be involved in. Can you give me his current address? Also, a list of the belongings that he picked up when he was released."

"Let me look at the file. He left with a wallet, some clothes, a set of keys, a couple of expensive gold chains and a fancy Rolex watch. He's scheduled to report to his parole officer once a month. I've got the address here where he's supposed to be staying now and the info on his parole officer."

"Thanks Dunn," Hobbs said.

"I hope this helps you. Keep me informed."

"Will do." After he hung up, Hobbs smiled reassuringly to Phil. "I'll check into this guy. Don't forget to meet me at the gym tomorrow morning at nine. I'll have some pals there that you've got to meet. And don't worry we'll get the missus back."

Phil accompanied Hobbs to the front door and closed it after he left. Muttering to himself, he slowly walked into the library. "Gotta get that ransom money. Friday will be here soon."

Raising his gaze upward, he whispered, "And please, dear Lord, watch over my Kelley."

Chapter 31

Just before nine the next morning, Phil entered Connors Gym wearing a blue warm up suit and carrying a gym bag. Inside he noticed several "No Smoking" notices posted. In the center of the room, with its rubberized floor, was a large sign that read "Team with the pros-without the blows".

The gym appeared to be well quipped and was extremely busy. Several men were lifting weights or dumbbells. Others were using kettle bells or cable pulleys. Upstairs on the balcony level, Phil could see people in the cardio room using treadmills and cardio bikes. The gym was clean and neat with the benches and padding in good condition.

Several large fans appeared to be doing an adequate job of removing the body odor from the sweating men who were working out. Phil decided it would be beneficial for him to join this gym in the future; a great place for a fellow to increase muscle tone, lower body fat, improve reflexes and upper body strength.

In the center of the gym was a platform four feet high with a standard size boxing ring. Two young men were sparring, occasionally knocking each other into one of the four parallel rows of ropes that were attached with turnbuckles to the corner posts.

Hanging from the ceiling on one side were three heavy weight punching bags. With their hands wrapped and wearing boxing gloves, three men were throwing punches and sweating profusely. On the other side of the gym, two young men, dressed in cotton shirts and gym shorts, were jumping rope.

Phil stood inside the door watching people working out. A man, who appeared to stand over six feet tall and weighing well over two hundred pounds, approached him. "You Willis?"

"Yes Sir." A muscle jerked in Phil's jaw.

"I'm Jilley Connors. I own the place. I was told to expect you." A grin broadened across his face. "Here's a key to a locker downstairs. You can change there. Anything you need, just ask. Any friend of Hobbs is a friend of mine."

Phil took the key from his outstretched hand. "Thanks. By the way, I'm looking for him."

"He's over there in my office. Waiting for you." Jilley pointed to a closed door at the back of the gym.

Phil entered the office and saw Hobbs sitting behind the desk, with his feet propped up on top of it, talking on his phone. He looked up, waved at him and continued his conversation. "Be here by eleven-thirty. Don't be late."

Hobbs hung up the phone, took his feet off the desk and smiled at Phil. "Morning Willis. You're in for a pleasant surprise this morning."

Phil plopped down in the chair across from Hobbs. "I hope so. I could use some encouraging news."

"First of all, Kelley gave us a great tip, mentioning that Rolex watch. It led us right to Benny Lotts."

Phil leaned forward, knowing he could not let his emotions get the best of him. "I know he was unhappy when I helped send him to prison for being mixed up in the killing of our neighbor. But why would he be involved in this?"

"Revenge is a powerful emotion. The warden said Benny left prison with a Rolex watch. I checked around with a few of my old friends. Finally I talked to a fellow who had been Benny's prison roommate for years. He said Benny talked nonstop about getting back at you and Kelley."

Hobbs leaned back in his chair, "This isn't just a coincidence, my friend. I believe that Benny Lotts is directly responsible for Kelley's abduction."

Phil lifted a doubting brow. "If he is, how are we going to find him?"

"Patience. Before I tell you any more, I want you to meet the team I've assembled to help us."

He walked outside of Jilley's office, opened the back door to the gym and ushered several people through the gym and into the office.

Hobbs grinned at Phil and shifted his gaze to the assembled group. "I think you know these people."

As if he had been slammed in the gut, Phil sat back in his chair momentarily, and then jumped to his feet. "Oh my God," he exclaimed.

Penny Gates, the retired police officer from Dolphin Springs was followed by the circus man of many talents, Fast Draw Pete. Next in walked Phil's uncle, Jack Walters, and finally a tall young man in his twenties.

Hobbs clasped the young man on the shoulder and shoved him toward Phil, "I think you'll remember this fellow. Last time you saw him he was a little boy. This is none other than, Paul Mathison, Jr."

Phil's heart hammered as he stared incredulously from one person to the other. Rushing over, he grabbed Penny's hands in his. "So good to see you again."

"Uncle Jack, I can't believe it's you. I thought you were still in prison." His uncle was now an aged, graying man with frown lines.

Jack hugged Phil and shook his hand vigorously.

"Got out early for good behavior."

Phil turned to Paul Jr. and clasped him around the shoulders. "I can't believe that this is little Paulie—all grown up."

"Good to see you again, Mr. Willis," Paul responded, with a big smile playing across his face.

Hobbs invited everyone to sit down. After discussing in detail Kelley's kidnapping and the demand for ransom, Hobbs shifted in his chair and looked at Phil, "I've been working on a plan to get Kelley back. The minute I called these people and said you needed their assistance, they agreed to rush to your aid. Now, why don't you all get re-acquainted? I've got some calls to make." He stood up and walked out of the room.

Glancing at Paul Jr., Phil could not get over how the youngster had changed. The tall young man was even more handsome than his father.

"And how are your parents doing these days, Paul?" Phil asked making an attempt at everyday conversation.

"Dad's doing great, now that he's given up the political life. Says he doesn't miss it at all. Said those two terms as governor of Florida was enough. They still live in Florida—in Key Biscayne actually. Mom's health is getting poor but she's hanging in there."

"And what do you do? Are you thinking of going into politics?" Phil asked.

Paul rolled his eyes. "No. I'm busy with a teaching job in the Tallahassee school district. I have a wife and two kids that keep me hopping."

Phil stood up, walked over to his uncle and put his hand on his shoulder. "So good to see you again Uncle Jack. I still can't believe you went off the track and got involved with that drug deal."

Jack shot him a twisted smile. "I did the crime. Then, I put in the time. Now, I hope that's all behind me."

Phil shook his head with confused dismay. "But, why

did you do it Uncle Jack?"

"Greed kid. Greed. Love of the damn money. I paid the price and now that I'm free, I'm determined not to have any more screw ups or schemes. I plan to stay on the straight and narrow."

"That's good. I'm glad to hear that," Phil said, as a feeling of relief surged through him.

"And you. I've been following your career and you've been doing well. I was so sorry to hear about Kelley's abduction. She's one sweet gal and I'm willing to do anything to help you get her back. You two always did make a great team." Jack relaxed back in his chair.

Phil turned toward Penny and Pete and talked with them for a few minutes about the past years before Hobbs returned to the room.

Hobbs stood in front of the group, his gaze direct and determined. "I wanted to give all of you the opportunity to visit briefly with Phil so that you could get reacquainted."

Choosing his words carefully, he added, "I feel I've assembled one hell of a team. But, I've still got a few more kinks to work out in my plan, so I'll call each of you when it's time to meet again. Stay close to your phones."

After the group left the office, Phil walked out into the gym, now relieved beyond measure. Jilley Connors approached him, rubbing his hands together. "Now, how about a little workout? Hobbs said to help you unwind a little."

Phil glanced around the gym. "Guess it wouldn't hurt me to do a little exercise."

"Let's start with the jump rope," Jilley instructed.

Dressed only in a T-shirt and shorts, after taking off his warm up suit, Phil started jumping rope slowly. With a grin on his face, Jilley stood nearby watching him as he began skipping vigorously, working up a sweat.

"That was pretty good," Jilley observed. Then he threw down a challenge. "Here's a pair of boxing gloves. Let's see how good you can do on the punching bag."

Phil shot him an amused look as Jilley helped him put on the gloves. Stepping up to the bag, he punched at it wildly.

"Wait, watch me," Jilley interrupted. "Don't try to kill the bag—just meet it. The bag should move gently."

Tap-tap-tap. Phil hit the bag slowly. First a right, then a left.

"That's it," Jilley said. "Now faster."

Before long, Phil had the bag moving like lightening. His exhilaration increased as his speed picked up. It was almost like he was actually punching Kelley's kidnapper.

"Okay. Take five," Jilley instructed. "You can finish your workout with the tread mill."

Phil was winding down on the tread mill when Hobbs re-entered the gym, walked up to him and shook him gently on the shoulder "Time to take a break Willis. It's Wednesday and you should be hearing something soon from the kidnappers. I'll see you at ten tonight. My plan for getting Kelley safely returned should be all in place by then. All I'll need from you is the time and place for the hand off."

Phil wiped the sweat from his face and agreed in a quiet voice. "Okay. I'll take a shower and head back home. On the way, I'll stop by my bank and inquire about my account. My stepfather said that he would transfer some funds into it as soon as he could get the money together."

Suddenly, Phil's cell phone jangled. Answering it he discovered that the voice on the other end was the same distorted one that he had heard previously. "So far you seem to have been following orders pretty good pal. How are you doing on getting the money together?"

"I'm working on it."

"Okay. I'll call you tomorrow to set up the exchange for Friday."

"How do I know that my wife is still alive?"

"Just a minute, I'll put her on."

After a few seconds, Phil heard Kelley say weakly, "I'm okay Phil."

The phone suddenly went dead.

A white-faced Phil choked and stared at Hobbs. "Kelley's still alive. The exchange is still set for Friday. I'm not sure where the drop will be."

Hobbs looked relieved. "See you tomorrow at ten."

Chapter 32

Thursday morning Phil rose shortly after six, dressed and took a jog around his neighborhood trying to keep himself calm. He had received a call from the kidnappers the night before informing him about the conditions of the money exchange for Kelley. It was to take place Friday evening at a charity auction at the home of Steve and Julie Winters in a suburb of Syracuse. After the phone call, Phil contacted his stepfather to make sure he could get the balance of the money needed for the ransom. Finally, he called Russell Hobbs and informed him of the time and place of the exchange.

After he returned from his run, Phil forced himself to eat a hearty breakfast, realizing he needed to keep his strength up for the ordeal ahead.

The workout yesterday had helped to relieve his mental stress, so having nothing else to do except wait for the meeting with Hobbs and the gang at Connor's gym, he decided to do some exercise there. Still wearing his jogging outfit he packed his gym bag with his everyday casual clothes and headed to the gym.

Arriving there about eight, he was greeted by Jilley. "Hi there Mr. Willis. Another workout?"

Phil laughed, "Got nothing better to do this morning."

"Want to do a little sparing?"

Phil shook his head. "Maybe some other time. By the way, thanks for letting me use your gym. Anything I can do to help you in the future, just let me know."

"Now that you mention it, there is something that you can do for me." Jilley shot him a grin. "See that skinny kid sitting over there." He motioned toward a boy of about sixteen, sitting in a chair, next to the boxing ring.

"That's my grandson, Timmy. Doesn't like school. Talking about quitting. Been in some trouble lately too. As an attorney, I'm hoping you could give him some good advice. I'd like you to explain to him what happens to a young kid if he gets into serious trouble. Describe life in jail to him."

Phil walked over to the boy and sat down beside him. "Hi. I'm Phil Willis. I'm looking for someone to work out with me on the heavy bag. How about it?"

Timmy shrugged his shoulders. "Sure. Why not."

They walked to the body bag. Phil donned the gloves and while the kid held the bag, he pounded it. When Phil finally stopped to take a breath, Timmy shot him an amused look. "Good job Mr. Willis. Now let me show you the right way to do it."

He put on the gloves and Phil held the bag for him. After they finished on the bag, they sat down and talked quietly.

Later, after Timmy left the gym, Jilley walked over to Phil, grinning from ear to ear. "Say Willis looked like the kid and you were connecting. Right?"

Phil rubbed at the stubble on his chin. "I explained to him what could happen to him if he didn't get a good education. Told him I'd take him to the police station and give him a tour when I get my present situation taken care of. Also, I'll take him to meet one of my friends at the courthouse. They need someone to do filing there on Saturdays for about four hours. He liked the idea of getting paid."

"Thanks my friend." Jilley reached over and clasped Phil on the arm. "You're always welcome here. No need for you to even join the club. In fact, consider yourself a permanent member. Right now, I've got to call the boy's mom. She'll be pleased to hear that maybe we're finally on track to getting this kid's life turned around."

"Good." Still struggling with his nervousness, Phil said, "I think I'll hit the jump rope for a while."

After a brief session with the jump rope, Phil discovered he was now calmer and had new energy. All this exercise was just what he needed to relieve his stress. He was ready to get back to the plan for getting Kelley back.

He sat in the sauna for a while, took a quick shower and got dressed in slacks and a casual open necked shirt. Now anxiety coiled in the pit of his stomach and turned into a choke hold around his neck as he took a seat in the gym and waited for Hobbs and the newly assembled rescue team to arrive.

Just after ten, Hobbs and his team strolled into the gym. Hobbs led them into Jilley's office, where he flipped each one of them a bottle of water and instructed them to sit down.

Hobbs swept his gaze up and down the group. "Glad to see everyone made it here on time this morning. Now, we'll go over the plan I've formulated to rescue Kelley."

"I'm anxious to get started. This sitting around waiting has been driving me nuts," Phil said as another quiver of nerves ran up and down his spine.

Hobbs walked over and laid a reassuring hand on Phil's shoulder. "We can all understand your frustration. But because Kelley gave us the clue about the watch, I'm almost positive it's Benny Lotts who abducted her."

Then in a strong confident voice, he added, "Rest assured we're going to get her back safe and sound."

Hobbs eyed Penny and lowered his voice. "The first part of the plan is for Penny to head to Benny's apartment this morning. Right Penny?"

"Yes. I'm going to walk his two dogs." She shifted to a more comfortable position and nodded. "I've arranged to substitute for his regular dog walker. That will give me the chance to check out Benny's apartment and the layout surrounding it. I'll try to take photos of the place inside and out."

She looked at Phil, "Did you get a call about where the money exchange will take place?"

"I heard from them last night. They said that would be the last time that I'd hear from them. I called Hobbs and told him everything that I knew."

"That was the news I needed to formulate our rescue plan," Hobbs said. "And Penny's the first step in our operation."

"So, what's the next step?" Jack asked, eyeing Hobbs with a cynical look.

"Friday night a charity auction will be held at the home of Steve and Julie Winters, a local society couple who own a jewelry store chain. The house is in an exclusive gated community in north Syracuse. The couple spends a lot of their time doing charity stuff. They expect to have a good size crowd. The who's who of local society, including the Mayor and a couple of Judges will be attending."

Hobbs reached over to Jack and handed him several sheets of paper. "Here's a list of the expected guests. I got you a spot on the private security force that's guarding the jewelry, art work and valuable items that are being auctioned off. You're supposed to meet with the security people at two o'clock this afternoon to go over things."

"I'm on it," Jack responded as he looked over the list.

"And what's my part in this caper?" Pete asked, sitting upright in his chair.

"Pete, I want you to work the parking lot. Take pictures of all the arriving guests. Remember one or two of them could be Benny's accomplices."

Hobbs glanced toward Paul. "I want you to accompany Phil inside to the auction itself."

"It sounds very ritzy. Do I need to wear my tuxedo?"

Hobbs shook his head. "No. The invitations didn't indicate formal. So just wear slacks and a jacket."

"And what will I be doing while you're attending this fancy affair?" Penny inquired.

Hobbs grinned at her. "Stake out. Your job is to stay glued to Benny. If he gets a rental car, get all the details on it. You know, make, model, license plate number and so on. That way if he tries to make a run for it, we'll have all the necessary information to give to the police."

"Hobbs, what will you be doing?"

"Before the auction, I'll be working in the kitchen, helping to serve appetizers and drinks. When the auction takes place, I'll be on stage with the security. Now does anyone have any questions? If any of you have any further concerns, you can reach me on my cell."

Phil waved his hand. "I'm on my way to the bank later this afternoon to pick up the money. What should I carry it in?"

"Glad you asked. I have a couple of duffle bags out in my car that I want to give you when we leave." Hobbs looked around the room. "If there aren't any more questions, I believe that we're done here. I'll see you all at the Winter's house tomorrow night."

They filed out of the room and headed for their cars. Phil walked with Hobbs to his SUV, where Hobbs opened the back door and handed Phil two large black nylon duffle bags. "These should be large enough to hold the money."

Phil stiffened and frowned, glancing down at the

bags. "Yeah. The kidnapper said to get the ransom money in fifties and hundreds. Guess he doesn't want to monkey around with small bills."

He put the bags under his arm and turned to walk away, when his cell phone rang.

"Hi Willis, its Gayle. I haven't heard from you. I'm anxious to learn what's going on. And, I think that it's time you gave me some answers." He could hear the anxiety in her voice.

"You're right. Where are you now?"

"At home. Come over for lunch and we can talk."

"Give me about a half hour and I'll be there."

Turning to Hobbs, he said, "That was my co-counsel, Gayle Tanner. I think it's about time that I gave her the real story on what's going on."

Hobbs regarded him for a moment, and then nodded, "That should be okay. I'm sure she can be trusted. Remind her that she shouldn't tell anyone about this."

A short time later, Phil and Gayle were seated in her kitchen with sandwiches and iced tea in front of them.

"Please accept my apology for keeping you in the dark so long Gayle. But, what I'm about to tell you now must be kept in total secret." His tone was firm.

As they ate, he explained why he had left the courtroom so abruptly and why he asked the Judge to postpone the trial.

When he finished the story, she sat there stunned, her temples throbbed with a thousand questions.

"What are you going to do? What's your next move?"

"At this point, I feel pretty confident we know who the kidnappers are. And with the help of a few of my old friends and the police, we expect to get Kelley back."

He put his hand on her arm. "I just hope you can forgive me for not telling you all this sooner. It was imperative that no word of this gets to the authorities. I don't know what the kidnappers might do to Kelley if it does."

"I understand. And, I think you did the right thing by not contacting the police."

"Now, let's talk about the trial," he said, changing the subject. "Where do you think we are with it?"

She hesitated, and then shrugged uneasily. "Nothing has changed. When we resume the trial, I'm ready to give my summation. I feel really confident about our chances of winning. And, Mrs. Cliff certainly deserves to get some compensation for all her grief."

"I'm glad to hear you say that," Phil replied. "I felt so guilty about leaving you and her hanging in mid-air, but I couldn't concentrate on anything except getting Kelley back."

"Believe me, I understand. I'll be praying for you both"

"Thanks. And thanks for the lunch." Phil stood up, unable to hide his nervousness. "Now, I'm heading for the bank to gather up the ransom money.'

Gayle clasped him by the arm as she followed him to the door. "By the way, you look pretty good considering what you've been going through these past few days."

"I've been trying to work off the stress at Connor's Gym. You should see me skip rope. I'm a terror at that."

"I'd like to see that. Call me as soon as you get Kelley back. I'll be waiting to hear."

"I'll do that. And I love you Gayle, my friend." Phil gave her a hug and kissed her on both cheeks.

"Save all that love for Kelley. She's going to need it after this." She tried to hide her feelings, but it was hopeless. Her eyes misted with tears.

Phil managed a faint smile. "I know. And after this, I'll never stop telling her how much I care for her. And remember not a word to anyone about this."

"You have my word."

Chapter 33

Sergeant Russell Hobbs had put in for a week's vacation time from his job at the courthouse so he could help Phil. Now, the team that he had assembled was ready to assist him in the task ahead. Each would play an important role in the upcoming operation, which he had named "Operation Return".

At this point, Hobbs had decided that all the evidence pointed to Benny Lotts as being responsible for abducting Kelley. It had been Phil's testimony at the trial that helped to convict Benny. As they led him out of the courtroom after the trial, he had looked at Phil and shouted, "I'll get even with you Willis, if it's the last thing I do."

Now, after serving only five years, Benny had been released from prison and seemed ready to seek his revenge on the Willis family.

Hobbs and Phil were determined to play out Benny's kidnapping plan and not bring in the authorities. Rather, they would proceed as directed and bring the cash to the Friday night auction. There, they hoped to get Kelley back alive. Her safety was their foremost concern.

At ten in the morning, Penny walked up to the door of Benny's apartment and knocked softly. The door opened slowly and a middle-aged, slender man, in a torn tee-shirt and with a jagged scar on his face opened the door slightly. From the description that she had received from Angel, the regular dog walker, she knew that this must be Doug, Benny's friend.

She exhaled slowly. "Hi. You Doug? I'm here to walk your dogs."

The man glared at her. "Yeah. I'm Doug. Who are you? Where's Angel?"

"Oh. She had to take her father to the emergency room." She took small measured breaths and continued, "I'm a registered dog walker too. Angel and I substitute for each other. I owe her because she walked a couple of my regulars last week. I'm Penny."

Doug hesitated and stood with his hands at his side, surveying the situation without expression. He snarled, "Don't just stand there. Get your ass in here."

"Okay." She stepped inside. The shades were drawn and the room was somewhat dark.

A voice called out from a back room. "Is that the damn dog walker?"

Doug gathered his brows in a scowl and yelled, "Yes."

Two medium size pit bulls came running into the living room and jumped up on Penny.

Leaning over she patted the first and scratched the second behind his ear. "Hi guys, you're going to have a good time with me."

Doug walked over to a nearby closet and pulled two leather leashes off a hook. He snapped the hooks of the leashes onto the collar of each dog. "Okay gal. You can get going now."

"We're going to be a while." Penny swallowed hard and then made up a lie so that she could look around further. "Any chance that I can use your bathroom first? I've been on the bus for a while and we have a long walk ahead of us. Can't use the ladies room anywhere with two dogs."

Doug sighed and looked over his shoulder and down the hall. "Guess it'd be okay." In a perturbed voice, he added, "Just make it quick."

Penny pulled her cell phone from her pocket and took a couple of photos as she walked down the hall toward the bathroom. As she passed what appeared to be a bedroom, she heard slight moans coming from inside. Then, the sound of a television blaring overpowered all other sounds.

She searched through the bathroom quickly, and was surprised to find a purse size woman's hairbrush with long red hairs on it. She took a couple of strands off the brush and put them in her pocket. After using the toilet and washing her hands, she headed back to the living room where Doug was standing by the door, with the dogs at his side.

He gave her an assessing glance and ordered in an exasperated voice, "Remember, you're supposed to walk my babies for an hour and a half. You know the area?"

Penny stared at him blankly and shook her head.

"Two blocks down, there's a dog park." Then he added, in matter-of-fact tone, "And, oh yeah. Don't feed them anything. They're on a restricted diet."

"Got it," she replied, with a placating smile, as she grabbed the dogs and headed out the door. Starting down the street with the dogs, she noticed a black van with rental plates parked next to the curb.

She took them to the dog park and unleashed them.

As the dogs ran around the almost deserted dog park, Penny called Hobbs. She told him she had heard moaning in Lotts' apartment and that she had spotted a hairbrush in the bathroom with long red hairs on it. "It looked like the color of Kelley's hair to me. I grabbed a couple of strands. Some guy called out from the back room too. Don't know if it was Benny or someone else."

When Penny returned the two dogs to the apartment, she spied two suitcases sitting just inside the door. She unleashed the dogs and said they had a nice run in the park. "You can send Angel your usual check for the walks. She and I will square up on our own." She managed a faint smile and said good-bye.

Leaving the apartment, Penny walked across the street to the bus stop bench. As her bus approached, she gazed upwards up at the apartment windows. The curtain moved in one of them and she spotted a man peeking out. The silhouette in the window indicated that he was a tall, heavy-set man, and she realized that this fit the description that she had gotten of Benny Lotts.

She called Hobbs again and told him about the man in the window.

With little emotion in his voice, he said, "We can't take a chance on trying to rescue Kelley from that apartment. We don't know how many people that Benny has in on this or how many are guarding her. Besides, the space is too confined and Kelley might get hurt."

"And, by the way, Hobbs, I noticed suitcases sitting near the door. And there was a black van with rental plates parked outside the apartment building."

"They might be on the way to making a move. We've got to be ready for them. Keep an eye on the rental van."

"You got it. Right now, I'm taking the bus back to where I parked my own van. I'll head back here in my vehicle and keep my eye on Benny and his friend. You're still on for the meeting this evening with the rest of the gang?" Penny asked.

"Yes. At the gym. It will be our final meeting before tomorrow night. After that, it will be "Operation Return"."

That evening at seven, they met in the back of the gym. Hobbs faced the group as he gave out final instructions. "Penny is continuing her stake out of Benny's apartment.

Phil, you and Paul should arrive at the Winter Mansion shortly before six tomorrow night. The auction is set to start promptly at seven."

Paul's eyes narrowed and he looked very solemn. "What's my role at the auction?"

Hobbs rubbed his chin. "You and Phil will each be assigned a paddle with your number on it. Just hold your paddle up to make a bid. If you win the bid for an item, you pay the auctioneer's clerk before you leave."

Anticipation surged through Phil. "The kidnapper told me to bid on a couple items. Then go into the garage to pay for them. That's where I'm supposed to hand over the two million in exchange for Kelley."

A short silence fell throughout the room. "I noticed from the brochure that there are some nice paintings in the auction. Even some original Thomas Kincaid's that a local gallery donated," Hobbs said. "You might want to bid on one of those."

"Good idea. My wife just loves his paintings. I just hope that all goes according to plan and that Kelley doesn't get hurt," Phil replied.

"Everything should run smoothly if everyone just stays calm, Hobbs said. "I'll be in the garage with the money. Paul, you accompany Phil to the garage and I'll hand the money over to him for the exchange."

"And what do you want me to do while this is taking place?" Jack asked.

"You'll be working security. Try to check every room and closet in the house before the auction if you can. Make sure that they haven't got Kelley stashed somewhere."

Jack replied, "They'll probably be bringing her in from outside somewhere so I'll come to the garage after the auction."

Hobbs nodded and then turned his attention to Fast Draw Pete. "You'll be outside parking cars. Your job will be to look out for Benny and his accomplices. They'll probably be in the black van that Penny spotted outside of his apartment. Try to determine if they have Kelley in the vehicle if you can, and keep an eye on it."

"Got it Sarge," Pete responded.

"Now gang. Let's set our watches." Hobbs looked down at his watch. "It's twenty-one hundred now. We should be all ready to operate tomorrow night."

Phil set his watch. The tremor in his voice wrenched the hearts of the others as he said, "I just want to get my Kelley back. It's been a long and crazy week."

"Don't worry my friend," Hobbs said, putting his arm around Phil's shoulder. "By this time tomorrow night, you should be holding your lovely wife in your arms."

Chapter 34

The next evening, Phil, with Paul seated beside him, drove up to Hobbs' van which was parked down the street from the gated enclave where the Winters lived. Phil jumped out of his car, walked around to the trunk and opened it. He pulled out the two duffle bags containing the ransom money and carried them to where Hobbs was standing next to his van.

"Is the money all here?"

"Yeah. It isn't easy raising two million in cash."

"Did you mark some of the money like I instructed?"

"My stepfather and I took care of it," Phil replied.

"Good. I'll see you inside the house," Hobbs said as he picked up the bags and threw them in the van.

Phil walked slowly back to his car and drove down to the guard house at the wrought iron gates leading into the secluded Fairfield Woods Community.

Paul reached into his pocket, withdrew the two invitations that had cost one hundred dollars apiece and showed them to the guard. He looked them over briefly and handed them a card to place on their windshield and gestured for them to follow the road to the house.

Phil pulled up to the circular driveway in front of the Winters' home and they exited the car. The parking valet directed them toward the front entrance of the three story mansion and drove their car away.

Behind the gated walls of the neighborhood were seven other houses in addition to that of the Winters. This section of the city was known as "Millionaire Haven" and everyone who lived here was actively involved in Syracuse's society and its many charitable events. The previous year, the President of the United States had attended one of the campaign fund-raisers in the community.

Walking toward the front entrance, Phil and Paul spotted Pete, who was standing in the street helping to direct the cars and keep the traffic moving.

The front of the pink stucco mansion was framed by six tall pillars and gigantic palm trees illuminated by spot lights. Beds of colorful crotons and azaleas framed the front walkway.

They followed the other guests up the stone steps that led to the double entrance doors. A huge balcony wrapped around the front of the house on the third level. From its black wrought iron railing, massive vines of colorful flowers trailed downward. The grandeur of this mansion could easily compete with the villas of Sicily, Phil thought.

Inside the entrance way a security guard frisked them briefly. Next, a maid directed them to a girl in her mid-twenties seated at a small table covered in a lace cloth. "Your invitations please, Gentlemen," she said.

Taking the invitations from them, she checked their names off against a list. She gave them each a name tag to wear. "Mr. Willis and Mr. Mathison, welcome to the Winters' Charity Event. Now, if you would, please proceed to the library on your right where the appetizers and drinks are being served. The auction itself will take place in the dining room to your left."

Julie and Steve Winters owned a chain of six designer jewelry stores called the "The Syracuse Gold and Diamond Store" where they sold only high quality merchandise. They also purchased previously worn gold and silver watches and fashionable jewelry. This gave their clientele a quick access to cash and the Winters made an immense amount of money reusing the fine metals. Their reputation was one of the finest in the jewelry business.

Phil and Paul walked through the entrance hall and could not help but admire the magnificent home which had been recently been featured in one of Syracuse's most prestigious home magazines. A huge chandelier hung from the third story ceiling and accented the entrance foyer.

Proceeding past the great room, they spied an ornate wrought iron elevator that went from the first floor to the third. A sweeping wrought iron stairway with a highly polished oak railing led to the second level of the house.

The imported Spanish tile on the floor was beige and brown with a circular mosaic set in front of the elevator. Massive tapestries on the second story walls accented both sides of the circular stairway. Tall bronze statues of ancient maidens flanked either side of the elevator.

Looking around, Paul shook his head in admiration, "I feel like I'm in Europe. I'd love to sit down with the Winters and hear about their travels."

Phil nodded, "The price tag for this place had to be in the millions. But, no time for small talk tonight."

Entering the library they looked at the far wall of the room, which was dominated by a two-story stone fireplace. A large, gold framed oil painting of Steve and Julie Winters hung over it. A beige leather sofa was placed in front of it and chairs with bronze and brown stripes flanked it sides. With small tables on either side of the chairs, the library looked like an inviting place to sit and read on a cool evening.

The side walls featured floor to ceiling book shelves.

In front of the book shelves two large tables were set up.
One was covered with silver trays filled with delicious
looking appetizers. The other table had silver buckets
containing various champagnes and wines. Standing in
back of each table was a waiter, dressed in a white dinner
jacket, waiting to serve the guests.

The Winters were known throughout the city for host-
ing many charitable events and it appeared as though
they had the staging for them down to a science.

"This place is even more elegant than the Governor's
mansion I used to live in with my folks," Paul said. "It
must cost these people a fortune to keep up this immense place."

Carrying their glasses of champagne, they walked toward the dining room where the auction would be held.
It was overflowing with elegantly dressed people—women
in silk pantsuits and beaded cocktail dresses and men in
turtle necks and sports coats.

Two large doors at the far end of the dining room led
to the living room, which was also filled with people milling around and talking. The ceiling of the dining room
was inset with mosaic panels and edged in solid oak
beams. Small chandeliers flanked the walls on all sides
and the large chandelier in the center of the room had
been raised to the ceiling for the event. The floor was covered in large blue Italian marble tiles and magnificent oil
paintings hung throughout the room.

The auctioneer's podium had been set up in the doorway between the living and dining rooms so that he could
be seen from either room.

The conventional furniture had been cleared out of
both rooms and rows of folding chairs had been set up to
accommodate the numerous guests.

The living room was decorated in shades of white and
gold with gold marble tiles on the floor. It's massive ceiling to floor sliding glass doors led out to the flood-lit patio

and the pool beyond.

Entering the living room, the auctioneer's clerk directed them to a table set up in front of the patio doors. Seated behind the table were six ladies with guest lists and numbered paddles sitting in front of them.

"Your name Sir?" one of the ladies asked.

"Phil Willis and Paul Mathison Jr."

She located their names on one of the guest lists. "Please sign next to your name. And print your address and phone number."

Each was given a numbered paddle that corresponded with their name and number on the guest list. "Oh, Mr. Willis, you have the lucky number of thirteen and Mr. Mathison your number is fourteen. If you wish to bid on something, please hold up your paddle."

They took their paddles and started to walk away. The woman waved at them, "One more thing gentlemen. Here's a program, listing the items that are to be auctioned tonight."

Taking their programs, they walked back into the dining room and found a couple of seats near the back of the room where a bar had been set up. A waiter walked up and asked, "May I refill your glasses? Would you care for appetizers?"

Both shook their heads.

"Please feel free to help yourselves to additional refreshments during the intermission," he instructed.

A short while later, all of the guests settled quietly into their seats, filling the chairs in both rooms. The auctioneer's clerk walked up to the podium. "The bar will be open for another twenty minutes. Then, we will start the auction."

Phil's uncle, Jack, approached them. He leaned over and whispered into Phil's ear. "Hi there. I checked out the house—nothing here. Hobbs just called and said to tell you that there was no sign of the kidnappers yet. He

has the duffel bags with the money and will meet you in
the garage when it's time for the exchange."

"Good. And Pete is working the parking lot?"

"Right. "He's supposed to alert us when he sees Benny's van drive in."

"Thanks." Phil's face was now drawn and weary, his
vigor suddenly gone. "Why don't you grab yourself a drink
before the auction starts, Uncle Jack?"

"Can't drink on duty, besides, I'm on the wagon these
days." Jack's face was set like stone. "I'll get myself a diet
coke and watch the action from the back of the room.

A short while later, Julie Winters stepped up to the
podium. "Steve and I wish to welcome everyone to this
special auction. Remember it's for a worth-while cause so
don't be afraid to wave your paddle with your generous
bid. Hope you have a drink in your hand and are ready
to help us purchase a new robotic machine for Syracuse
Hospital. It will help them perform miracles."

Phil gazed in admiration at the beautiful Julie Winters, dressed in an elegant white silk pantsuit covered in
elaborate silver crystals twinkling in the lights. It seemed
to accentuate her long black hair and dark eyes. Standing at her side, was her tall and distinguished looking
husband with dark hair that was slightly gray at the
temples. Phil could see why they had been honored last
year as one of Syracuse's most well-dressed and powerful couples.

Looking around the room, Phil saw there were countless celebrities present, including local athletes, politi-
cians and well-known local television personalities. A local newspaper society editor was present and her camera
man was taking a few photos of the attendees. The publisher and his assistant from a local magazine were also
covering the event.

Steve Winters took a step forward. "In your program,
you'll see that we have forty items for sale tonight. After

you have purchased your items, you can pay for them at the auctioneer's booth in the garage. Also two security men will be available out there if you need any assistance. If you wish to ship your items somewhere, we can make arrangements for that."

Julie stepped forward once again. "Now, the auctioneer's clerk will briefly review the bidding procedure and introduce our auctioneer, Lester Van Dyke. I hope that everyone will get in the spirit and generously give to this great cause."

Chapter 35

The young clerk stepped up to the podium and explained the bidding procedure. After she finished her short speech, she introduced the auctioneer, Lester Van Dyke. Wearing a tuxedo, the tall, gray haired man with a neatly cut gray beard and wearing horn rimmed glasses took his place in front of the group.

In a deep baritone voice, he announced, "We'll begin our bidding with item number one, which is a Buckingham Wallace antique silver tea service, made in London in the sixteenth century and once owned by the Duchess of Kent. As you can see from your program the tea set has been authenticated and papers accompany it. It's difficult to put a definite value on this item, but let's show lots of spirit as we start the bidding. Please follow your programs as we continue on to each item. And finally, remember that the money is to help the hospital purchase new and advanced equipment, so be generous in your bids."

Paul carefully read the description listed in the program, then leaned over and whispered to Phil. "My mother loves antiques and she hosts a lot of afternoon teas for her lady friends. I'm certain that she'd just love this for their fiftieth wedding anniversary."

Phil shot him an amused look and nodded, "Give the

bidding a shot."

Before Paul had a chance to deliberate any further, the bidding started.

"Do I have five hundred?" Van Dyke shouted out.

A paddle went up in the back of the room.

"Yes. I have five hundred. Now six hundred. Now nine hundred." Van Dyke was now animated as his eyes swept around the room.

Paul raised his paddle after Van Dyke asked for a bid for a thousand dollars.

A lady in the front row raised her paddle, at the request for fifteen hundred.

When Van Dyke asked for two thousand, something glittered deep in Paul's eyes and he waved his paddle vigorously in the air. He was determined to not lose this precious gift for his parents special anniversary.

"I have two thousand dollars. Do I hear three?" Van Dyke demanded.

When he received no further bids, Van Dyke announced, "Going-once. Going-twice. Sold to the gentleman in the back row with number fourteen. Sold for two thousand dollars. And, may I say, Sir, you've got yourself one magnificent tea set."

The clerk wrote down the bid and Paul's number as the auctioneer continued on with the next item.

Paul leaned over and whispered, "I'll be back soon. I'm going to pay for the tea set and see if they can ship it to Mom and Dad."

Phil nodded as the auctioneer continued. "We now have a fifteen-day cruise to South America for two. We'll start the bidding at five thousand dollars."

The auction and the bidding continued for the next hour as Phil waited impatiently to bid on the original Kincaid painting he had decided to purchase for Kelley. He knew that after their trip years ago to Carmel, California, Kelley had been enchanted with Kincaid's gallery.

The painting was scheduled to be one of the last items and the anticipated time for the auction to end was around nine-thirty or ten.

The rescue plan was that Hobbs would accompany Phil to the garage where Pete was waiting with the bags of money. Phil would pay for the painting and wait to hand the ransom money over to the kidnappers.

Penny was staked out at Benny's apartment waiting for him and his friend to leave in the van with Kelley. She was prepared to call Hobbs and inform them when Benny made his move.

Pete was in the garage with the duffle bags of money, watching for the van to arrive. And Jack was in the house and would follow Phil and Hobbs to the garage for the money exchange.

At the intermission, Phil and Paul got up and strolled casually towards the bar. Standing next to it was Hobbs. Phil walked up to him and said, "Boy, the time is really dragging."

Hobbs smiled reassuringly. "Yes. But soon it'll be over. You'll have Kelley back. We'll recover the ransom money and have Benny under lock and key."

"I hope so." Phil's expression was empty.

"As soon as you get Kelley safely in your arms, I'll have an ambulance here to take her to the hospital to get her checked out," Hobbs replied.

Phil pursed his lips as he considered that statement. "If we pull this off and get Kelley back safe and sound, I'll be forever grateful to you my friend."

"This will all work out. Just trust me," Hobbs said as Paul walked up. He handed Phil a drink and gave Hobbs a Coke.

Hobbs grinned and smiled his thanks. "Now, gentlemen, go back to the auction. And hell, spend some money Mathison. It's for charity."

After a momentary pause, Paul smiled. "I'm already

out two grand for a tea set. But I appreciate your advice."

Settling back into their seats, Phil clenched his fists as he felt his confidence build back up. We can do this, he thought. Yes. We can do this.

The auctioneer wrapped his fingers around the microphone, "The next item in the program is a fourteen-day Hawaiian vacation for two. Plane trip from New York to San Francisco, then on to Hawaii. Hotel and sightseeing included. Now folks, let's hear those bids. This would be a great gift for your kids for their honeymoon or for a second honeymoon for you and the missus."

As the auction continued, Phil noticed the Winters standing in the back of the room, watching. Julie had changed her outfit from the white pantsuit to a short clinging red satin dress with spaghetti straps. Steve had donned a bright red shirt that matched her ensemble. Both were smiling and talking quietly with a couple of guests as they saw the amount of money being raised for their charity steadily climbing.

Van Dyke flipped through the pages of the program and said loudly, "It's almost time to bid on the final items for the evening. The first will be a three-foot by four-foot original painting by Thomas Kincaid. Since his death, Kincaid's paintings have increased in value tenfold. Following that, ladies and gentlemen, the best is yet to come—the Dali collection. But before we take the bids on the last few items, we will have a fifteen-minute break. And this will be the last call for drinks and hor-dourves."

Only a few members of the crowd left the room to obtain more refreshments. Most seemed to be anxiously awaiting the bidding on the Kincaid and Dali paintings.

After everyone had taken their seats once again, Van Dyke pointed to the Kincaid painting placed on an easel to his left. "Now, who will start the bidding on this original? I would like an opening bid of five hundred?"

Phil's hand trembled as he raised his paddle.

When Van Dyke asked for a thousand, a woman in the front row quickly flashed her paddle.

"Do I have fifteen hundred?' Van Dyke asked.

Phil looked cautiously around the room. Only he and the woman appeared to be bidding for the oil painting. He raised his paddle and held his breath as he waited to see if the woman would outbid him. She put her paddle on her seat, got up and walked to the bar.

"Going once. Going twice. Sold for fifteen hundred dollars to the gentleman with number thirteen." Van Dyke slammed his gavel and nodded toward Phil. "I believe you just purchased a valuable painting."

Phil lowered his eyes, hiding the sly gleam of satisfaction that he knew must be in his eyes.

"Next item up for auction this evening will be an original sketch by Salvador Dali," Van Dyke announced.

After the auction ended Phil and Paul headed to the garage to pay for Phil's purchase.

"It's time to get Kelley back," Phil whispered to Paul with excitement in his voice.

Glancing at his watch, Phil saw that it was about nine-forty-five. Following the other patrons into the garage, he waited until they had paid for their purchases and left before he headed to the table where two of the auctioneer's clerks were seated.

"I'm Phil Willis, number thirteen. I purchased the Kincaid painting." He put his paddle down on the table before the clerk.

The clerk looked up his number on her list. "Oh, yes. You bid fifteen hundred for it. How were you planning to pay for it? We take cash, checks or credit cards."

Phil reached into his pocket, pulled out his wallet and removed a credit card.

After running the card though a scanner, the clerk handed Phil a receipt and ordered one of the security men to go into the house and get the painting.

A few moments later, he emerged with the painting, wrapped it in bubble wrap and placed it in a large cardboard box. "Do you need help taking this to your car Sir?"

"No. Just have the valet bring my car up."

While Hobbs stationed himself next to the duffle bags of money, Pete got Phil's car and helped the security guard place the painting in the trunk.

"I'll pull your car off to the side of the driveway," Pete whispered to Phil. "I know that you fellows are waiting for the kidnappers and Kelley to get here."

Phil bit his lip as he nervously realized that he probably had to wait until most of the other guests had vacated the premises before Benny would bring Kelley in and make the exchange.

Chapter 36

Phil and Paul were standing side by side, in the garage, talking quietly, when they noticed Hobbs approach carrying the two large duffel bags.

He strolled casually over and set the bags down on the floor next to them. He slid a glance in Phil's direction and asked, "Where's your painting?"

"Oh. I paid for it already and put it in my car. Pete parked it out in front."

Hobbs nodded, but his attention suddenly shifted as the phone in his jacket pocket vibrated. He pulled it out and turned to the side as he listened to the voice on the other end. "Yes. Yes. Good work."

He snapped the phone shut, jammed it back in his pocket and grinned. "That was Penny. Said that Benny and his friend, Doug, just left the apartment. They pushed a small black-hooded person in front of them into the van. Penny couldn't see if it was Kelley, but, she's almost certain that it was."

"Thank God. I can't wait to get this over with." Phil's eyes were filled with anguish.

Hobbs sighed and grimaced. "My feelings exactly. They should be here in about fifteen or twenty minutes."

Trying to divert the onslaught of emotions that were surging inside him, Phil turned to Paul and suggested,

"Why don't we step inside and say a quick good-bye to Julie and Steve?"

"Good idea," Hobbs said. "If you see Jack, tell him to come out here. We might need his help. I have the ambulance waiting in case Kelley should need it. After we make the switch, you may need to rush her to the hospital for a checkup."

Phil stood a step backwards, as cold fingers of fear crept up his spine. He whispered, "I just pray she's okay."

He took a deep breath trying to calm himself, before he looked at Paul. "Now let's go thank our hosts."

Steve and Julie were standing just inside the house, near the exit door to the garage, talking to a small group. When there was a little break in the conversation, Phil approached them. "Mrs. Winters, we want to thank you for inviting us to this lovely affair."

"Please, call me Julie." She smiled warmly. "You're Phil Willis. I saw your picture in the paper about the trial with the Gypsies."

"Yes, and this is my friend, Paul Mathison."

"We both enjoyed the auction immensely," Paul said.

Grinning proudly, Steve said, "Glad to hear it. How about joining us at the bar for a farewell drink?"

Phil stiffened and glanced over at Paul. "Sorry, we don't have time right now. Paul and I have some important business to take care of."

Julie winked at them. "Must be really important—to turn down a drink."

A shudder rippled through Phil. "It is. Very important."

"Well, if you must leave, please make sure we have an address for both of you," Julie said. "I'd like to send you an invitation for the Cattlemen's Ball, it takes place in a couple of months. Steve and I are the chairpersons."

Looking at their ring fingers, she chuckled and added, "And, oh yes, you must bring your wives this time."

Phil offered her an impish smile. "I'm certain that my

wife would enjoy that. She'll be ready for some fun."

"And what about you, Mr. Mathison?" Julie asked.

Paul gave a brief shake of his head. "Won't be able to make it I'm afraid. Going back to Florida soon. And by the way, I'm certain my parents will love the antique tea set I got for their fiftieth wedding anniversary."

"And you, Mr. Willis. I understand you purchased the lighted Thomas Kincaid original," Julie inquired with some interest.

"That's right. It'll look great over our fireplace. I'll look forward to that invitation to the Cattlemen's Ball. But, now, if you will excuse us, we have to be going."

They shook hands with Steve and turned to re-enter the garage, where Hobbs was patiently waiting for them.

"Looking forward to meeting your missus at the ball," Steve called out to Phil as the men walked away.

Phil's stomach started to churn. He looked upwards and prayed silently. "Please Lord, let Kelley be okay."

"You guys ready?" Hobbs asked.

Both nodded as Hobbs added, "And remember Phil, we'll give the money over only after we have Kelley in our hands. These are desperate men and they'll probably have guns. Don't rush things. Just follow their orders. We won't worry about following them out of here. Penny put a tracking device on their van."

Phil merely nodded as Hobbs continued, "Once we have Kelley and they have the money, we'll let them take the lead."

The men stood waiting inside the garage. After a short time, Hobbs' cell phone rang. "Thanks," he replied. "That was Penny. The black van is minutes away and she's right behind them."

Jack entered the garage, at the same moment, from the corner of his eye, Phil saw the black van drive up.

He stepped forward as the van pulled up to the open garage door. Hobbs grabbed him by the arm, pulled him back and handed the two bags of money to Phil.

"Wait," he snapped. "Don't rush it."

The two large coach lights outside of the garage were the only light in the driveways as the doors to the front of the van flung open. Two men in dark hooded sweat shirts, one of which Phil recognized as Benny Lotts, jumped out. Benny peered into the garage and saw Phil, Paul, Hobbs and Jack standing inside.

Walking up to the entrance he called out in a voice that was all the more dangerous because it was so unnaturally controlled, "Bring me the money Willis."

"Not until I see Kelley. Where is she?"

"In the back of the van." Benny snarled to his accomplice. "Get the girl."

He walked to the back of the van, opened the doors and lifted the bound and blind-folded Kelley out.

Phil stepped cautiously forward with the bags of money in his hands. "Bring Kelley here," he said icily.

For just a moment Phil wavered as he saw that Benny and Doug each had large guns aimed at him.

Benny glared at Phil. "Shit Willis. You weren't supposed to bring the law in on this."

Phil's mouth curved into an unexpected half smile. Then it faded away as he answered calmly, "No law. These are just a couple of Kelley's close personal friends who wanted to come along for the exchange."

"Tell her friends to step back. It's you and me, Willis."

Dragging Kelley behind him, Doug followed Benny into the garage. Benny walked over to Phil, grabbed hold of the bags, set them on the ground in front of him and unzipped each one.

"Looks like about two million," he snarled at Phil. "Better not be marked or have a dye pack."

"Trust me. Would I risk my wife's life for money?"

Benny pulled Kelley toward him and then pushed her roughly into Phil's outstretched arms.

"Let's go," Benny yelled to Doug. He picked up the duffle bags in one hand while the other hand held the gun that was pointed at Phil and raced toward the van.

He threw the duffle bags into the passenger side of the van. Doug climbed into the driver's side and started the engine. Benny jumped in, slammed the door and the van shot out of the driveway and around the corner with a squeal of the tires.

Penny ran up as Phil, with a relieved sigh, quickly whipped the blindfold off Kelley's face. Hobbs untied Kelley's arms.

Putting his arms around Kelley and drawing her to his chest, Phil whispered, "Thank God. I've got you back. Are you okay Kell? Did they hurt you?"

Kelley hesitated, a trifle nervous and then slowly shook her head. "I'm all right. The only things worse than the food, were the ass-holes who kept me tied up."

Phil made a big effort to get hold of his emotions as he put his arm around her, led her out of the garage and to where the ambulance was waiting.

Two medics hopped out of the vehicle when they saw them approaching and lifted a stretcher from the back. In spite of Kelley's repeated refusals, they placed her on the stretcher and loaded her in the ambulance.

"I'm okay. I don't need to go to any hospital," she said, feeling out of sorts and distinctly off balance.

"I want you to get checked out, Honey," Phil insisted in a low voice. "I'll follow you to the hospital in my car. Syracuse General Guys?"

"Yes Sir, Mr. Willis."

As the ambulance, with Phil's car following, left the Winters' residence, the other members of the Hobbs gang gathered in the driveway.

"I've got the tracking device planted underneath Benny's van, just as you instructed," Penny told Hobbs.

"That's good. But, most likely they'll ditch the van

somewhere."

"If they're as smart as I think they are, I believe they'll eventually try to head to Buffalo and cross the border into Canada," Jack said.

Hobbs nodded. "Now, that we've got Kelley back safely, it's time to get the Feds and the local police involved."

"I've got the other end of the tracking device installed in my van so I can keep tabs on Benny Penny said.

"We should have plenty of time to track them," Hobbs pointed out. "I doubt if they'll make a run for the border just yet. Pete, you go with Penny and follow the van. Stay with them. Paul, you and Jack, come with me."

An hour later Hobbs', phone rang. It was Phil giving him an update on Kelley's condition.

After talking for a while, Phil asked, "And where do you think Benny is headed?"

"Probably back to his apartment for the night. They'll lay low for a few hours," Hobbs replied. "They won't try to cross the border tonight. If anything changes, I'll give you a call. Otherwise, we'll plan on getting together in the morning. The gang wants to be there for the capture."

Phil began to breathe more easily. "Keep me posted."

"Hug Kelley for us. Over and out," Hobbs said.

After he finished talking to Phil, he looked at the others. "Kelley is dehydrated and they have her on an IV. Otherwise, she's just fine. They want to keep her overnight and check her out. Phil's going to stay with her. We'll keep him updated."

The others sighed with relief. Kelley Willis was safe in the arms of her husband.

Chapter 37

The next day, Pete and Agent Penny Gates were staked out at Benny Lotts' apartment waiting for him and Doug to make a move. They sat in their van talking and watching the door of the apartment. The time passed slowly.

"Thank goodness we stopped to pick up food and coffee before we got here," Penny said, her face lined with tension.

"I can't believe that Hobbs isn't trying to nab Lotts this morning at the apartment, now that Kelley's safe," Pete said in perturbed voice.

"He decided to let them try to skip the country with the money. That way they can be picked up by the Feds and will face a lot more charges. If Lotts leaves the state they can get him for jumping parole among other things. Hobbs wants to put this guy away for a long time so he can't try anything like this again."

"Have the Feds been notified?" Pete asked leaning back in the passenger seat and shutting his eyes for a moment.

"Yeah. Hobbs called them," Penny answered, rearing upright in her seat. "Look Pete. A frozen food delivery truck just pulled up in front of Benny's apartment."

She pulled a pair of binoculars from under the seat. "It says 'Edmonds Frozen Foods—we deliver to New York and Canada' on the side. I'll bet that Benny is planning on switching to that truck and heading to Canada with the money."

Her tone of voice changed as she picked up her cell phone and called Hobbs. "I think we've got a problem. It looks like Benny may be switching vehicles and we won't be able to track him. He's got a frozen foods truck outside his place. It delivers to New York and Canada."

"That's okay. I expected him to ditch the and switch to Plan B. Does the truck have a phone number on it?"

"Yeah, It's got the address and phone number painted on the side," Penny said, her gaze never leaving the truck.

"See if you can find out where that truck is headed." After a brief pause, Hobbs added, "Just don't follow too closely. We don't want him to know you're tailing him."

With her heart beating rapidly, Penny dialed once again and called the dispatcher for Edmonds Frozen Foods. This was the part of her life that she liked best—action with its adrenaline pumping excitement

After talking with him, she said to Pete, "I told the dispatcher I was interested in getting a delivery to Niagara Falls sometime soon. He told me it's about a three and a half hour drive from Syracuse to the Canadian border and their trucks go there twice a week on Wednesdays and Saturdays. It's headed there now."

They watched as the driver got out of the truck, strolled up to the door of Benny's apartment and knocked. Within a few minutes the door opened and the driver entered.

"Looks like that guy knows Benny," Pete said, squinting out the window.

"Right." Penny picked up her phone again, called Hobbs and filled him in on what she had just observed.

Before she had a chance to finish, the door to the apartment opened and three men emerged.

Benny and Doug were each carrying a duffle bag and a suitcase. Pete recognized the duffle bags as the ones that held the ransom money.

The truck driver had a large manila envelope in his hands. He threw it into the truck before he climbed into the driver's seat.

Benny and Doug walked around to the back door of the truck, opened it and threw the duffle bags and suitcases inside. Benny climbed in the passenger side. Doug went to the van they had been using, the one with Penny's tracking device underneath, and jumped in.

Both the truck and the van started to pull away from the curb. "Looks like our friends are on the move," Penny said.

She hung up the phone and threw it down on the seat as her eyes darkened noticeably. "Let's go. Hobbs said to follow them, but not too closely. We're going to nail those suckers."

Pulling away from the curb, Pete eyed her doubtfully, "How're the Feds going to tie the money they have on them with the actual ransom money?"

Penny laughed, though the sound was as humorless as the hammering in her head. "The bills are marked."

They followed the frozen food truck and the van to the outskirts of Syracuse. The vehicles took a sharp turn into a junk yard. Keeping a careful distance, Penny pulled over down the street and waited patiently.

A short time later, the frozen food truck spun hastily out of the junk yard. There were now three men in the truck.

"Looks like they dumped the van in the yard," Pete said.

"Yeah, that's what Hobbs thought they would do. Benny is smart enough to know we reported this to the authorities already and that the locals will have a BOLO out on that van."

As the truck drove down the street, Penny and Pete followed them a safe distance behind. She gave Hobbs a quick call and told him the van was now in Stacy's Junk Yard. "By tonight," she said, "those three should be apprehended and Phil will have his money back."

Pete's eyes narrowed and it took him a long time to respond, "You know we really did well on this case."

While Penny and Pete were following the truck, Hobbs called Phil to update him.

"Willis here."

It took several minutes for Hobbs to bring him up to date on what had taken place.

In a soothing tone, he added, "So you can see Phil, it's almost over."

"Thank God. My heart is still beating a hundred miles an hour."

"How is Kelley this morning?"

"The doctor said she's doing just fine." Hobbs could hear the joy in Phil's voice. "She ate a good breakfast and I brought her a change of clothes, so as soon as the doctor releases her we're out of here. I just wish we could be with you when you catch up to those bastards." His tone had changed to one of deep anger.

"Well, as a matter of fact, the Feds helped me to commission a helicopter for you. It will be on the roof of the hospital in half an hour. You two can join us and be in on the final action."

"Love it," Phil shot back. "I don't know how I can thank you for all that you've done for us Hobbs."

"Don't think anything of it. And don't worry, we'll have the ransom money back in no time. I'll be waiting for you at the small private airport in Buffalo. We're all set to go."

"Terrific. Where's the rest of the gang?" Phil asked, all fired up now.

"I've got Paul and Jack with me. Penny and Pete are following the three guys in the truck. We should all arrive at the border about the same time."

At approximately twelve-thirty that morning, Hobbs, Paul and Jack met Kelley and Phil at the airport, just ten minutes from the Canadian border.

From there, they drove in Hobbs' van to the border where they found enormous crowds of people milling around, almost in a carnival atmosphere.

Having been alerted to watch for the kidnappers and the ransom money, the Buffalo police as well as Federal Agents were posted on the American side while the Canadian Federal authorities were waiting on the Canadian side.

Exiting their vehicle, they spotted several American Border Patrol agents standing nearby.

"I'm Russell Hobbs. Looking for a Captain Miller."

One of the officers nodded. "I'm Captain Miller. I was notified by central command to be on the lookout for you. I understand you're here looking for a couple of kidnappers and some ransom money?"

Hobbs reached over and shook his hand. "You've got that right. We can use all the help we can get." He nodded toward Kelley and Phil, "This is Mrs. Willis and her husband, Phil. She was abducted several days ago. We paid the ransom money to get her back safely, but her abductors are on the run and headed toward the border in a frozen food truck."

Captain Miller nodded in acknowledgement toward them. "Well, you picked one hell of a time to come looking for some criminals. We've got thousands and thousands of people coming here. Tonight the famous tightrope walker, Nik Wallenda, is going to attempt to walk across the Falls on a tightrope, so already the spectators are lining up to watch him."

Jack nudged Hobbs in the side. "Look over by the entrance. There's an Edmonds Frozen Food truck."

Hobbs looked puzzled. "I just got a call from Penny. She said they were behind them in the truck and were about twenty minutes away from the border."

"Maybe, they got here early," Jack added coldly.

With Border Patrol agents accompanying them, the group approached the truck.

Captain Miller pulled his gun from the holster, walked up to the truck, and ordered the driver to come out with his hands in the air.

The driver croaked angrily as he climbed out, "Say, what's going on? All I've got in the truck is a big load of frozen lobsters. Headed for the Big Top Hotel just over the border in Toronto."

"Sure. Sure," Miller responded. "Let's take a look."

The agents walked the driver around to the back of the truck and instructed him to open the doors. One of the agents jumped inside and looked around. With a touch of disappointment in his voice, he yelled out, "He's right, Captain. Only cases and cases of lobsters in here."

Hobbs' cell rang. "Hey Penny, still with that truck?"

"Right. They stopped at a diner for a short while. On the move now. We should be at the border in about ten minutes."

"Yeah. That's what you said before. You still got the three guys in your view. Right?"

"Yup. Just leaving the diner now."

Beginning to sound rather irritable, Hobbs said, "Well, don't let them out of your sight."

"Yes Sir. Over and out."

Chapter 38

A few minutes later, a second Edmonds Frozen Food truck pulled in the border parking lot near the mob of sightseers who had lined up to watch Nik Wallenda prepare for the evening's performance. A large number of media vans with their television antennas reaching high into the sky were parked nearby.

Once the Edmonds truck stopped, Hobbs, the police and the Border Patrol raced over to it. Peering into the cab, Hobbs saw the driver and two strange men. Benny and Doug were nowhere to be seen.

He threw open the driver's door, grabbed the man by the shirt and yanked him out. "Where's Lotts?" he shouted, his voice crackling with annoyance.

The truck driver wrenched his shirt from Hobbs' hands and glared at him. In broken English, he said, "Don't know Lotts. These are my cousins."

Penny and Pete ran up to the truck. "I heard what you just said—that's a lie," she hissed at the driver. "We followed you all the way from Syracuse and Benny and Doug were with you." She turned to Hobbs. "Maybe they're in the back of the truck."

Hobbs pushed the driver to the back of the truck. "Open up, pal," he ordered.

The driver shrugged his shoulders, stepped toward

the back door. "Okay. I do. Got nothing to hide."

He opened the doors. The truck was filled with boxes of frozen food, but, no sign of Benny or Doug.

An ugly sensation gripped his gut as Hobbs turned and looked at Penny with an outraged stare. "Are you sure they were in the truck when it left the restaurant?"

She felt herself growing rather hot, and answered after a brief hesitation, "I thought so."

She turned to Pete. "Did you see them in the truck when we left the restaurant?"

Pete flinched and thought for a few minutes. "I can't say for sure. I saw three guys get into the truck. I just assumed that it was the driver, Benny and Doug."

"Oh shit," Penny exclaimed. "Maybe, they switched with these two guys at the restaurant and they're still back there."

Hobbs felt his nerve ends twitch. Then disturbed, he wrenched his gaze away from Penny and instead looked at Phil and Kelley. "Get the directions from Penny and head back to that restaurant in her van. Check it out. In the meantime, I'll have Jack and Paul look around here. Maybe, they're coming in another vehicle."

As they turned to follow Penny, Hobbs called out. "Wait a minute. You better take some weapons with you. Penny, hand your gun, shoulder holster and cuffs to Kelley. Phil, you take mine. And here, take this picture of Benny, so you can show it to people in the restaurant."

Hobbs' face became grim. "In the meantime, we'll go through the truck. This guy might have part of the ransom money stashed somewhere inside. We'll keep in contact with each other."

Kelley and Phil ran with Penny to her van, as she shouted out directions to the restaurant and motel. She handed her keys to Phil and he jumped into the driver's side. Kelley ran around to the passenger side and slid in. Within seconds they were on the interstate and on their way back to the restaurant.

Arriving at the restaurant, Phil whipped the van into the parking lot near the entrance. Kelley jumped out and ran inside while Phil headed toward the motel office next door.

Walking into the restaurant, Kelley saw it was busy with the noon-day lunch crowd. From the conversation, she determined that many of the people were on their way to the Falls to observe the high-wire walk.

A poster beside the cash register at the entrance had a photo of the thirty-four-year old, sandy haired Nik Wallenda, dressed in a red jump suit, announcing that he was going to walk on a thin wire stretched high above the treacherous Niagara Falls.

A framed newspaper article on the nearby wall, indicated that he was an American acrobat, aerialist, daredevil and high wire artist and the walk came after a two year legal battle, involving both sides of the Canada-United Stated border to gain approval. For this walk, he was going to be wearing a safety harness for the first time in his life.

A hostess with a clipboard in her hand walked up to Kelley, "Table for one?"

Kelley gave her a slow warm smile. "No. I'm not staying. I'm looking for someone. Do you recognize this man?" She pulled the photo of Benny from her pocket and flashed it.

The hostess studied it briefly and put her hand on her hips. "Listen Miss, do you have any idea how many men I've seen in here today?"

Kelley shook her head.

"No? Well, in this business everyone starts to look alike after a half hour. My job is to seat people and make sure no one sneaks out without paying their bill. Why don't you check with the cashier over there?" She pointed toward the woman seated behind the register.

Kelley walked toward her. Out of the corner of her eye she spied a tour bus pulling up in front of the restaurant. The driver jumped out, strolled briskly into the restaurant and walked up to the cashier.

"Hi Jim," the cashier struggled to pin a smile on her face. "How many today?"

"Just thirty," the driver answered.

"Your group will be seated in the back room as usual," the cashier tried to answer in a pleasant tone.

The occupants of the bus hurried into the restaurant. Some of the women looked around for restroom signs and quickly made a dash for them. A small group crowded together behind the bus driver. All of this just added to the already chaotic atmosphere in the restaurant.

After the bus travelers walked away, Kelley approached her and showed her the photo of Benny. "Can you tell me if you've seen this man in here today?"

"You've got to be kidding lady." She lifted her head and glared at Kelley. "How can I remember seeing anyone today in the midst of this zoo?"

"Damn," Kelley swore softly as she pocketed the photo and walked away. Now desperate, she decided to check out the restaurant herself. She walked hastily down one aisle and up the other. No sign of Benny.

One man jumped up from his seat and knocked Kelley to the side as she was passing by. "Sorry, lady, I need to get to the restroom."

Kelley paused for a moment as she watched him enter the men's room. Then, muttering another cuss word under her breath, she decided to follow him inside.

The man's brows drew together when he saw her enter. "Hey lady. Can't you read? This is the men's john."

Kelley silently opened the side of her jacket and showed him the gun that was in a holster. The man took a rapid step backwards and regained his composure with surprising speed as she pulled the gun out. "Forget it lady. I didn't have to go that bad." He scurried out of the room.

Kelley saw four porcelain urinals lined up against the wall. Past them, were three enclosed stalls. The last one was marked for the handicapped.

A man standing at the furthest urinal looked up when he saw Kelley with gun in hand. He gasped in fear, quickly finished his business, zipped his pants and ran out.

Kelley checked out the first two stalls. No one was inside. From under the door of the last stall, she could see a pair of shoes. With her gun in a ready position, she knelt down and waited for the person inside to exit.

The door abruptly opened. There stood Benny Lotts. Before he had a chance to react, Kelley gave him a swift karate kick to the groin. "We meet again Mr. Lotts. Only this time—on my terms." She grinned broadly at him.

She reached forward, yanked him out of the stall by his shirt and threw him to the floor. She planted her foot on the pit of his back, while she took the handcuffs out of her pocket. Kneeling down, she drew his hands behind his back and cuffed him. "You're my hostage now," she snapped tersely.

The door to the men's room opened and two young men stood in the doorway, staring at Kelley and Benny.

The astonished men stood there with their mouths wide open. Kelley looked up at them and smiled sweetly, "Federal Agent. Don't just stand there, fellows. Help me get this guy to his feet. He's under arrest."

"Sure lady," one mumbled as they pulled him up.

Everyone stared at them as she pushed him in front of her walking through the restaurant and out the front door. From behind her, Kelley heard a voice yell out, "Hey, who's going to pay his tab?"

Just then, Hobbs and an officer pulled up in front of the restaurant and got out of the squad car and walked up. "Hey Kelley, nice collar," Hobbs said with a chuckle.

Kelley gave him a tremulous smile. "Nothing to it."

"Where's the money and his accomplice?" Hobbs asked.

"You mean his lovely friend, Doug," she answered with undisguised sarcasm. "I guess he must be in the motel somewhere. Phil's over there checking it out."

Hobbs pushed Lotts over to the officer, who shoved him into the squad car.

"Let's head for the motel office." Hobbs' mouth turned down at the corners.

They went over to the motel office and questioned the owner about Doug.

"I told that other fellow who just asked, that a guy in blue jeans checked in a while ago. He's in the last room down there. Number sixteen." He pointed to the end of the row.

With their guns drawn, Kelley and Hobbs walked hurriedly to room sixteen. Without knocking, Hobbs kicked the door open and rushed in with Kelley behind him.

Both Phil and Doug were lying on the bed. Doug was face down, his cuffed hands pulled behind his back. Phil was sitting beside him with a gun pointed at his head.

"This guy didn't put up much of a fight," Phil said grinning broadly.

"Great. But, where's the money?" Kelley asked.

"Haven't had time to get to that yet," Phil choked on a laugh. "Why, don't you check out the closet for starters?"

Kelley ran over to the closet, opened the door and looked inside. "Hello," she exclaimed with happiness.

There, on the floor, were the two duffel bags. She dragged them out and unzipped each one.

"Yes!" She exclaimed as she put her fist up in the air and pulled it down quickly. "And it looks like it's all here."

Chapter 39

"Your day isn't over yet, folks," Hobbs said. "I have a surprise for you. I've arranged with Nik Wallenda's production manager to get you two front row seats on the observation deck so you can view Nik's walk over the Falls tonight. They're going to have complimentary drinks and appetizers in the glass enclosed deck before the walk. And Nik is going to stop in and greet the guests."

A shot of excitement ran up Phil. "That's something I wouldn't want to miss. What are we waiting for? Let's head back to the Falls. It's show time."

Hobbs's head shot up in amusement. "First, we've got to see Lotts off to jail. We should have plenty of charges for the D.A. to pile on him. Let's see: breaking parole, kidnapping Kelley, and who knows what else. He and Doug probably even stole the van. Say Attorney Willis, how would you like to prosecute this case?"

"It should be a slam-dunk," Phil answered, grinning from ear to ear.

"Personally, I think I've seen enough of Benny and Doug," Kelley added with anger in her voice.

"Well, now it's time for some fun," Hobbs said. "We have a couple of hours before Nik is scheduled to make his walk. I talked to your Uncle Jack and he wants to take the whole gang out to an early supper to celebrate.

The rest of the group are driving over here and meeting us inside the restaurant. After that the three of us will head to the Falls."

After the meal, Phil stood up and thanked Hobbs, Jack, Penny, Fast Draw Pete and Paul Mathison for their assistance in getting Kelley back safely. "You guys made up one great team," he said.

Kelley walked around the table, hugged everyone and thanked them for rescuing her.

Hobbs bid good-bye to the rest of the team and turned to Phil. "Now, let's head back to the Falls. After Nik's walk, I have a helicopter ready to take you back to the hospital, where your car is parked."

It was twilight when they drove up to the Falls. Captain Miller was waiting for them in a roped off section of the crowded parking lot. The Captain and a couple of his men quickly escorted them to the observation deck.

Hobbs went to the mini bar and got drinks. Phil and Kelley walked toward the glass enclosure that overlooked the cascading Falls. Her voice could barely be heard over the roar. "Looks like it's a little foggy and misty tonight. Maybe that will make the walk even more dangerous."

The door opened and Nik Wallenda walked in; behind him were his wife and their three children. He walked around the room, talking briefly to the guests, celebrities and the media.

He stood in the front of the room and shouted, "I want to thank everyone for coming. Unfortunately, I can't stay. My manager is checking everything over as we speak. So I need to leave and take a little walk."

The crowd laughed as he waved and left the room.

Sometime later, Wallenda climbed onto the rope with the pole in his hands and walked slowly across the Falls in the mist. Everyone held their breaths as he completed the world famous feat over the treacherous waters.

For Kelley and Phil, it was the climax to an exciting

day and one that they would never forget.

"It's time to leave folks," Hobbs said. "I just got word the helicopter's here."

He led them outside and over to the side of the parking lot, where the helicopter was waiting. After a brief hug and kiss, Kelley jumped into the helicopter with Phil behind her. They could see Hobbs waving to them as the copter lifted off the ground.

Phil picked up their car at the hospital and drove home. Kelley laid her head back against the seat and thought about how thankful she was that her ordeal with Benny Lotts and Doug was finally over and that the kidnappers were now on their way to jail.

"I can't wait to get home, Phil. Please don't leave my side in the future." Her voice quivered with emotion.

"It's a promise," he responded in a soothing voice, as he pulled into the driveway of their home. He walked around to the passenger side of the car and helped Kelley exit. Then he pulled a handkerchief from his pocket. "Here. Let's put this over your eyes."

Kelley stared at him, momentarily panicking as she recalled her recent kidnapping ordeal. "You've got to be kidding," she muttered.

"No. Trust me. It won't be for long and everything will be okay." Phil's reassuring gaze swept down at her.

She smiled weakly, squeezed her eyes and held the handkerchief over them as he led her up the front steps to the house. "No peaking," he instructed firmly.

In front of the door, he said, "Okay. Open your eyes."

Hanging above the doorway was a large sign that read, "Welcome Home Kelley."

She stared at the sign, and then struggled to take it in. Realizing she was finally safe and sound at home, tears filled her eyes.

"You like it?" he asked drawing her into the comfort of his arms.

Catching her breath, she offered him a brilliant smile. "You bet. Remember what Dorothy said in the movie, 'The Wizard of Oz'? There's no place like home. She was so right."

Phil opened the front door, reached down and picked her up in his arms. "From now on Mrs. Willis, we're on our second honeymoon. And I expect it to last forever."

He carried her inside, gently placed her on her feet and tenderly kissed her. Suddenly, loud shouts rang out. "Surprise. Welcome home."

Alan and Ashley, both who had been away at school, came running down the hall toward Kelley, followed by Phil's parents, Kaitlin and Dexter McLane.

Kelley sighed in contentment and threw her arms open. "You guys come here. I need a group hug."

After they exchanged hugs and kisses, Alan said, "It's time for a special celebration, Mom. Come into the living room. We have a bottle of wine all chilled and waiting for you. It's one of Dad's special ones he gets from Sicily."

With her arms around Ashley, Kelley followed the others into the living room. "You guys are just too much. And it's so good to be home."

After everyone sat down, Alan opened the bottle, filled the glasses and held his glass in the air. "I get to make the first toast. Salute. To my wonderful parents."

Kelley touched him gently on the cheek. "And to our wonderful children who are now young adults."

Dexter stood up and offered a toast. "To our amazing Kelley, who's back in our arms once again."

Kelley put her wine glass down on the coffee table and stood up. "If you don't mind, I'll hurry and change into something more comfortable."

"Take your time my dear," Kaitlin's eyes shimmered with emotion. "The evening is yours."

They sat in the living room, enjoying the wine and talking about the events of the past week.

Finally, Dexter stood up and said, "You young people, just relax. Kaitlin and I will wash the wine glasses and put on some coffee. Your mom brought your favorite dessert for you, Phil."

"Thanks Dad," Phil said as he pulled Kelley over closer to him.

Before Phil had a chance to give Kelley a kiss, they heard a knock on the front door. "You guys sit down and relax," Phil said. "I'll get the door."

He went to the front door, and opened it. To his surprise, Gayle Tanner was standing outside.

"Did I catch you at a bad time Phil?" Gayle asked anxiously.

With a laugh of happiness, he waved her inside. "No. Not at all. I just got home with Kelley. And the kids and my folks are here. We were celebrating Kelley's safe return. Please join us."

"I heard on the news that Kelley was rescued and that her kidnappers were apprehended. I'm anxious to talk with you, but my cell phone died, so I couldn't call you. But can you spare me a few minutes?"

Phil nodded and led her into the living room, where she threw her arms around Kelley and said, "I'm so glad that you're safe."

Phil introduced Gayle to Alan and Ashley and then to his parents, as they entered the room.

"So sorry to interrupt your celebration," Gayle said with some hesitation. "But I needed to speak to Phil for just a moment."

"You're not interrupting us." Kaitlin said. "We were just about to have dessert. Would you care to join us?"

"Thank you. But, I'm in a bit of a hurry." Her eyes flashed back to Phil. "I must speak to you in private."

"Sure thing, let's go into the study."

He led the way into the study and they sat down.

"What's going on Gayle?" Phil asked. His expression was filled with concern.

"I wanted to speak to you about the Burjan case. It's still on the court docket for Monday at nine. I had a closing statement prepared. But, I'd prefer for you to handle it if you're available now."

Phil let out a loud whoop and his face broke into a big grin. "Great. I'm available and anxious to do it. Now that I have my Kelley back, I'm ready to jump back into action. I'm certain we'll take those shysters down and get Edith Cliff her well deserved restitution. I'll be at the courthouse at least half an hour before the case is scheduled to resume."

"That's what I came to hear," she said as she patted him on the hand. "I'd love it if you took over the final summation. Here are my notes."

"Thanks. And I won't let you down," Phil replied, fired up with anticipation.

"Now go back to your family celebration and I'll see you on Monday."

"You're welcome to stay for dessert."

"No. I just wanted to be sure that Kelley was okay and that you could get back to the case. I hope you'll take tonight to rest up after your ordeal. You can look this folder over tomorrow." Her eyes lit up as she added, "And I'll see you Monday at eight-thirty."

Phil took her hand and held it. "Sure you don't want to stay for Mom's dessert. I think that she made her killer chocolate cheesecake."

"That sounds mighty tempting. But, I'm trying to lose a few pounds and I need to go upgrade my cell phone."

She stood up and added, "After this case is over, you need to give me a blow by blow account of Kelley's adventure."

"Will do."

He led Gayle to the front door and bid her good night, then returned to the living room where the family was talking quietly and waiting for him.

They walked to the dining room for dessert, when Alan said, "I have some special news to tell all of you. After graduation this spring, I'm going to apply to the police academy. I just hope that I can pass the entrance exam."

Phil looked at Kelley. "Well, one down and one to go."

Ashley put her hand on her father's arm and grinned, "Wait just a minute folks. I want to make an announcement too. I'm scheduled to graduate early and I've been accepted to Georgetown Law School. I'm going to study to become a lawyer."

Dexter walked over to Ashley and put his arms around her. "We're so proud of you." Then he looked over at Alan and smiled, "And you too, Alan."

"Yes. I can see the sign now. Willis and Willis, Attorneys at Law," Kaitlin added.

Ashley's smile broadened. "That's a long way off Grandma." Turning to Phil, she added, "I love watching you work Dad. I just hope that I can become half as good a lawyer as you are."

Kelley put her arm around Phil as they walked over to the dining room table. "Both of my youngsters will be out on their own soon."

Kaitlin and Dexter went into the kitchen and a short time later she returned to the dining room with a large tray filled with plates of her famous chocolate cheese cake. Dexter followed behind her with the coffee pot, cups and cream and sugar.

As they enjoyed their coffee and dessert, Kelley looked at the McLane's. "I was so surprised to find you here, Mom and Dad. I didn't notice your car anywhere around."

"We wanted to surprise you so we left it parked down

the block. We'll head back to Florida in a day or two."

"Of course, you're staying over with us while you're in town," Kelley said.

"Thank You. We were planning on it," Kaitlin replied. "In fact, our open suitcases are in the guest bedroom."

"And Ashley and I are glad to be back in our old rooms for a couple of nights," Alan said.

"When do you two have to be back at school?" Phil asked.

"By Wednesday for finals," Ashley answered.

"I start finals on Thursday," Alan added. "So, I'll only be staying for a few days."

"Well, you're all welcome to stay as long as you want. I know I'll just be glad to be sleeping in my own bed tonight," Kelley said with tears in her eyes. She looked around the table. "God, I missed all of you so much."

"And since the four of you are going to be here for a few days, I've got a surprise for you," Kelley said. "My dear friends, the Wilders gave me tickets for the Sunday matinee performance of the circus at Madison Square Garden's in New York. Thought we could all go together. What do you say kids?"

Ashley looked at Alan with a sly grin. "Only if we can get popcorn, hot dogs and all that junk that you used to treat us to when we were little."

Phil laughed loudly. "It's a deal. And I'll even buy cotton candy for everyone."

Kaitlin stood up and picked up the dishes. "Dexter and I will put these in the dishwasher and then head up to bed, if it's okay. We've had a busy day for old people."

"Wait," Phil said suddenly. "I just remembered I have one more surprise for my lovely wife. Alan, come with me."

With Alan behind him, Phil hurried outside. He opened the trunk of his car and pulled out the boxed Thomas Kincaid painting. Glancing at his son, he directed, "Alan, you grab the step ladder and bring it inside."

They walked back into the house. "Follow me," Phil instructed everyone as he headed to the family room. "Now everyone sit down and close your eyes," he ordered.

"Alan bring that ladder over by the fireplace and take that old painting down"

Alan put the ladder up in front of the fireplace and removed the faded painting that had been hanging up there for years. Phil took the Kincaid out of the box, unwrapped it and handed it up to Alan to hang.

Alan hung the picture. After straightening it, he climbed down from the ladder and moved it aside. Phil walked over and turned on the battery operated light that was attached below the Kincaid canvas.

Suddenly, the lovely winter Kincaid scene was illuminated. It looked like a winter in Vermont with its charming old cottage and glistening snow covered trees.

Phil, excited, then said, "Okay everyone, you can open your eyes. Kelley, this is your welcome home present. I hope you like it."

Kelley took a long look at the painting, then jumped up and threw her arms around Phil. "Oh, my God. Is this what I think it is? An original Kincaid?" She blinked rapidly, trying to clear her eyes. She couldn't see through the mist of tears.

"That it is, Sweetheart. The minute I saw it, I knew it was meant for you."

She shook her head as she walked over to the fireplace and looked up at it. "I just love it. Thank you."

Everyone spent considerable time admiring the painting. "We've got a big day planned for tomorrow," Phil said. "I think it's time for all of us to head upstairs to bed. Let's plan on breakfast together and then we'll attend mass. In the afternoon, we can head into New York City for the circus."

"Sounds good to us, Dad," Ashley and Alan responded as they followed Kaitlin and Dexter out of the family room.

Phil looked at his father and said, "Oh, the ransom money is being held by the Feds as evidence. We should get it back in a week or so."

Later, Phil and Kelley were cuddled closely together in bed. She leaned over and whispered, "Let's hope that our days of wild adventures are finally over."

"Right," Phil said as he kissed her. "I think it'll be our kids who will seek justice from now on. Maybe, we'll even see 'Final Justice'."

Author Bio

Ray Weaver is a resident of Clearwater, Florida. He and his wife, Ellie, have been married for over fifty-four years and have two children and six grandchildren.

Ray has been writing for eight years and has numerous short stories and articles published in magazines and newspapers.

He is very proud of the stories that he has had published in the *Chicken Soup for the Soul* books.

His first novel, *Tightrope to Justice* was published in 2010 and his second novel, *Miami Justice* in August of 2011. His third book, *European Justice* was published in May of 2012 and his fourth novel, *Justice 4 Willis*, will be on Amazon, EBooks and Nook in 2013.

The fifth and last book in the series about the Willis family is titled *Final Justice* and will feature Kelley and Phil's grown children. Ashley, their daughter follows her father's footsteps and enters the courtroom as an attorney. Alan, their son, commands a swat team and encounters many adventures.

Email-raymondellie@aol.com

Articles and Short Stories
by Ray Weaver

"The Past Sixty Years" published in *Chicken Soup for the Soul: Twins and More*, March 2009.

"A Star is Born" published in *Chicken Soup for the Soul-Inspiration for the Young at Heart*; August 2011.

"The Cell Phone" published in *Chicken Soup for the Soul-Inspiration for the Young at Heart*; August 2011.

"It's a Poem" published in *Chicken Soup for the Soul-Inspiration for Writers*-May 2013

"A Grandfather's Dream", "the Wieliczka Salt Mines", "Ground Zero in New York", "So this is Canada, Eh", "Ray and Ellie visit Lourdes" among articles published in the Safety Harbor Florida, newspaper, *The Tropical Breeze*.

"So this is Sterling" published in the Dunedin Florida's newspaper, *The Highlander*.

"Make your Memories" published in the "Seniority Section" of the *St. Petersburg Times*.

Second place in "June Times Remember Section" of the *St. Petersburg Times* with a story about his granddaughter.

Story about Grandpa Weaver's 1902 Grocery Store, published in *Bend of the River* magazine.

Numerous articles published in the Suncoast Hospice newsletter.

Articles in the Francis Wilson Playhouse newsletter.

COMING SOON

The last in the series of the five adventures of Kelley Ryan Willis, her husband, Phil and their two children, Ashley and Alan.

"FINAL JUSTICE"

Ashley Willis, Kelley and Phil's daughter, follows in her Dad's footstep as a top attorney, practicing in Florida.

Their oldest child, Alan, goes right to the top of his profession as the Captain of a prominent Swat Team, directing his team mates through wild escapades.

The adventures of these two will keep you turning the pages of this, my fifth novel.